# Ten Things My Husband Hated

# Ten Things My Husband Hated

*Pauline Wiles*

This novel is a work of fiction. The names, characters, places, publications, and incidents portrayed are the product of the author's imagination. Any resemblance to real persons, living or dead, is purely coincidental. Magnus Monkton, Brissinghorn & Beem, Kern Kitchens, and *Cornice* magazine are entirely fictional entities.

# Author's Note

In keeping with its English setting, this novel uses British spelling and grammar conventions.

# Acknowledgements

Like my previous novels, *Ten Things My Husband Hated* owes thanks to a diverse group who helped with research, encouragement, and more.

For information on topics within the book, I'm grateful to Sue Johnson, Andrew Carter, Kimberly Purcell, Cynthia Miller, and Lauren Mang. They were generous with their time and knowledge; any misrepresentation of what they told me can be assumed due to artistic license.

I helped myself to small plot points from various friends. I hope Rosemary Butcher, Martina Munzittu, and Marg & Peter Dalziel will recognise their contributions and forgive me.

The book in your hands is considerably improved over the version which landed with my intrepid beta readers Tracey Gemmell and Martha Reynolds. And proofreader Wendy Janes added further polish, for which I'm most grateful. Any lingering errors are mine.

Further writing friends offered much-needed encouragement not to give up, and the role of Chief Morale Officer was once again filled by the long-suffering Darius Wiles. He juggled his wife's writerly emotions with one hand, while untangling her technology woes with the other. He won't be surprised to learn that when he's gone from home, I leave all the lights on, play Classic FM on the radio, and eat stinky cheese in bed.

# Ten Things My Husband Hated

## Chapter 1

I needed a stone.

Although, I wasn't sure whether I wanted to bludgeon someone with it, or crawl under it and not emerge for a year.

My smile wobbled, then froze into a lopsided grimace. My borrowed evening dress instantly shrank two sizes, preventing any oxygen from reaching my lungs. And all around me, acquaintances were hooting, pointing, and laughing.

Not with me, though. At me.

~~~

Two hours ago, when we'd gathered for champagne cocktails in the opulent ballroom of Saffron Hall, I'd felt a flutter of nerves, but nothing more. The award ceremony, to recognise outstanding businesses in the Cambridge area, was abuzz. Everyone who was anyone was here, and I was a moth in a swarm of vibrant butterflies.

Outside, March rain pattered against the windowpanes, but in here, the radiators were keeping bare shoulders warm. Expensive perfumes mingled with the scent of lilies from the elaborate arrangement on each table. Air kissing and effusive greetings muffled the string quartet in the corner.

Once the painful mingling was over, we sat down to a sumptuous dinner of crab salad and beef Wellington. That was much more enjoyable: the caterers had excelled themselves and wine flowed freely. I could concentrate on my food and chat with Vincent, without worrying about being charming or clever.

Over dessert we applauded the preliminary speeches and some minor award winners.

My ex-husband, Colin, was nominated in the category of best environmentally conscious renovation. He seemed confident of a win, because he'd splurged on not one, but two tables of friends to witness his potential glory.

I was there as Vincent's plus one: his wife was at home with a sick child. Colin had pressured Vincent to bring someone, and since we'd all been friends since back when Vincent first started working for Colin, I was a reasonable choice.

'It's not too weird is it, Maggie?' Vincent had asked me on the phone earlier in the day, when he'd issued the last-minute invitation.

'Of course not,' I'd replied, thinking it would do me good to get out. Especially if my ticket was paid for. My social life in the sleepy village of Saffron Sweeting was mundane at best.

Everyone knew Vincent and his wife doted on each other, so there'd be no sniff of scandal there. He was Kenyan, his wife was Scottish, and their kids were gorgeous. And Colin and I were amicably divorced, so there'd be no awkwardness on that front, either. My mind was already on what to wear: no way could my wardrobe handle this.

'Good.' Vincent had said. 'We'll be at the second table, so you don't have to sit next to Keiko or anything. But Colin thinks this could be his night.'

And it was. My ex-husband's instincts, as usual, were spot on. Colin knew people. Yes, he did excellent construction work – when he wasn't cutting corners to cut costs – but his true skill was in networking. Colin could work a room better than a British ambassador could handle a cranky colony. If success in life is half down to what you know, and half down to *whom* you know, Colin had fifty per cent in the bag without even trying.

I'd reached the dregs of my coffee when the chairman of the nominating committee – and, surprise surprise, an old friend of Colin – began his speech outlining the emphasis the organisation placed on respecting our precious planet. He mentioned the importance of not buying more stuff than we need, which I noticed drew a special nod of appreciation from Colin's new wife, Keiko.

And then I missed the next bit of the speech, as I stole another look at Keiko's slim figure in her black satin sheath dress. I would never be able to wear a cut like that. It's not that I'm curvy, exactly... I'm more of a practical pear. My burgundy velvet dress borrowed from my friend Grace wasn't a bad fit, but I felt a bit awkward in it. Keiko's hair, too, was tamed in a precise chignon, whereas mine was threatening to frizz from the wet weather.

In fact, everything about Keiko was chic and starched, not thrown together at short notice like me.

Beside his new wife, Colin looked sharp, too. His black tuxedo combined with his dark hair made a striking combination. He was still in really good shape: not surprising, given his job. Tonight was the first time in ages I'd studied him. As our marriage had deteriorated, first imperceptibly and then irreversibly, his physical attractiveness hadn't been top of my mind.

The committee chairman attempted another joke, and the audience laughed dutifully, although my friend Amelia, who was seated a few tables away, rolled her eyes. She'd missed out on the award for best independent estate agent, and although she would claim not to mind, I think she was disappointed. She'd invested in a new midnight blue dress for tonight, and her long auburn hair shone. I made a note to seek her out after the formalities were over, in case she needed cheering up.

How ironic.

'And it gives me the utmost pleasure to present this award. Actually, I'm going to make him come up here and stand beside me while I tell you all why he won it. It gives me great pleasure to announce the winner as Colin Kern, of Kern Kitchens!'

My table, and the one where Colin was sitting, erupted in a mixture of pride and alcohol-induced festivity. There was much back-clapping and a few whoops. Colin planted a smacker on Keiko's cheek, then, beaming, swaggered the short distance to the stage. Once there, he shook hands with the chairman with enough force to dislocate his buddy's shoulder. They even shared an awkward hug, which in Colin's line of work, was saying a lot.

I clapped too, of course. Colin might be a smooth operator, but he worked hard. And although I'd helped him build the business up, in the last couple of years, he'd come on in leaps and bounds.

Someone let a helium balloon go, and it drifted up to the high ceiling of the ballroom, as if to get a better view of the proceedings.

'Now wait, wait, before I give this gent his award, I need to tell you why the committee chose Kern Kitchens.' The chairman consulted his notes before reeling off a few impressive certifications, plus clients including two Cambridge colleges and a famous novelist, who lived in nearby Grantchester. 'And it's not only the work he does – everyone who comes across Colin knows you couldn't hope to meet a more decent bloke.'

I stole a glance at the room and found there was general nodding. I knew a bit more about Colin than most people, but even I had to admit, he had a way of making friends wherever he went.

'You won't find anyone with a bad word to say about him.' The chairman almost echoed my thoughts.

At this, Colin attempted to look bashful, but he was swelling like a peacock.

'Clients love him, his employees love him...' The chairman paused for Colin's team, all of whom had just enjoyed the feast he'd paid for, to cheer. 'Other people in the industry love him, and that includes the planning inspector.'

We all laughed, assuming that was the punchline. But it wasn't.

The committee chairman beamed around the audience and left a moment for perfect comic timing. Then he proclaimed, 'Heck, I have it on the *best* of authority that even his ex-wife is still in love with him.'

At this, the room exploded in laughter, and every head turned to seek out the object of the joke.

Me.

Friends, acquaintances, and even perfect strangers chortled or sniggered, and in some inebriated cases, actually guffawed.

The helium balloon popped, and the scent of flowers suddenly choked me.

I looked around wildly, taking in their mirth, seeing only Amelia's uncertain face amongst the mockery.

And I tried to smile back, I really did. I tried to be a good sport, and not spoil Colin's glory, or allow my face – which by now matched my dress – to crumple.

But inside, my whole universe collapsed with humiliation.

## Chapter 2

The silence which fell when I arrived at Amelia's house the next evening was unmistakable.

'Okay, I can tell you've been talking about me,' I said, as my three friends threw each other awkward looks. At least I knew these women well enough to be direct; it wasn't usually one of my traits.

Grace, the quiet and empathetic one, came over to me. 'How are you feeling, Maggie?'

I looked at Amelia. 'You told them, then?'

'Started to.' Amelia owned the estate agency in the village, knew everyone, and was both the best-dressed and most confident woman in Saffron Sweeting. Now, though, her grimace was sympathetic. 'You looked like you'd been hit by a train, darling.'

Nancy, our American friend, handed me a glass of wine. 'So, other people think you're in love with your ex-husband? But you say you're not?'

I shook my head. 'Absolutely not. But Colin and I... we stayed on friendly terms.'

Amelia gave a half chuckle. 'You're a better woman than me. How you can divorce someone and continue to send birthday cards, I'll never know.'

She'd been divorced a few years ago, but had bounced back stronger than ever.

'It's nice that you're friends.' Grace sat down on Amelia's cream leather sofa and tucked her legs under her. 'Anyway, I could never hate James.'

'You could if you found he'd drunk the last of your wedding champagne in your bed, with another woman,' Amelia said.

'Okay, okay.' Nancy flapped her hand at the other two. 'Maggie, you're happily divorced, bravo.'

'It was so mortifying,' I said. 'His new wife, all our friends...'

At least, all the people who *used* to be our friends. I'd dropped out of contact with several couples after the divorce, seeing how awkward it was when the husband was pals with Colin, but the wife claimed allegiance with me. And I was terrible company, too, not witty or entertaining like my ex-husband. After a while, most of them had drifted to spending time with Colin and Keiko, cutting me out of arrangements. It seemed like Vincent was the only pal I had left from my former life. And even he'd been bashful, after that awful speech.

'They don't think that,' I'd protested last night, once my heart rate came down from the cardiac arrest zone. 'Do they?'

Vincent had squirmed in his seat. 'Er, well, a few of them might, Maggie.'

'Really?' I'd turned to him in horror. 'They actually think I've still got a thing for Colin?'

He hadn't met my eye. 'One or two rumours, nothing much.'

Rumours? Nothing much?

As soon as I could, I'd slunk away from the dinner, head down. I'd trudged the mile back home in the worsening rain, without noticing that my shoes were rubbing my feet raw.

Tonight I'd brought an umbrella, and worn plimsolls. I'd kicked those off the minute I'd hobbled across Amelia's threshold.

'You need cake,' she said.

There was an appropriate reverent silence while Nancy divided the carrot cake – an early celebration for Grace's birthday – into eight modest pieces. I didn't have much appetite, so I waited while the others raved about its moistness, and the tang of the icing.

Grace noticed my silence. 'Remind us, how long were you married?'

'Technically, ten years. But we were separated for a chunk of that. Initially, it was so I could nurse my dad, then...'

They didn't need details of my time in Yorkshire, and the subsequent fizzle of my marriage.

'You were young, then?' Nancy licked her cake fork.

'Yeah. I was twenty-two when we tied the knot.'

'And your divorce took a while?' She had sharp, bird-like eyes and a brain to match. 'I thought it was amicable?'

Maybe I did want cake, after all. 'I, er, may have dragged my feet a bit with the decree absolute.'

The others exchanged glances.

'It was a load of boring admin! That doesn't mean I'm pining for Colin.' I got up and helped myself to the cake. 'I don't know why that hateful man made that joke last night.'

'Okay, so the awards ceremony was awkward,' Amelia said. 'You'll get over it, darling.'

I hung my head. 'It's only I had no idea everyone thinks I'm still moping around after him.'

'Are you sure you're not, hon?' Nancy pointed her fork at me.

'No!' I prodded my cake. 'Well, not much.'

'You've totally moved on?'

'I'm sure I have.' I cast my mind around for an example. 'Colin's vegan. He hated me eating meat. Today, for lunch, I had a big steak.'

'You've lost me.' Amelia's expression suggested I'd lost myself, too.

'No, I get it.' Grace laughed. 'A little act of defiance!'

'There's more to building a new life than eating sirloin, though,' Nancy said. 'I mean, how about changing your name, or getting a new job? New haircut? Maybe a new man?'

The others were silent. They knew I'd done none of those things in the year since my divorce became final. Amelia, who claimed her hairdresser transcended any therapist, had even offered to pay to bring my shoulder-length sandy curls into line. But I'd declined, preferring instead to tie my hair back and ignore it.

If the truth be told, I'd ignored a few things.

'Have you even unpacked fully, since you moved here?' Nancy prodded.

I sighed. How did she know about the boxes stuffed in the cupboard under the stairs, and in the miniscule second bedroom of my cottage?

'As I said, I had steak.' I cast around for more. 'Oh, and I painted my front door.'

Amelia clicked her tongue. 'Darling, are you feeling okay? Because I thought you said you painted your front door. Don't you mean, you went out and bought new shoes, or slept with an Italian waiter, or gorged on custard tarts?'

It was easy to picture Amelia resorting to all of these, possibly at the same time.

'No,' I said. 'I did my door. Today. It's pink.'

Grace, who's an interior designer, failed to hide her grimace. 'Really?'

'Well,' I amended, 'sort of a dark pink.' I wasn't good with colours, but I liked my new door.

'She's had too much wine,' Amelia said.

'No, I haven't. Colin, you see. He can't stand pink, or lilac, or lavender, and especially not on houses.' My ex-husband preferred understated style. 'So I found this lovely glossy pink and slapped it all over my door.'

This time, Grace attempted a laugh. 'Well, that sounds... fun.'

Clearly she'd chosen the kindest adjective she could find.

'Now the penny drops.' Amelia licked icing off her cake fork with relish. 'You're trying to show the world you're over Colin. So you're finding sneaky acts of rebellion to get back at him.'

'Doesn't sound very evolved.' Nancy, who'd surely had loads of therapy under her American healthcare plan, pursed her lips. She probably wanted to tell me I was being passive aggressive, but stopped short.

'I don't care if it's evolved,' I said. 'There I was, thinking we were all grown up and amicable, and it turns out people are laughing at me.'

'Well,' Amelia said, 'you need to show them you're a new woman. You should do other things which would get under Colin's skin.'

'Like what?' asked Grace.

Amelia thought about this. 'Could you paint your whole house pink?'

We laughed.

'What else would annoy him?' Grace asked.

'Ooh, yes, let's brainstorm,' said Amelia. 'What would *totally* give him kittens?'

'Really, you guys?' Nancy held up her hands. 'This doesn't sound mature. If Maggie needs to move on from her marriage—'

'Then she needs to assert her independence,' Amelia said. 'Starting with a bunch of things which would wind Colin up. Grace, grab a pen.'

Grace giggled and fished in her handbag. 'It could be fun,' she said. 'I mean, when James is away, I light all my scented candles, and eat stinky cheese in bed.'

'You see!' Amelia gestured with her glass of wine, almost slopping it over the edge. 'Maggie, you need to scoff Stilton in bed.'

I had to smile. 'No, Colin wouldn't care about cheese. Maybe a sausage roll, though.'

'Terrific!' said Amelia. 'We're getting somewhere. Number one, paint front door. Number two, change your name. Number three, adopt carnivore habits in bed.'

Even Nancy had to smile at this. 'You Brits have a strange idea of emotional healing.'

'So we do,' I admitted.

'What else winds him up?' Amelia wanted to know.

'Well, he hated shopping for clothes. And hoovering.' I thought for a moment. 'And getting a flu jab... and when I made jam.'

'Jam?' Nancy asked.

'I find it kind of therapeutic.' As I said it, I realised I hadn't done this in ages. 'It takes hours, turns the whole kitchen into a sticky mess, and the house smells fruity for days. Colin used to go bonkers.'

Amelia frowned. 'Actually, these are kind of sissy, Maggie. You need to think bolder. What about dating Hugh Grant, getting a part in *Game of Thrones*, and engineering a hostile takeover of Colin's company?'

The others grinned.

'Could this really help?' Grace asked. 'Some silly rituals to help Maggie move on?'

'Absolutely.' Amelia grabbed the pen from her and produced a pad of yellow paper. 'Especially if we make sure Colin finds out about some of them. Don't you think, Mags?'

I had to admit, the glossy pink front door had given me a boost. Perhaps I could look out for a pink barbecue on which to sear my meat, and install it in my front garden?

'Yes.' A knot had eased in my shoulders. 'Yes, I think it could help.'

'Fantastic,' said Amelia. 'Let's make a list.'

~ ~ ~

Ten Things My Husband Hated:

1) Pink houses
2) Heights
3) Karaoke, especially Queen and Abba songs
4) Doctors, needles, and hospitals
5) Tattoos on women
6) Dogs, especially yapping dogs
7) English beaches
8) Golf and cricket
9) Live theatre
10) Television cooking shows

## Chapter 3

For the start of April, the wind wasn't too chilly as I walked down the slight hill towards Sweeting School and turned right along the high street. The village itself was pretty enough, with several quaint thatched cottages and a dignified medieval church. The old-fashioned streetlamps seemed to bow their heads to keep an eye on things, and conveyed an air of gentle tradition.

When we first owned the cottage, though, some of the businesses were struggling and a couple had closed altogether. But in the interim, the village had found its feet. Grace told me the arrival of lots of American families, with jobs at the nearby Cambridge Science Park, was the catalyst.

'There were all kinds of fireworks those first couple of years,' she'd said. 'Literally.'

These days, you were as likely to hear a Boston accent in the post office as Suffolk. And the village generally celebrated Mother's Day twice: once in March, for the local folk, and then again in May for those who preferred the American calendar. On the one hand, the pub clung to its British menu, whereas Brian at the bakery had cheerfully added pumpkin pie to his autumn repertoire.

I liked the mix: there was always something going on and since I'd never been to America, it made me feel more cosmopolitan. I was no culture vulture, but there was a cheerful air in the high street.

Obviously, on a nippy Monday morning, people weren't standing around outside chatting. But a mistle thrush trilled as I passed, and daffodils in window boxes waved bravely in the breeze. The new beauty salon was open, and there were already a few pushchairs parked outside the second-hand children's clothes shop. No doubt its little coffee corner was a big part of its success.

I turned left there, and headed for the estate agents.

~~~

'I phoned Vincent on Saturday. He thinks I've been a bit *too* friendly towards Colin,' I said to Amelia, as soon as I'd closed the door to Hargraves & Co behind me. 'I was determined to be cordial, and people have taken it the wrong way.'

'*People* can be so tiresome.' She leaned back in her chair and stretched. 'You've had a heart to heart with him, then?'

'Colin? Crumbs, no.'

'I meant Vincent.'

Vincent had hummed and hawed, and protested that he was trying to watch the Grand National on TV.

'Then, he admitted that *people* thought I'd popped up in places Colin frequented once too often. And they saw my offer to temp, while his assistant had shingles, as over-keen.' How would Amelia view these unfortunate coincidences? 'And then, the time my car broke down outside his house, it was, er, there all weekend.'

'All weekend?' She pursed her lips.

'I'd popped over with a birthday basket for his mother. Couldn't get a mechanic out on a Sunday. It was completely innocent.'

'I see.'

'So, you think so too? That I've been too... genial?' I fussed with the property leaflets on the table next to me. Thursday's humiliation was lurking just below the surface. 'Nobody gave me a handbook on this.'

Amelia shook her head. 'It doesn't matter what I think. Or other people, come to that.' Before I could respond, she continued, 'But it *might* matter what your ex-husband thinks. Did Vincent give you any clues on what Colin makes of it all?'

One of the leaflets rewarded me with a deep paper cut. 'Ow!' As my finger shot to my mouth, I blamed the stinging for the way my eyes filled.

'He wouldn't say.'

Amelia's eyes flicked away. She agreed, then. Vincent's failure to reassure me meant that Colin thought like everyone else: I was moping over my failed marriage.

Then she sighed. 'Come on. I'll make some tea.'

But even tea was not straightforward that morning. The sink in her tiny office kitchen gurgled and refused to drain.

Putting thoughts of Colin's disdain to one side, I grabbed a bucket and found a spanner. Then I got down on my knees. 'Where's your usual maintenance bloke?' She had a small army of people she called on, to help with properties she was selling.

'Paternity leave. Short notice. So tedious.'

I peered at the plumbing in dismay. 'Oh boy. I think you've got rats.'

This hadn't been in the morning's plan. But at least it was a distraction from my reputation: this, I could do something about.

'Bloody hell,' Amelia shrieked, and I raised my head in time to see her dashing to safety in the front office, as fast as her kitten heels would carry her.

Great, I thought, that's friendship for you.

Before my marriage ended, I was Colin's office manager, bookkeeper and trouble-shooter. I still did some bookkeeping around Saffron Sweeting, but, with nine years' experience nurturing a small business, I'd learned to be adaptable. And recently, my clients had been asking for more practical jobs. Today, at the estate agency, I was supposed to be helping with Amelia's taxes and totting up the VAT she owed. But I couldn't afford to be picky. If she had rats, I'd tackle them instead.

After all, I really needed that cup of tea. It was a pity Amelia didn't feel the same.

But I was wrong. Within moments I heard the returning click clack of heels. As I wriggled out from the lower kitchen cabinet, there she was, brandishing a broom. With her red hair and black sweater, the effect was witch-like.

'Okay!' She adopted a stance which combined fencing and snooker. 'I'm ready for the little buggers.'

Her voice wasn't quite steady and my estimation of her climbed two notches.

'Hang on.' I screwed up my face and reached into the pipe. Good grief, bring me a tax return any day. 'It's probably dead. There.' I dropped the wet, lifeless form into the bucket.

Amelia gripped the broom tighter and craned her neck to look in. I took in her wrinkled nose and puzzled expression, and pulled myself up to look too.

'Ohhh!' She was like a child on Christmas morning. 'I was *wondering* where that went!'

Before I could stop her, she'd flung the broom aside and reached into the bucket, coming up with the rat dangling from one hand.

'Amelia—' I began, then stopped. It looked more like a red squirrel – or at least, the tail of a squirrel – than a rat. And it didn't seem to have a head. 'What is it?'

She was already rinsing the item under the tap, before brandishing it. 'It's my hair piece.'

'Your what?'

'You know, darling: a fake ponytail. I was wearing it last week when a friend came over for... dinner. Well, I say dinner, I'm not sure we ate much.' She gave me a salacious wink. 'This must have come off in the, er, commotion.'

'In your office kitchen?' I couldn't help saying. Colin and I never once did it in the kitchen. Now I came to think of it, we never had sex anywhere, once we were married, except the bedroom. 'Er, never mind,' I added.

Amelia was in her late forties, although she was notoriously vague about how *late*. That put her around fifteen years older than me, but she was having masses more fun.

'Maggie.' She beamed at me. 'You're brilliant. I don't know what you did and I don't want to know, but you're bloody brilliant.'

'Well...' I was taken aback by this praise. 'Let me put this back together and see if that was the problem.'

'Of course it was the problem, you clever old thing. Where did you learn a trick like that?'

'Colin, sort of.' I disappeared back under the sink with my spanner. 'You remember, he's a builder.'

'So he taught you?'

'No, actually. Haven't you heard about cobblers' children?'

'What?'

'They're the kids with no shoes.' I couldn't see her, but the answering silence told me to explain. 'Colin was always busy fixing up other people's houses. He had no time for ours; kept promising to do odd jobs but never did. I got fed up waiting.'

It wasn't long before I could put up shelves which were both sturdy and straight, and I could unstick a stubborn door with one hand tied behind my back.

'Poor you.'

'Oh, no.' I tightened the last fitting. 'I like it.'

I made it sound like I'd acquired these skills from necessity, but the truth was I'd always enjoyed making things, from the first day I got my hands on my brother's Lego set. Repairs were a natural extension and almost more satisfying, knowing that something had been saved.

'You like grubbing around under people's sinks? I had no idea.'

I shimmied my way out, so I was lying on my back on the kitchen floor looking up at her. 'Well, apart from rats, yes.' I propped myself up on my elbows. 'I suppose I do.'

It was a pity, though, that I wasn't doing a better job of fixing my own life.

She put her head on one side. 'Can I put more business your way? My bloke – the one whose wife had twins – he'll be gone for weeks.'

'For your houses, you mean?' It made sense that, when selling property, there would be minor repairs to take care of. 'I suppose so. Sure.' I wasn't in love with bookkeeping and, with the UK tax year about to end, demand would tail off. And I could definitely use the cash for all the work my own cottage needed.

'Marvellous! That's a load off my mind. What a pity unblocking sinks isn't on your hit list.'

'My what?'

'Can I try this?' She gestured to the tap and I nodded. We both watched, satisfied, as the water drained. I might get my cup of tea after all. Seeing my expression, she clarified. 'You know, your list of things to make you a new woman.'

'Oh. That.'

Amelia filled the kettle. 'Which brings me back to our earlier conversation. You must admit, Maggie, the evidence is stacking up that you need to take control of your life.'

I was silent.

'We were having a laugh the other night, but you said it yourself, you've barely moved on at all. And if your ex is poking fun at you too...'

'I get it.'

Her office kitchen was unbearably tiny.

'Don't look so stricken. That list you made is fun. Use it! Paint the town red. Or pink, even.'

I opened the upper cupboard, finding mugs and a big box of teabags. She was right. I needed a springboard to a new life, and the list might as well get me started. 'Okay.'

'Promise?'

'I promise.' I dropped a teabag into each mug, then, for luck, added an extra to mine.

# Chapter 4

On Tuesday, I surveyed the little house I'd never expected to call home.

When I first got to know Saffron Sweeting, it was a docile village with little going for it. Colin and I certainly didn't set out to buy a second house there.

'You've got to be kidding me,' I'd said, when he came home one night and announced we were now the owners of a narrow cottage in a tiny lane.

'I took it as payment from that Russian bloke.' Colin had reached for the fridge so he could glug milk from the bottle.

'You what?!' I'd been so horrified, I hadn't protested the milk infraction.

'There's no way he'll pay, otherwise. They're going to freeze his assets any day.'

We'd suspected all along the Russian casino mogul was dodgy. And I'd been furious with Colin for not insisting on interim payments for a project renovating his English country home. As the crime squad had closed in, the invoices I'd sent had been a waste of paper.

The news of the cottage had started another marital fight. I'd been unable to make him understand that cash flow, not cottages, was the critical currency for his business. But the deal was done. When the dust settled, we found two graduate students to rent the cottage. I made yet more personal sacrifices to make ends meet, and pretty much forgot about Saffron Sweeting. That was until Colin and I separated, when a habitable asset became much more interesting.

With last week's spontaneous choice of front door paint, the cottage looked more cheerful. There was no getting away from the extensive maintenance it needed – the roof, for starters. I had three different buckets catching leaks in the attic whenever it rained, which this year, seemed to be all the time. There was never enough hot water, and there was a worrying bounce to the upstairs floorboards, which might be damp, or even – ugh – have woodworm. But the stone structure was solid, and the windows – although draughty – were sound.

The bathroom was dated, but in a fairly charming way, with a roll-top bath. The kitchen, however, needed to be torn out, unless someone with more imagination than me could wave a magic wand.

In other words, the cottage needed about a million woman-hours of work. But the front door was a start. I stood there, head on one side. What else would go with that colour? Maybe I could plant some lavender in the front garden, too? And something pink. Roses?

My heart gave a little lurch, which after a second I recognised as excitement. Could there be something in this? Might my friends have a point? Was that crazy list actually a way to move forward, and have some fun? I wasn't sure I remembered what fun felt like.

I gave my magenta front door a little pat. Then I locked it and set off to the bus stop.

~~~

The shop window was crammed full of line drawings.

'Inspiration, presumably,' Grace said in a hushed tone.

'Crumbs,' I replied. 'I don't want an anchor, or a heart, or Betty Boop, and certainly not one that says *mum*.' I inspected the premises for signs of grime and was relieved to find it looked clean.

'So, what *were* you thinking?' Grace asked.

'I dunno.' This had troubled me all morning. Having taken the decision to get a tattoo, I was alarmed I couldn't think of a single defining icon or passion. 'My mind's blank,' I confessed. 'What about you?'

'Not sure. Maybe a butterfly, or a hummingbird. I like hummingbirds. Or a teacup, if they can do it.'

'Do you think it'll hurt much?' My divorce had been a dull, aching process: I didn't fancy trading it for acute pain.

Grace grimaced. 'A bit. Maybe. Yes.'

'Bum.' Then I rallied. 'What about Amelia? Was she telling the truth?'

Amelia had refused point-blank to come with us. 'Sorry, darling, already got one.'

'What of?' I'd asked, at the same time Grace had said, 'Where?'

But Amelia had just smirked. 'Absolutely not telling.'

'What if I get something and hate it?' I said to Grace now. 'It's not like repainting my front door.'

She tilted her head, considering. 'I don't think removal's all that bad, these days. But still, you should pick something you've got a chance of liking until you're eighty.'

'I think I'll get it in the small of my back. That way, if it's awful, I don't have to look at it.'

'Good plan.' She stepped aside for a large, male customer to leave the shop.

'Piece of cake,' said the man, who was bald, but no older than forty. He was dressed in black leather trousers which stretched over his considerable girth, a T-shirt, and a black leather gilet. I couldn't help noticing his arms, where there wasn't an inch of undecorated skin. None of those tattoos looked fresh, so I surmised he'd moved on to other body parts.

'What did you get?' Grace asked him. From her stiff expression, she was pretending to be more blasé than she felt.

'Yellow-eyed penguin.' He grinned. 'Souvenir of my trip to Dunedin.'

'Oh.' I did a terrible job of hiding my surprise. 'Is that how you choose things? Places you've been?' I hadn't been anywhere interesting for years. I wasn't sure what Devon was famous for, and whatever the symbol was for Lyon, I didn't want my mother's adopted city emblazoned on me.

The leather-clad man looked me up and down. 'First time?'

I thought about fibbing, but then looked at my shoes and nodded.

'It's simple,' he said. 'What's your happiest memory?'

The first thing that came to mind was sitting in the treehouse with Matty, when I was no more than seven years old. We'd play up there for hours, content in our secluded world. I was hardly going to get a tree engraved on my back, though: too many complex branches.

'Or, what have you done in the last month that brought you joy? You know, made you feel at one with the universe?'

I looked at him sceptically. He didn't strike me as a guy who would be in touch with his higher bliss.

'She painted her front door,' Grace offered.

'There you go, then. Nothing to it.' The man set off down the street, whistling.

'Come on.' I gave a sigh of melodrama. 'Standing around out here isn't helping. Let's get it over with.'

~~~

We'd staggered about fifty yards from the tattoo shop when Grace sagged onto a bench outside a church. Fortunately, the morning's showers had given way to watery sun.

'Ow,' she said. 'Ow, ow. I took three paracetamol beforehand but it should have been more.'

'Are you okay?' This was a pointless question. In fact, she'd gone a bit green and was shivering. 'Are you having some kind of reaction?'

'Dunno.' She put her head between her knees.

Jeez, I thought. She's got blood poisoning, or something. She's going to pass out, or worse. And then it won't be *my* husband who's on my mind, it'll be hers. James will probably kill me.

'Should I call an ambulance?'

She grunted, shook her head, and mumbled, 'Just sit here... a bit.'

Maybe it was nothing more than the pain. My own tattoo was smarting like crazy.

I looked around the street: a cafe, a hardware store, a newsagent's... and a chemist's. 'Okay. Stay there. Don't move.' That last part was redundant.

I nipped across the road, dodging three bikes and a slow-moving bus, then hurled myself into the chemist's. The front of the shop was full of useless things, like toiletries and ancient gift sets of hand cream. The good stuff – the prescription medications – would be at the back.

I trotted in that direction, grabbing a couple of standard painkiller brands as I passed, and nipped straight up to the counter.

'Hi, hello, do you have something stronger than these?' I waggled the boxes at the pharmacist to get her attention. 'Please, it's rather urgent.' I leaned across her counter, hoping to look both trustworthy and in a terrible hurry.

The pharmacist blinked a couple of times but before she could respond, a self-righteous cough came from beside me.

'Sorr-eh,' began a nasal tone which could have been male or female. 'But there's a queue here, miss.'

I looked, and found the speaker was an elderly man in a knitted cap, thick glasses, and beige raincoat. He was occupying one of the plastic chairs for customers waiting for prescriptions.

'Oh! Sorry!' I said automatically, although I wasn't.

'He's right, this *is* a queue, *actually*.' This came from a tired-looking woman with a baby in a sling.

'I'm terribly sorry,' I said again, then turned my back on them to address the pharmacist. 'But my friend's outside, she's not well, she really needs something. *Now.*'

The duo in the chairs tutted.

The pharmacist hesitated. 'Well, what are these for?' She eyed the boxes I'd plonked on the counter. 'What's the condition?'

I wasn't going to tell the whole shop Grace and I had paid good money to squirt ink into our bloodstream. 'She's just not well. Please, can you give me something stronger?'

From the corner of my eye, I noticed the third person stand up.

'For heaven's sake,' I barked. 'Can you give me a minute while you all wait for your laxatives or whatever you're here for?'

The person coughed. It was a male cough. 'If somebody's been taken ill, I have some training.'

I jerked around, to find a young guy with brown hair. He was taller than me by a few inches.

'Are you a doctor?' I noticed his casual clothes and at least three days of stubble.

He shook his head at the same time as the pharmacist said, 'This is all I can do, without a prescription.'

'Really?' I tried not to snap. 'Please? My friend's in agony out there.'

'Well, why are you in *here* then?' said the elderly man.

I swore under my breath, before throwing a ten pound note on the counter for the pills I'd already got. As I turned, the guy with the stubble was right there.

'I'll come and have a look,' he said. 'If you like?'

Armed only with painkillers strong enough to subdue a mouse, I nodded. 'Okay.'

I led him outside and across the road, avoiding the worst of the puddles. I was relieved to see Grace was still on the bench, and conscious.

'I brought you some Nurofen,' I said, realising we didn't have anything for her to swallow them with.

'Thanks,' she mumbled. 'Doughnut might have been better.'

Thank heavens, I thought. If she can joke about cakes, she'll live.

The guy from the chemist's crouched down. 'I'm Finn. Can you tell me what's wrong?'

Grace looked up at me, and I shrugged. 'He's not a doctor. But he says he can help.'

I snuck a look at him. He wore a grey, long-sleeved T-shirt, jeans, and work boots. I guessed he was in his late twenties, or maybe early thirties at most, a little on the skinny side, but undeniably attractive.

'Where does it hurt? Are you dizzy?' The guy – Finn – was waiting for information.

Grace shook her head and gestured to her back. 'Sorry to be a bother.'

Another good sign: she was apologising.

'So, what happened? Did you fall?' Finn was losing patience. He had, after all, lost his place in the queue, although he looked far too healthy to need a prescription.

I sighed. There was no shame in it. 'Er, we just got tattoos. Grace might be having a reaction.'

Finn glanced up at me. 'Tattoos?'

I nodded. Then I remembered to be defiant. If we wanted to brand our bodies, that was our business. 'Who are you, anyway? If you're not a doctor...'

'I'm a nurse. Sort of.' His attention was on Grace. 'Can you show me?'

Grace grimaced and pulled her T-shirt out of the way with her left hand. Her right shoulder blade was pink and angry, wrapped in some kind of plastic film. 'Ouch.'

'What did you decide on?' We'd been in different cubicles for our tattoos and I felt bad for not being able to tell. 'That's not a hummingbird, is it?'

Grace shook her head. 'Teapot.'

I looked at Finn. 'Is it okay?'

He frowned. 'It's not my expertise. But it doesn't look too bad.'

I thought it looked blooming awful, but I kept quiet. 'So would a painkiller help her?'

'Sure.' He sat down on one side of Grace, while I lowered myself gingerly on the other. Then I delved into one of the little pill boxes.

Seeing I was going to give it to her to chew, Finn pulled a water bottle from his rucksack. 'Here.' He offered it to Grace. 'You won't catch anything.'

'Thanks.' She took two of the pills, and I glugged one back as well, for good luck.

'Does yours hurt too?' Finn leaned around to ask me.

I nodded. 'Once she can walk, I'm heading for a pub and a double brandy. Although I might have to drink it standing up.'

Finn smiled.

'Will it sting like this for long?' I asked, but he shook his head.

'No idea. You might try a topical pain reliever. But keep an eye on her, especially if she gets a fever, yeah? Get help fast if she does.'

'Okay. Thanks.'

'You're talking about me like I'm not here.' Grace sighed. 'All I need is a nice cup of tea and I'll be right as rain.'

I patted her knee. 'That's the spirit. We'll find somewhere for a cuppa in a minute.'

'So what did *you* get?' Finn asked, meaning me.

'Never you mind,' I said.

'She got a moon.' Grace presumably wanted to be helpful to this kind stranger.

'Can I see?' From the way Finn's eyes danced, I doubted it was a medical enquiry.

To be safe, I glared at him. The tattoo was a classic side profile of the man in the moon, with a shower of stars falling.

He read my look. 'Never mind. I shouldn't have asked.'

'It's pretty,' Grace offered. Mine was finished after hers, so she'd seen it.

It *was* pretty, at least I hoped it would be, when the redness on my upper thigh abated. I'd gone for my leg in the end, not my back, as the tattoo artist said it would hurt less.

'So, why'd you get a moon?' Finn sat forward on the bench so he could see me better.

I paused. He was a complete stranger, not a doctor but a sort-of-nurse, and although he seemed nice enough, he might be a total nutcase for all I knew. 'Shouldn't you be getting back? To the chemist's? For whatever you...'

He shrugged. 'Yeah, in a bit. I was waiting for my gran's blood pressure pills.'

'Okay,' I said. 'We'll be fine, now.'

'So, not laxatives.' His eyes twinkled. They were an unusual golden brown, almost amber. 'Just to be clear.'

Not only had I jumped the queue, I'd snapped at an old-age pensioner, and accused everyone of needing pills to help them poop. 'Right, er, sorry about that.'

Grace didn't understand the joke, but colour was returning to her face. 'Yes, come on, Maggie, why *did* you choose a moon?'

I shrugged. It was no big deal, was it? 'It's my maiden name. Moone, with an E.' It was time I went back to using it.

'It suits you,' Grace said. Then, for no obvious reason, she told Finn, 'She's divorced.'

At the other end of the bench, Finn nodded. 'Nice to meet you, Maggie Moone.' His accent was soft and rolling, not from the Cambridge area. 'Sounds like an Irish name,' he added. 'Are you Irish, Maggie?'

It felt strange to hear my maiden name after so long. I probably hadn't heard it since my wedding day, way back when Pluto was a planet. But I liked the way it sounded, especially from him.

'No.' I realised where his origins must lie. 'From Yorkshire, originally. Sorry.'

Bah, I added mentally: must stop saying *sorry* for no good reason. There was nothing wrong with where I came from.

'That's a shame,' he said. 'You even look Irish.'

I had no idea what he meant by that. It couldn't be my eyes, which are a dull brown, not green. Could it be my pale skin? Or my troublesome hair, escaping from its ponytail? I found myself touching a strand, and dropped it.

'Still.' He turned back to Grace. 'What possessed the two of you to get yourselves branded, now?'

Grace gave him a half smile. 'As a sort of dare.'

'Oh, no, not really a dare.' I didn't want to tell a stranger that I'd marked my body in a grumpy rebellion against my ex-husband. 'More, er, a celebration.'

He smiled, showing white teeth. One was chipped, a tiny bit missing.

I decided a change of subject was needed. 'How are you doing?' I asked Grace. 'Can you walk to a teashop? Or a pub, maybe?'

My friend rolled her shoulder and winced. 'If you don't mind, I'd just like to go home and sleep.'

'Okay.' I ducked my head to check her watch. 'There's a Saffron Sweeting bus in twenty minutes. Or should I phone for a taxi?'

Parking in Cambridge was notoriously impossible, but now I cursed the decision to leave our cars at home.

She shook her head. 'Bus is fine. I'll be all right.' Then, she leaned in towards me and stage whispered something about my fist.

'My what?' I hissed back.

'Your *list*. Doctors.' This was accompanied by an unsubtle jerk of her head.

Oh no. She had to be joking. Anyway, he wasn't a doctor, he was a sort-of-nurse. Whatever that meant. Perhaps he was a caregiver, or physiotherapist, or something.

'Come on,' she whispered again. 'He'd be perfect. He's sexy.'

Finn was looking at us curiously.

'You're right.' I raised my voice to normal level. 'You're quite right, there was another bus we just *missed*.' I grasped her good elbow to coax her off the bench, trying to ignore the shooting pain in my thigh and praying I had some brandy at home. 'It was nice to meet you,' I added, not looking at our Irish acquaintance.

'Thanks for the help.' Grace turned to him, despite my vice-like grip on her arm.

'Yes,' I muttered. 'Thanks.'

'Hope you feel better, Grace.' Finn got up too, pulling his rucksack onto his shoulder. 'And you take care as well, Maggie Moone.'

From the corner of my eye, I caught his smile.

# Chapter 5

As spring nudged into East Anglia, the bluebells in the woods at Saffron Hall were not the only harbingers of fine weather. The villagers of Saffron Sweeting took on a collective urge to spruce up their homes and surroundings. With faint April sunshine peeking through windows, and back doors flung open for the first time in months, there was a surge of activity. In the space of a week, I bumped into the local chimney sweep twice, and saw a roof thatcher begin his fascinating but painstaking work at the Old Forge.

News of my handywoman capabilities spread like weeds after rain.

First was the vicar, wringing his hands over the jammed latch on the churchyard gate.

'Bless your heart, and your hands,' he said, as I braced my good hip against the gate to work on the mechanism. My other thigh – the one with the new tattoo – was still tender, a bit like sunburn, but not bad, considering. Grace, too, had confirmed her pain had abated by the next morning.

'Last Sunday,' the vicar went on, 'I thought we were all going to have to scale the wall.'

I laughed. 'You're very welcome, vicar.' He'd not been with the village long – he was shared with two other parishes – and he didn't need a mutiny amongst his fresh flock. Then I made my escape before he could inquire about my own churchgoing habits.

From there, I was needed to mend a squeaky floorboard above the post office, and to change a washer on a leaky tap at the pub. An old lady who lived next to Amelia had no fewer than four extinct light bulbs. Those took me ten minutes and naturally, I didn't charge her a penny. To my surprise, I found I was enjoying myself, but it did make me realise how much work my own cottage needed too.

'Darling, you can't be serious?' Amelia said, as I finished changing the locks on an empty house she was selling. 'I know you have a knack for it, but surely you're not *liking* these odds and sods?' She made it sound as though I was embalming corpses at the morgue, or cleaning public toilets.

'Actually,' I replied, 'I do. It's nice to be useful. And the results are so... tangible. Not like taxes.' It was strange how much relief people expressed over minor household repairs. I suppose a blocked loo is kind of a big deal when you're ninety, with elbows too weak to work a plunger.

'Anyway,' I continued, 'it's not just odds and sods. Kenneth wants me to glam up his whole kitchen.'

'Kenneth? From the library? What does that old fart want with a fancy kitchen?'

I smiled. 'He's not that much of an old fart.' I helped him occasionally with the library's accounts and we'd had some interesting chats in the cool, musty silence. He kept a re-homed parrot there, in the children's section, but had promised me the bird was discreet. 'Apparently, he's met someone. They're getting serious, but she loves to cook. She says there's no way she's moving in unless he rips out his kitchen.'

'Good grief, Kenneth in love, perish the thought.' She paused. 'Is his kitchen a disaster?'

I grimaced. 'It's not good. I'm hoping Grace might have some ideas. You know... paint, or something.'

'Or a bulldozer. Rather you than me, darling.'

'It'll be fine,' I said, and crossed my fingers.

~~~

Grace and I crossed the road by the duck pond and continued at a steady pace along the high street, towards the malt house. We'd anticipated parking would be a nightmare, and opted to go on foot.

'How's your tattoo?' I asked. It was a fortnight since our adventures at the wrong end of a needle. 'No complications?'

'It's fine, thank goodness. Swollen as heck for the first week, though. How about you?'

'Same.' I'd spent much of the first ten days peering at it. The oozing and scabbing had frightened me, but once it peeled, the moon underneath was lovely. 'Glad it was a small one, though. How did James take it?'

'He wasn't too fussed. I was surprised. I don't suppose Colin's seen yours?'

I shook my head. I'd overlooked how I might casually inform Colin of my new tattoo, or better still, show him. It wasn't like we'd be bumping into each other at the swimming pool, after all. I loved to swim, whereas he avoided it. In fact, that was a drawback to my whole plan: how was I going to make sure he found out about my antics?

'This certainly wouldn't be here without Amelia,' Grace said, as we arrived at the malt house. Now the pride and joy of Saffron Sweeting, the ancient building had been gravely threatened. Amelia had led the efforts to save it.

'It doesn't quite seem like her thing.' I admired the imposing building, formerly vital for processing grain into malt. Today, it was decorated with bunting. 'I mean, I see her more at the opera or somewhere, in London.'

'You're right,' Grace said. 'It was a surprise. But she got all competitive about it. She's friends with the man who wanted to turn it into flats, but nonetheless, she enjoyed thwarting his plans.'

So, I wasn't the only one who got a kick from doing the opposite of what a man wanted. 'But it seems a bit twisted to deliberately mess with a friend.'

Grace shot me a sidelong look. 'It was complicated.'

And, hats off to Amelia, the renovated malt house had been a huge success. Against the odds, her zealous team had not only saved the dilapidated structure, but managed to turn it into a centre for artists, crafts, and special events.

That's precisely what was happening today: a healthy living exhibition was in full swing.

We paid a pound each for admission and plunged into the throng of stalls, crafts, wellness offerings, and chattering visitors. The malt house was packed and conversations bounced off its wooden walls.

'Where shall we start?' Grace raised her voice to be heard.

'Let's work in a circle, shall we?' I gestured to my left, to a stand of yoga clothing.

From there, we progressed past a chiropractor, nutrition coach, and the Women's Institute. We browsed offerings including organic vitamins, candles, and meditation chimes. Grace stopped to chat with her friend Bella, who had a stall promoting her flapjack business. She introduced us to her boyfriend, Leo, who was the master craftsman behind the gorgeous wood restoration inside the malt house.

Today, he was helping her, and they were struggling to keep up with the demand for her free samples.

'Caraway and fig!' Bella announced. 'Thanks to you, Maggie.'

I'd been out to her little factory-warehouse the previous week, to install new shelving. Presumably, the work was too mundane for Leo to bother with, but it was a good match for my skills.

Bella had been testing new flapjack recipes, which I had to admit was more fun than drilling into walls. Together, we'd contemplated caraway combined with apricot, cherry, or fig.

Now, I chewed on the little sample. 'It's good.' The fig was a clever addition.

Sustained by flapjacks, we encountered further stalls selling crafts. Their links to healthy living were more tenuous, but they were pretty, nonetheless.

'Oh, look!' Grace stopped. 'Dream catchers.'

I was only partly familiar with the concept, but admired the pretty objects dangling from a display of wooden branches.

'Should I get one for my cottage?' Apart from the front door, I hadn't done much yet to personalise the place. It wasn't my strong suit.

'Why not?' Grace replied. 'Hey, a moon!'

I looked, and saw a small crescent moon, made of crisscrossed wires and a cluster of teal-coloured feathers. I reached out to touch it, not sure why it appealed to me.

'It's handmade,' said the stallholder, a young woman with blue eyes and hair in a pixie cut. She unhooked it from the branch, encouraging me to touch it.

'You should get it, Maggie,' Grace said.

'Wait,' said the stallholder.

My hand hovered in mid-air as she snatched the dream catcher back.

'This one's sold.' She reached under the table for wrapping tissue.

I glanced at Grace, confused. 'But—'

'Sorry, sold,' the woman repeated, making a deft little parcel. Then she held it out. 'To you.'

'I don't understand.' I eyed the dream catcher. Was this the ultimate in pushy selling? 'I don't think—' I hadn't even checked the price, after all.

'It's a gift.' The stallholder smiled and I tentatively took the package. Then she continued, 'A friend of mine stopped by earlier, while we were all setting up. He said, in the event that a young woman named Maggie showed interest in a moon, that he would like to buy it for you. So there it is. It's yours.'

My mouth dropped open.

'No way,' said Grace. 'How cool! Who do you think—?'

I swallowed hard. Things like this never happened to me. 'Friend of yours...?' I managed.

'That's all I'm allowed to say.' The stallholder placed a finger over her lips.

I shook my head. I had hardly any male friends, and nobody mysterious who traded in dream catchers. Vincent came to mind, but this wasn't his style at all.

'So how do we thank him?' Grace had her wits together. 'Will you tell us his name?'

'Nope.' The pixie-haired seller shook her head. 'But he said he'll be waiting in the car park.'

'The car park?' This was getting bizarre.

'Yep. In the car park. Look for the big white van.'

~ ~ ~

Grace's eyes lit up and she practically dragged me out of the malt house towards the car park in the adjacent field.

'No!' I protested, heels digging in as best I could. 'No way am I pursuing any strange men in white vans!'

'We can just look.' She was undeterred by my dragging weight. 'It's romantic!'

'It's not romantic,' I said. 'It's creepy.'

Even so, my mind was reeling. Who could it be, and how on earth did he guess I'd want one of those dream catchers?

We arrived at the field, and thanks to a few dry days, it wasn't a total quagmire. Grace's frantic pace slowed. 'I don't see any white vans,' she said.

I swivelled my head, aware that we might have been misdirected. Maybe the creepy moon guy was watching from across the street. But I saw nothing unusual. No one loitering, no lurkers in cars, no drones overhead. Heart rate slowing, I turned back to the field of cars.

'You're right,' I agreed. 'Nothing.' There was a tiny prick of disappointment.

'Unless that counts.' Grace pointed.

'What?'

'There. The blood donation thing.'

I looked. At the far end of the car park was a small white lorry, with a bold red stripe down one side. It was emblazoned with the NHS logo and two interconnected hearts.

'Seriously?' I gave a half laugh. 'The blood wagon? No way.'

'Well, it might be.' Grace shaded her eyes, scanning the cars one last time. 'There's nothing else. Come on, let's go and see.'

'No.' I stood firm.

'Why not?'

'It's a trap,' I said, somewhat illogically.

Grace laughed. 'Hardly. It's the National Health Service.'

'I don't care. It might be... he could have—'

'What?' Grace shook her head. 'You think a crazy vampire guy stole a mobile blood unit, and made up a ruse with a moon, so he could kidnap you and suck your blood?'

I sniffed. Okay, that did sound outlandish.

'I'll come with you,' Grace said, but before I could begin arguing again, a man appeared at the top of the van's steps. He was wearing what looked like surgical scrubs: a dark turquoise top with navy trousers. The next moment, he spotted us. To my amazement, he waved.

'Oh, look!' Grace let go of my arm. 'Isn't that—?'

'I think so. Yes.' I felt a jolt of surprise as the penny dropped. This time, as Grace tugged my arm, I didn't resist. By the time we'd picked through the muddy grass to the van, the man was leaning on the railing attached to the small flight of steps, watching us approach.

'Well, hello there, Maggie Moone.' He grinned.

It was the Irish guy, from the day we got tattoos. Finn.

'Hello,' Grace called up to him. 'Fancy seeing you here.'

'Hi.' He smiled at her too. 'Feeling better?' Then he looked at me again. '*You* look a wee bit pale, Maggie.'

'I'm fine,' I said feebly.

Grace looked from him to me, no doubt wondering if she should fill the gap in a conversation that hadn't even started.

Finn's smile faded. 'Er, we met in Mill Road, remember?'

I nodded. 'But, er, what are you doing here?'

'You got your moon, then?' he said, not answering my question.

I nodded again. 'But I'm a bit confused.' I tried again. 'How come you're here?'

He shrugged and came down the steps of the blood van.

'I took a bit of a chance,' he said. 'I remembered, you mentioned you were getting the bus to Saffron Sweeting, and thought maybe you lived here. And then work,' he gestured to the van, 'needed folk for this, and I figured I'd give it a shot.'

'And... the dream catcher?' Grace prodded, finally understanding how freaked out I was.

'Ah, yes, I admit, that was an impulse. I didn't think you'd come and hang out here otherwise.' He pointed again at the blood unit.

'So you *are* a doctor?' I tried, although I was pretty sure I hadn't hit on the right term. And I was still processing the information that he'd engineered another meeting, or at least taken a gamble that he'd bump into us again. Or me. Had he spotted Grace's wedding ring?

'Charge nurse,' Finn said.

Did I imagine it, or did he glance at me for my reaction? I kept my face neutral, and in any case, I was trying to make sense of the dream catcher.

'You collect blood for a living?' Grace asked him.

'That's right. You interested? You get a free cup of tea, after.'

Grace hesitated. 'Er, not sure... sorry...'

Serves her right, I thought, for dragging me across this field. If she has to roll up her sleeve and spill a few pints, maybe she'll think twice in future. Mischief tugged at me; I was fed up playing the passive friend today.

'I can donate,' I said. 'I don't mind. Come on, Grace.'

Finn turned to me. It would be a cliché to say he looked good in uniform, but I wasn't immune to the clean crispness of the look. He hadn't shaved, though, which added a touch of incongruity.

'Ahh, Maggie... sorry, but no.'

'No?'

'That won't work.' He shook his head, but his eyes were teasing.

'Why not?' I felt a flash of irritation. 'What's wrong with me? I'm healthy.'

Grace looked intrigued, too. 'I bet it's the tattoos. Are we banned because of those?'

Finn smiled. 'Good point. I'd forgotten about those. But, in any case... well, I'm afraid it wouldn't be ethical.'

'What wouldn't?' I asked, which was probably what he intended.

He shrugged. 'For me to stick a needle in your arm, it wouldn't be right, now.'

'Why not?' For some bizarre reason, I suddenly wanted to give blood. Very much. My pulse had even quickened, in anticipation of doing my civic duty.

Finn looked at the ground. 'Well, let's just say it's best if I don't.' He took a breath, then met my eye with a mixture of playfulness and uncertainty. 'Because I'm about to ask you on a date.'

'You're a genius,' I said to Grace, as she completed her assessment of options for turning Kenneth's ancient kitchen into a pleasant space.

'Happy to help.' She handed me her list.

Considering Kenneth's budget was tiny, we'd only been able to afford a one-hour consultation at her friends-and-family rate. I'd be on my own from here. But Grace had given us loads of ideas. Her recommendations included painting the cabinets, changing the lights, and swapping the dingy curtains for a roller blind. Considering Grace was so mild and agreeable when I saw her socially, at work she was surprisingly assertive.

'That *might* leave some budget for a new fridge,' Grace said. 'Ideally, replace that small one with a dishwasher. Get rid of that wonky little table, and put a tall fridge there instead.'

'Goodness.' Kenneth's eyes were wide behind his glasses. 'You really have looked at this place with fresh eyes.'

'I'd never have come up with this on my own,' I agreed. 'I don't have the knack for it.'

Grace pulled a ream of paint swatches from her shoulder bag. 'Well, Maggie, if you can actually make this stuff happen, then that's its own kind of genius.' She frowned. 'Don't suppose you can change the taps, too?'

I shrugged. There were many hours of work here, but it would be fun to attempt the makeover. 'Don't see why not.'

Grace's gaze continued to rove. She pointed to a motley collection of pans, vases, and baskets stuffed in the space above the cabinets. 'Kenneth, you need to declutter. Get rid of stuff you're not using, okay?'

This was what Colin's new wife Keiko did for a living: bullied people into getting rid of their junk. She called it professional organising, though. From what I heard, she excelled at it and her clients worshiped her. But most people were attached to their stuff, right? I mean, I'd hardly been able to look at Dad's place when he died. I waited for Kenneth to object.

'Yes, dear, all right.'

Wow, he must really want to make his lady friend happy. That was sweet. I noticed he'd followed Grace's gaze to the stack of magazines on the table where the new fridge was supposed to go. 'Oh my, yes, I'm behind on my reading.' Then he caught my eye. 'Bit of a guilty secret, Maggie. These are library subscriptions, but I wanted a quick peek first.'

I looked at the pile too, noticing the magazine on top. 'Are you a railway fan? My dad was crazy about trains.' It would have been his birthday today. The magazine had a feature on an upcoming auction, billed as a once-in-a-century opportunity for collectors.

'Oh, no, not per se,' Kenneth said. 'But I like old things. Sometimes I sneak into the back of auctions, and try to guess what things are worth.'

I picked up the heavy magazine and began to flick through its glossy pages. The antiques and collectibles world was, it seemed, eagerly awaiting the upcoming sale of railway art and memorabilia at a small auction house in Bury St Edmunds. I listened with half an ear as Grace asked if I could replace the kitchen flooring.

'Probably.' I was deep in the magazine now, but the floor looked like vinyl, so I could lay something fresh.

'Super.' She consulted her paint colours. 'Now, Kenneth, how do you feel about this one, called Lichen? And on this wall, I'd love to do Green Smoke.'

'That's appropriate,' I said, as my gaze fell on a half-page spread of a painting of a steam train. The engine was a deep bottle green, and it was belching out clouds of smoke and steam as it climbed a hill. I turned the page, then flipped back. 'Well, I never.'

'What?' Kenneth asked me, perhaps delaying his agreement to Grace's rather bold colour choice.

I peered at the page, and smiled. 'My dad had this painting.'

Kenneth came to look over my shoulder, but Grace was still holding paint swatches up to the walls.

'Over his fireplace.' I tilted my head to stare at the familiar scene. 'A print of it, obviously. Not the original.'

It had hung in his study in Burwell, then later, when he'd moved back to Yorkshire, above the mantelpiece in his little terraced cottage. A spot which every kid senses as pride of place. Seeing it again was so strange. It had been a daily fixture in my youth, something I'd barely glanced at. Now, I realised that every detail was familiar to me: the big, green steam locomotive, labouring up the hill, with three young boys running beside it on a farm track.

'*Chasing the Train*,' Kenneth read, from the caption beside the picture. 'Very nice. That's the kind of thing that counted for entertainment, back then of course. Trying to beat a train up a hill.'

'Wow.' I ran my finger over the magazine, amazed at the effect it had on me. The muted browns and greens of the countryside and steam locomotive weren't just familiar; it was as if they'd chugged off the page, bundled me into one of the carriages, and puffed and hissed and whistled me back to Yorkshire. This painting was practically in my DNA.

'Are you all right?' Grace asked, tearing herself away from her Farrow & Ball paint reverie. 'Maggie, you look like you've had a blast of steam up your skirt.'

'Let's see what it might fetch.' Kenneth leaned in, then gave a surprised grunt. 'For that? Well, I'll be damned.'

I found the price in the accompanying text, and couldn't help but laugh. 'Pity my dad's was only a print. He had a Monet upstairs, too.'

I gave the magazine back to Kenneth, who clearly found it more interesting than imagining his new kitchen.

'I wonder who's selling it?' He turned the page, looking for the full auction listing, before announcing the name. Then he added, 'Never heard of him,' and threw the magazine on the table. 'Shall I make some tea for you, ladies?'

My stomach lurched. 'Say that again, could you?'

'Say what?'

Had I heard him right? 'The person *selling the painting.*' My words were clipped and urgent.

Kenneth had already moved to the sink. Grace gave me a funny look, but seeing that I appeared frozen to the spot, reached for the magazine. 'Okay, hang on, where is it?' She ran her finger down the page. 'Er, *Chasing the Train...* offered at auction by Brissinghorn & Beem. Seller is Colin Farris, private collector.' She read on, oblivious to my reaction. '*Stolen in the infamous Harrogate heist, and never recovered. Miraculously came to light last year in the Pickering attic of a train enthusiast.*'

By now, there wasn't just steam in the painting, but it had puffed off the page and was swirling around my eyes. I sagged against the cupboard behind me.

'Maggie?' Grace's voice came through the white cloud. 'Are you okay?'

I wasn't okay. The steam in my vision was joined by a whistling in my ears.

'Hey, Mag!' Grace's voice sounded high up, so perhaps my knees were already buckling.

'I think,' I said, as my bottom encountered the doomed vinyl of Kenneth's floor, 'I'd really like to sit down.'

~~~

Later, as Grace and I braved the drizzle and headed for the bakery for a much-needed sugar infusion, I said, 'Thanks for your help. I owe you big time.'

'No worries. I won't forget you can do all these nifty DIY jobs, once I start tarting up my place.'

'Oh yeah? When?'

It was a running joke in the village that Grace designed stunning spaces for her clients, yet her own cottage was coming along at a snail's pace. That could be why she spent so much time at Amelia's: she was the only one of us three whose roof was watertight.

But, like the good friend she was, my attempt to divert the conversation didn't work.

'Never mind that.' She moved her umbrella so she could see me better. 'What happened with that magazine? And the painting?'

'I think it's my dad's.'

'Yes, but he had a print, right?'

I took a breath. 'When Dad died, I couldn't face clearing out his cottage. I'd been up there, living with him and helping, for the last year of his life. But it was simply too much for me, I was exhausted. He, er, collected things... a *lot* of things. I had total decision paralysis. Couldn't let anything go.'

With no wife to protest, Dad's house was jammed full of books, old timetables, and railway paraphernalia.

'Okay...' One of Grace's biggest strengths was listening.

'And Colin is so much better at that kind of thing. I think that's why he's so compatible with Keiko. Anyway, he eventually offered to do it for me. We divided things up: I got the empty cottage here in Saffron Sweeting, and he took Dad's place, including the contents.'

'I see where we're going,' Grace said. 'Your dad was an art buff?'

I shook my head. 'No. Not art in particular. But he loved railways, especially steam trains.'

He'd moved from Cambridge back to Yorkshire when he and Mum split up. As a fourteen-year-old, I didn't question it, but later I saw that the major attraction had been the proximity to Pickering railway station, where preserved steam trains still ran. It was close enough that we could hear their whooshing and tooting.

'So he had a painting of a train...'

'...Which I always assumed was a copy. You know, a cheap print. Worth less than the frame it was in.'

'And it looks like it *wasn't* a print?'

'No.' I sighed. 'It seems it wasn't.'

'But who's selling it, then? Who stands to benefit?'

This was the part I had trouble believing myself. 'My ex. Farris is his mum's maiden name. He uses it for privacy sometimes.'

I didn't mention that he occasionally used Farris in business dealings he wanted to keep under wraps, too.

'The magazine claimed it turned up miraculously,' Grace said.

'Miraculous is a strong word.'

We paused outside the bakery window to admire the display of pastries and cakes. The weather had fogged the glass, but we could see an array which included Chelsea buns, millionaire's shortbread, and mini fruit pies.

'I mean, a miracle is a cure for cancer, or a predictor of tsunamis,' I said. 'Or even finding someone to help you locate the size of screw you want in Homebase on a Saturday afternoon. Not an ex-husband on the make.'

Grace looked at me in the rain-splattered reflection of the window. 'Are you furious?'

'I don't know, honestly. A bit stunned, I guess. But not furious. Not yet, anyway.'

'Did Colin know all along, that the painting was valuable?'

I shrugged. 'Hard to say. But if he did, he's made a right fool out of me. Again.' I winced as I said this. The award ceremony had been a public humiliation, whereas this was private. But the money at stake stung. We'd been so civilised, so careful to be fair in our divorce. Had Colin really pulled a five-figure trick on me? If the estimate of the painting's price was anywhere near correct, the proceeds would cover the cost of my new roof. And probably new central heating, too.

'Well. All the more reason for you to go out with that Irish guy.'

'Sorry?'

'Your list, remember? For asserting your independence?' Grace pushed open the door of the bakery. 'If Colin's making fun of you and selling your family assets, it's time for you to make fun of him back. Phone up that hunky Irish bloke, go on a date. And make sure you have the time of your life.'

~ ~ ~

Before I went to bed that night, I decided to review the list of things which would wind Colin up. My cottage was so chaotic, it took me a while to hunt it down.

I found it, eventually, in the bag I'd taken with me to Amelia's. I only used three bags regularly. There was my practical rucksack: the grey one from Black's. There was my smart rucksack, a nice metallic brown, with the requisite straps for keeping my hands free. And there was the mini rucksack. This one was black nylon, and I liked to kid myself it served as an evening bag.

'For Pete's sake, Maggie,' Colin used to say. 'We're going out to dinner, not up Scafell Pike.'

He didn't like my clothes, either. 'But they're comfortable,' I would say, when he complained about my tough cotton shirts. 'They wear well and they go straight in the wash.'

All right, so maybe a woman doesn't need a dozen flannel shirts in varying checked patterns, but I loved my shirts. They were warm and reliable, unlike my husband.

My bed wasn't warm enough on that late April evening, either. I lay awake until late, the wind rattling my window, trying to make sense of what had happened. After midnight came and went, I switched on the radio beside my bed.

At first, I dwelt on the painting, going over in my head the chaos after Dad died, the horrible timing of my divorce, and Colin's offer – which truly had seemed like he was being helpful – to sort out Dad's house in Yorkshire, if I took the place in Saffron Sweeting. Had he known about the value of the painting? How could he?

My brain swirled around and got nowhere, and my thoughts turned to Finn. When I'd last seen him, standing outside his blood donation lorry at the wellness fair, I'd been non-committal about a date. After all, it was about a dozen years since the last time I'd been properly asked out, and I suspected it wasn't in the least like riding a bike.

However, I'd agreed to put his phone number in my pocket.

On the one hand, I wasn't the type of person who picked up men on the street, or in a chemist's shop, for that matter. Although, Grace had needed some help that day, so perhaps the encounter could be put down to chance.

But then there was the unlikely aspect of Finn turning up in Saffron Sweeting. Was that flattering, or just far-fetched? The way he engineered our meeting with the dream catcher, what was he, psychic? That had rattled me more than anything: the fact that he'd taken a chance like that, and I'd walked right into it.

Yet I had to admit, as the Radio 4 Shipping Forecast began, he didn't *seem* creepy. I mean, he was a medical professional, that must have meant loads of background checks. Could it be as simple as... he liked me, he'd taken a gamble?

The notion of him liking me didn't sit easily. Never mind my last date as a teenager. Since my divorce, I'd barely attempted any contact with men.

Yes, there was the time – when, last autumn? – that I'd tried the online thing, but that didn't last long. The first guy had been nice, but then his mother in Lockerbie fell ill, he dashed off up there, and that was the end of that. The second man had recently been made redundant. Every time he had a drink, he started talking about his ex-employer, and on one occasion broke down and cried in the middle of a pub. And my final effort, the third guy, was a building safety inspector by profession. Every time we went somewhere, he unnerved me by peering at the roof, or jiggling a fire exit door, and then sucking air through his teeth. I couldn't relax around him. The final straw was when he came to my ramshackle cottage for dinner one night. I swear he couldn't get out fast enough.

So after my trial period of online dating expired, I hadn't bothered to renew it. And that had been that.

The Shipping Forecast ended and I lay there in the darkness, calculating how long it was until my alarm would go off. I couldn't get my thoughts away from the two encounters with Finn. If, as it seemed, he liked me, I was forced to admit I liked him too. His manner was so relaxed, I hadn't been sure he was flirting until he'd asked me out. There was nothing predatory about him – unless you counted sticking needles in people for a living. His voice was attractive, but there was something more than his lilting accent. Maybe it was the way he said my name, Maggie Moone. My new name.

There was no denying, Colin had moved on miles from our marriage. Not only did he have a new wife, he was blithely auctioning off my family heirlooms. It was time I made some changes, too.

And Finn might just fit the bill.

## Chapter 7

'I'll have to cancel!' I wailed. 'There's no way I can go.' I leapt up from where I'd been sitting on my bed, surrounded by clothes.

'Rubbish.' Grace was on the floor, trying to untangle a pile of my belts. 'Amelia, tell her she has to go.'

'Of course you'll go.' Amelia reached out one long finger, placed it with terrifying accuracy on the soft flesh by my collar bone, and pushed me back down again. 'Why on earth wouldn't you?'

'Because I'm newly divorced!'

'You're not newly divorced,' Grace said, splitting hairs as usual.

'And it's only a daytime jaunt,' Amelia added, holding up the blue tunic I'd worn yesterday. 'Is this it?' She pulled an exaggerated face. 'A dozen checked shirts and a blue top?'

'We should go shopping,' Grace suggested. 'Amelia's brilliant, she'll get you kitted out.'

'No time.' Amelia looked at her watch. 'I have to open in a minute.'

It was a Saturday, always her busiest day at Hargraves & Co. As it was, she was running late.

'Oh, jeez.' I put my head in my hands.

'Look.' Amelia put her hands on her hips. 'Which are your best jeans? The darkest, tightest pair?'

I pointed. We were now in early May, but there was a nippy breeze today. Jeans would be fine.

'Put those on.' She stuck her head into my wardrobe and started pulling out single shoes. 'Grace, darling,' she waved a summery wedge, which I never wore, 'see if you can find the other one of these. Maggie can walk in them, but they'll look like she made an effort.'

'And how about this?' Grace joined in on the bullying. 'It's your lucky colour, after all.' At the back of my small –

and jammed – wardrobe, she'd found a magenta T-shirt with a scoop neck.

'I never wear pink.' I shook my head.

'Clearly.' Amelia nodded. 'The labels are still on.'

~~~

So there I was, propelled towards my first date with Finn in a new top and wobbly shoes.

At least it was a lovely day, I thought, as I waited at Cambridge station, watching the crowds of tourists weaving around, looking either for the right platform if they were outbound, or the best route to the city centre, if they'd just arrived.

I wondered what it would be like to live in a city which wasn't a magnet for visitors. One-dimensional, probably. The time I'd spent in Yorkshire, first as a teenager from a broken home, then nursing my dad, had left me restless. And yet I didn't need the bright lights of London. This was a happy medium for me. I could only guess at what had brought Finn to Cambridge.

'Well, hello, Maggie Moone.' On cue, he interrupted my thoughts with that soft voice which invited the listener to lean closer.

'Hello.' I turned to him, shy. How long had it been since I'd met a man at a railway station? Come to that, had I ever met a man there?

'I wasn't sure you'd be showing up today.' He pushed his brown hair back. At my questioning look, he continued, 'I was pretty certain I'd spooked you with the blood wagon stunt.'

'It was certainly...' I searched for a word. 'Memorable.'

Despite myself, I smiled. I *had* been spooked by Finn popping up in Saffron Sweeting. But a detail like that wasn't going to stop me proving to Colin that I'd moved on.

In any case, Finn wasn't in his blood-sucking uniform today. He was back in jeans, with a cotton shirt that looked so worn, I decided he hadn't had wardrobe help from friends. He had, however, shaved.

Then I chastised myself for noticing details like that, and for speculating about his preparations for our afternoon. It wasn't as if I was *interested* in him and his flirty Irish accent, after all. This was just a bit of fun.

'So, what did you have in mind?' I gestured around us, aware that if he wanted to go for a long walk, my shoes would mean trouble.

'Well, I was hoping to reassure you I'm entirely average, and definitely not a vampire.'

'I never said you were a vampire.' But he'd guessed my doubts.

'It's okay. I'm used to it. So, to show you I'm completely normal, how about we start off with some casual animal abuse?'

'Huh?' My mouth dropped. Sure, Colin was vegan, but I wasn't about to hurt anything with four legs, simply to get back at him.

'Eel throwing, to be more specific,' said Finn.

'You what?' Good grief, *what* was that? And what kind of man suggested it for a first date? Or any date, for that matter?

'Relax.' He laughed. 'I know how it sounds. It's over at Ely. Today's their eel festival and if we hurry, we'll be in time to lob some cuddly fakes around. We might win something.'

'Really?' I must have looked doubtful.

'And my gran's running a cake stall. Fundraiser... I sort of said I'd go.'

I breathed out. The eel throwing involved stuffed toys, we'd be at a public event, and there would be cake.

Finn was waiting for my response.

'They're not selling eel-flavoured cookies, are they?'

He grinned. 'I've no idea. Want to find out?'

Three eel-packed hours later, I asked if we could sit down for a bit. My wedge shoes did indeed look just right, and they'd even coped with the grass on Palace Green where the stalls had been set up, but my calves weren't used to heels.

'Well.' I sank onto what might be the only empty bench in Ely. 'That was a first.'

'You're right there. Hope it wasn't too weird.'

We'd watched a procession led by a giant carnival eel, locally known as Ellie. We'd sampled eel-inspired dishes, including smoked eel with beetroot, pea soup with eel, and an electric eel mocktail. I'd declined the eel appletini but risked a brownie with a sugar eel decoration on top. And I'd been reminded that the city of Ely had been named after the Isle of Eels. These, apparently, used to be a staple of the local diet.

'I must suggest to my friend Nancy that she comes here on a non-eel day.' I glanced at Finn. 'She's American. She'd go nuts over the cathedral.'

'And how is your pal with the tattoo? Grace? All okay?'

I nodded, but was impressed that he'd remembered. Before he could ask again to see mine, I changed the subject back to the day's events.

'You were so close to winning, with your eel throw.'

'Ack, I was robbed,' he replied. 'Sixteen metres, and no prize. For shame.' He was pretending to be crestfallen.

'Imagine... grown men queuing up to launch stuffed toys at a target.' I couldn't quite believe the eel throwing had been an actual activity.

'You're right. We should have used real ones.' But he was smiling. 'So will you be ordering eel, next time you see it on the menu?'

I shook my head. 'I'll pass, if you don't mind. But your gran's lemon courgette cake was top notch.'

He nodded. 'She's a grand baker.' He shot a sidelong glance at me. 'I think she liked you, too.'

I checked to see if he was smirking. As we'd walked up to his grandma's cake stall, Finn had placed his hand briefly on the small of my back, but then dropped it before I could decide if I liked it. His grandmother had been formidable, clearly from no-nonsense Irish stock. She'd looked at me like I was no more appealing than one of the poor eels heading for someone's pie.

After a few seconds, I opted for honesty.

'Well, she scared me no end.'

He laughed. I liked the way his eyes danced when he was amused. Today, they really did look amber.

'She was in a good mood, actually. If you want to see her being scary, you should come to bingo.'

'Bingo?'

'Yep. She plays with her cronies, every Monday without fail. It's life and death, basically. I help out, sometimes.'

I digested this. 'They play for... money, then?'

'Lord, no. A tube of Pringles, at most. But still...' He leaned closer to me and grinned. 'If you'll see me again, I thought we might give it a whirl.'

'What, and be beaten to a pulp by a bunch of octogenarians?' I shook my head. 'It was nice knowing you, Finn...'

But as he caught my eye and winked, we both suspected I was only joking.

# Chapter 8

'Bingo? Gee, that's a first,' said Nancy.

'Dump him, he's clearly off his trolley,' said Amelia, at the same time.

Grace paused, then added, 'You must admit, light gambling isn't very romantic.'

It was Monday evening, and I'd allowed myself to be hustled to the pub for a debriefing. Grace's husband was over in the corner playing darts, rarely glancing our way.

'Like your chap, you mean?' I tipped my head in his direction, and she grinned before stealing one of my crisps. 'Anyway, he got the hint I was only lukewarm,' I added. 'So no bingo for me. At least, not yet.'

'You're seeing him again, then?' Nancy asked.

I looked down at the table. 'Oh, I dunno. I enjoyed the day out, but... well, it's weird, you know?'

'What, being with someone new?'

I nodded. 'And he's probably too young for me. If I was looking, I mean, which I'm not.'

Nancy asked, 'How young is he?'

'Thirty.' Finn exuded so much youthful energy, I'd been surprised to learn he'd reached this milestone.

'And that's a gap of...?' Nancy prompted.

'Three years. Going on four.'

Amelia snorted. 'Hardly a chasm, darling. If he were eighteen, you might have a point. But thirty? Tally-ho!'

'I thought you just told me to dump him.'

She shrugged. 'For bingo, yes. Not for his age.'

'Well, at any rate, you can tick doing a doctor off your list,' Grace said. 'Good work!'

Amelia frowned. 'No, you can't.'

'Why can't she?' Nancy asked.

'Well, you didn't *do* him, did you?' Amelia smirked.

'Eww! Amelia!' This was from Grace, whereas Nancy put a hand over her eyes in mock horror. 'Ladies,' she said, 'we don't need to know.'

I blushed. 'Of course I didn't!' It was an excellent time to change the subject. 'Grace, is eggshell finish okay for kitchen cabinets?'

A little while later, when we'd all ordered fish and chips and were halfway through another round of drinks, Amelia started scrolling on her phone. That wasn't unusual, except it went on for much longer than usual.

'Is everything okay?' Nancy was into mindfulness, and did a digital detox every Saturday.

'Sorry, darlings.' Amelia didn't look up. 'It's the new sales listings, and they're late.'

'What's she talking about?' I asked the others.

'She means it's a report of local houses which have just come on the market.' Grace had worked for Amelia at one point. 'She pounces on them every week. Claims it keeps her ahead of the competition.'

'Always good to know who's moving,' Amelia muttered. 'And I like to check mine are showing up properly, too.'

'Anything big and expensive?' Grace asked.

'All of it's expensive, regardless of size,' Nancy said. She'd been wondering about taking a long-term contract with her company, but had ruled out buying property in Cambridge. 'It's nuts around here,' she'd complained. 'The price per square foot makes Manhattan look cheap.'

I suspected it didn't, but I did empathise with her finances. If I hadn't been able to move into my crumbling cottage during my divorce, I'm not sure where I'd have gone.

'West Lane, Burwell. Isn't that where you used to live, Maggie?' Amelia looked up and took a swig of her wine. 'Looks huge.'

'How did you know that?' I asked, surprised.

'She's got a photographic memory for who's lived where,' Grace said. 'If you mentioned it once, that's all it took.'

'Well, in that case, yes. West Lane. Not any more, obviously.' I looked at Amelia. 'So, what number's for sale?'

She shook her head. 'It doesn't say. There's a photo, though.' She pushed her phone across to me. I took one look and dropped it on the table with a worrying clunk.

'Careful, darling.' Amelia snatched for her precious gadget.

'Sorry,' I gulped.

'What's the matter?' Grace saw my frozen face. 'Or can I guess?'

She exchanged a look with Nancy, who asked, 'Is it your house, Maggie? I mean, was it, before your divorce?'

I nodded, unable to say anything.

'No wonder you're a bit upset.' Grace patted my arm. 'End of an era?'

'Well, yes, I am upset.' I exhaled. 'Very. But not about the house.'

~ ~ ~

The next morning, I couldn't help myself. I had to see if Amelia's information was correct.

I waited until I thought Colin would have gone to work before driving the narrow country roads from Saffron Sweeting to Burwell. My route was lined by hedges and cow parsley, no doubt encouraged by the spring rain. At one point, a green woodpecker swooped across the road. Only later did I realise its mocking laugh would set the tone for my morning.

Colin had always liked to start work early – standard in his trade – so I figured half past nine would be safe.

It wasn't. I'd barely parked opposite my old home in West Lane, when the front door opened and he came down the drive towards his van. He was dressed as usual in black jeans and a black polo shirt with his company's logo on. The colour suited him, and his clothes fitted well.

Beside me, a dog chased a squirrel up a tree with a frenzy of yapping. I shrunk lower in my seat but it was too late: Colin had spotted me.

He paused for a moment, hands on hips, then, even from this distance, I saw him sigh. He shook his head and crossed the quiet road towards me.

'What are you doing, Maggie?' he asked, after I'd rolled down the window.

He was right to be puzzled. Our divorce had been low on drama and I wasn't in the habit of stalking him.

*Well, I was just passing, and I thought I'd make sure you don't think I'm still carrying a torch for you.* Seeing him brought the humiliation of the awards ceremony flooding back. Yet, rehearsing those words in my head made me cringe. Could I simply gloss over it and pretend that evening hadn't happened?

'I'm not in love with you,' I blurted. Apparently, glossing wasn't for me today.

He took a step back. 'I never said you were.'

'Good – coz, you know, at that dinner in March, the speech, that pompous friend of yours said... and that would be bad, so I just wanted to...' I trailed off. 'Oh, congratulations by the way. On your award.'

Colin frowned. 'We were all a bit drunk that night. What did Lester say?'

Scarlet-faced, I repeated the gist of it.

'Huh. He was only having a laugh. Forget about it.' But he didn't meet my eye.

And in any case, what help was *forget about it*? I'd been stewing for weeks over being the laughing stock of Cambridge, and he brushed it off like dust? Well, it was all right for him. He wasn't the one people were poking fun at.

Still, picking at this painful scab wasn't going to help. I got out of my car and gestured at the for-sale sign stationed in our front garden. No, *his* front garden. 'You're... selling the house?'

'Yup.' He looked over his shoulder, even though he knew which one I meant. 'Time for a fresh start.'

Colin had grown up in this house, a few doors down from where I'd lived. But his dad had died young from a heart condition, and his mum dealt with her grief by redoubling her efforts to become an actress. When she got regular work with a cruise ship company, Colin and I got the house to ourselves. And a few years later, she moved to Los Angeles and put it in his name altogether. We were incredibly lucky to start married life in such a nice home, and I couldn't remember him ever showing any dislike for the house.

So that must mean... 'Keiko doesn't like it?' I looked up at him.

'She wants something smaller. Says we accumulate clutter, living with four bedrooms.'

But Keiko's aversion to clutter didn't interest me. 'So what are you doing about the treehouse?'

I couldn't see it from the road, not with all the lush May foliage and his neighbour's huge lilac in my way. I craned my neck anyway.

Why, oh why, had I not thought about this sooner?

'The what?' Colin asked.

'The *treehouse*,' I repeated. Surely he hadn't forgotten where the three of us – he, Matthew, and I – had spent so many hours, as kids? Although it was in the garden of the house Colin had grown up in, the lofty structure felt like another world, *our* world. In that kids-only zone, with no adults allowed, we could ignore the fact that none of us had a parent in our life who gave a damn about where we were and what we were doing.

'Oh, that.' He scratched an ear. 'Sell it with the house. The estate agent says it's a plus point.'

It wasn't a *plus point*. It was a unique part of my past. 'You can't sell it! I want it.'

'Eh?'

I took a breath. 'Since you're selling the house anyway, I'd like... er, the treehouse.'

'And do what with it?'

'Move it.'

'You what?' Colin let out a laugh.

It wasn't until I'd said the words that I realised moving the treehouse would indeed be ambitious. But I couldn't backtrack now.

'You're bonkers,' he said. 'Moving it would be a total nightmare.'

Since he was selling Dad's painting, which was apparently worth a small fortune, he could afford to give me the treehouse. But I decided not to mention that. Not yet, anyway.

'But—' I swallowed. Darn it, if he wouldn't give it to me, I could buy it, surely? 'I can pay you. I'll make you a good offer.' Maybe I could sell my car.

He narrowed his eyes, but then shook his head. 'Sorry. No can do.'

'Please?' I tried.

'I have to go.' That was Colin's answer to everything, right through our marriage. When things got tricky, or tough, he absented himself, claiming business pressures.

He'd turned away and was halfway across the road, towards his own vehicle.

'It's not up for grabs, Maggie. It's in the house details, included in the sale.'

I caught my breath. If he sold his house with the treehouse included, I'd never set foot in it again.

'Will you think about it?' I called, as Colin swung himself into his van and closed the door abruptly. 'Please?'

I'm not sure if he heard me as the engine started. Then he pulled out of his parking space, and didn't look back.

# Chapter 9

Ten days went by, during which I kicked myself for not tearing into Colin about the painting. If he was going to be difficult about the treehouse, maybe I should get stroppy about Dad's art.

And despite my ambivalence about seeing Finn again, I had to admit my ego was a little bruised that he hadn't been in touch. Not only was he a handy way to take a swipe at Colin, but he'd been fun company. Maybe I should have seemed more keen, flirted, even? But really, I'd been out of circulation for so long, how was I to know what men expected these days? I decided he must have taken his laid-back Irish charms elsewhere.

But I didn't have a lot of time on my hands to dwell on either of these things.

As well as finishing Kenneth's kitchen, I fixed drips, a shelf, and a door for Amelia's clients. This, in turn, led to me repairing a broken garden gate for a neighbour, and rewiring a faulty plug for the people over the road. The money was trivial – thirty pounds here, forty there – but I enjoyed being useful. At this rate, though, it would be a while before I could afford a new roof.

One new customer told me she was ninety-three. The brave old lady wanted grab bars in her bathroom.

'But I can't service your gas boiler,' I told her, when she gripped my elbow and tried to lead me to it. Gas was a total no-no. 'I'll send Vincent. He's qualified, and he'll do you a good price.'

Vincent had worked for twenty years as a gas man; the night of the awards ceremony had been one of the few occasions I'd seen him out of his blue overalls. At one point his wife was ill, and I'd bailed them out with childcare. Somewhere along the line, I knew I'd made a friend for life.

'Don't tell Col I'm helping you out,' he said, when I phoned about the old lady. 'He gets funny about stuff like that.'

Colin was indeed loyal to his team, and he expected the same in return.

'He won't mind.' I laughed. 'He's got nothing against me, after all.'

At that point, Vincent had gone quiet and I found myself protesting, once again, there were no undertones between me and my ex.

'All the same,' Vincent concluded, 'no need to mention it.'

~ ~ ~

We celebrated the successful completion of Kenneth's kitchen with his engagement party. A throng of villagers attended, and we ended up spilling outside into dappled May sunshine. For the money spent, his kitchen looked amazing. This had the unfortunate repercussion that the daunting and demonic Mrs Worthing informed me she'd be my next client.

She collared me at Kenneth's front door and demanded that I 'spiff up' her kitchen next.

'Mr Worthing has been unwell,' she said. 'I shan't bother him with a big expense at the moment. What can you do for three hundred pounds?'

I gulped and resisted the urge to say 'bugger all,' followed by 'bugger off.' Money was money, after all.

That's how, a few days later, I found myself in a new kitchen, with a new client.

Nobody in Saffron Sweeting knew Mrs Worthing's first name. Everywhere you went, people accorded her the respect she demanded. She walked around in all weathers with a headscarf firmly tied, and her chin half an inch higher than it should be. The corners of her mouth, on the other hand, never lifted at all.

So here I was, along with Grace, who'd taken her life in her hands to help with ideas again. In return, I'd be stripping floorboards in my friend's cottage when she was ready. Given how helpful she'd been at Kenneth's, I could hardly refuse the deal.

The moment Mrs Worthing was out of earshot, the two of us went into a huddle.

'It's women like her who made Hitler afraid to invade us,' Grace said.

Coming from her, that was strong stuff.

'Could we sedate her with paint fumes?' I checked again that my client had indeed retreated to what she called her morning room. Then I jumped as my pocket vibrated.

'Well?' Grace asked, three minutes later. 'Do I assume that was the Irish guy? You're looking dreamy.'

'No I'm not.' But I didn't bother to fight the smile. 'Well, yes, actually. Date on Sunday.'

'And you like him?'

'Oh, I dunno.' I wasn't looking for anyone to *like*, after all. I put my phone back in my pocket. 'But he's funny and kind and... seems uncomplicated.'

'Uncomplicated?' Grace echoed. 'Sounds like a keeper.'

She waited a moment, then saw I wasn't going to gossip about Finn while I was supposed to be assessing a scary client's kitchen.

Grace bent back over her color chart. 'Do you think Mrs W would go for Sudbury Yellow? It's practically mustard, but I feel like it would suit her.'

~ ~ ~

'Surely punting's for the tourists?'

I eyed the Scudamore's sign which proclaimed we had to leave half our net worth as a security deposit. Too many tourists hired a punt without knowing the flat little boats were harder to control than a bull on Viagra. I knew the mayhem which could ensue as soon as we were let loose with nothing but a pole, a paddle, and our wits to ensure our safe return.

'Not in the least!' Finn handed the attendant his credit card. 'Haven't you ever been?'

'Not for years,' I replied.

Not since I was at school, maybe. I was terrible at it then, narrowly avoiding an unscheduled swim in the Cam.

'Want me to go first, then?'

'Definitely.' I teetered to a safe sitting position, as the Scudamore's man began untying the long, low punt.

Spring had truly arrived in Cambridge: the trees were in full leaf and I spotted a family of ducklings too. It was early morning, because although Finn said he was a competent punter when it was just him, he 'wasn't too dapper at steering round other eejits.' And the eejits – or idiots – tended to take to the water later in the day. So we glided under Silver Street Bridge, Finn's face a picture of cautious focus.

Surreptitiously, I studied him, trying not to compare him to Colin, but failing. Finn's hair was much lighter brown, and straighter. His skin tone was lighter too, not least because he worked indoors whereas Colin was outside much of the time. My ex-husband's chin was pointy, whereas Finn's was more square. Finn's eyes were more twinkly, and his lips... well, they were hard to judge, because he was biting them in concentration.

Later, when I was alone, I might mentally compare the rest of him to Colin, too, but for now, I'd better make conversation.

'So you've got good balance, then?' I watched his slight wobble each time he pulled the pole up from the riverbed.

'Not really,' he replied, jaw clenched.

'But you're a good swimmer?'

'Not really,' he said again. 'Are you?'

'I am, actually. I like to swim. Not in the river, though, if I can help it.' The Cam flowed so slowly, all kinds of nasties lurked. There was even a name – Cam Fever – for the resulting stomach upsets. Then again, given that most of those dunkings were alcohol induced, the symptoms might be mainly hangover.

'So if it comes to it,' Finn asked, 'will you save me from drowning?'

'Don't count on it.'

At Amelia's urging, I'd finally adopted a pricey conditioner in my minimal beauty routine. For the first time in years, my hair was imitating loose curls instead of frizz. Obviously, if Finn's life were in danger, I would intervene. But nothing short of a disaster would induce me to plunge into the river today.

'You're a tough woman, Maggie Moone.' He shook his head and laughed, then wobbled.

'The trick,' Finn said, after he'd regained his equilibrium, 'is not to get this bit wet.'

I looked at where he was standing on the small raised platform at the back of the punt. 'It's a huge puddle.'

'*Exactly.*' He injected so much warmth and self-deprecating humour into that single word, my stomach flipped over.

We were passing King's College, and I leaned back to take in the iconic Cambridge view.

'You were right.' I admired the college chapel, the cows, and the scattering of other punts on the river. 'This is a lovely way to travel.'

'Sometimes,' Finn stilled the pole to let the punt drift for a minute, 'we don't appreciate what's right under our noses.'

A little farther on, at a quiet spot on the river where a few ducks and a solitary swan were our only companions, he steered us to the side. 'Do you want to have a go? While we're going with the current?'

'Oh, I don't know... last time I tried, I was pretty rubbish.'

'I won't laugh.' He stepped down from the back. 'Or scream. And if you fall in, I will absolutely jump in and save you.' His eyes danced with this last part.

'Okay.' I scrambled carefully towards the back of the boat. It wobbled as Finn and I swapped places, and we clung to each other for a moment.

'Sorry,' I said.

'No worries.' He was still holding onto me, even though the rocking had stopped. 'Okay?'

I nodded. My knees were rather shaky, but surely that was from the lapping motion on the water.

He handed me the pole. 'Right you are, Maggie Moone.'

It weighed a tonne, but I had more bicep strength than when I was a teenager. I managed to heft the pole up and then into the water, without too much trouble.

'Do you want advice?' Finn asked, when he'd settled himself in the boat facing me. 'Or should I keep my trap shut?'

'No, no, advice would be good,' I replied, as the punt set off at an angle across the river. It was nice of him to ask, though. Colin never hesitated before giving his opinion.

'Okay, well, first, drop the pole straight down so it goes in vertically, not behind you. That way you don't waste any of the power.'

I tried again.

'And I can't remember where the muddy bits are, but if you twist it a bit as you pull it out, that reduces the chances of it getting stuck.'

'Thanks.' I had witnessed plenty of other punters – tourists, of course – lose their poles. Each boat was supplied with a paddle for this eventuality, but it always caused mirth on the river when it happened.

'How do you steer?' I called, as we approached the bank again. As I said this, a punt coming the other way – one of the expensive ones with a professional guide – changed course to glide around us.

'Aha.' Finn leaned forwards. 'That's the clever bit.'

With much hand waving and pointing, and me getting my lefts and rights mixed up, he explained that I could move the pole in the water at the end of each stroke, to guide the punt.

'If you push the pole to the right, the back of the boat – where you are – goes left. So the front goes right.'

'What?' I almost crashed us into the bank. This is the part, I thought, where Colin would have lost patience entirely.

Finn, however, grinned. 'Sorry. Look, all you have to do is move the pole to the side where you want the boat to go.'

I tried again, hefting the pole up, dropping it to the riverbed, pushing off, and then leaving it in the water to steer us. 'It works!'

'Of course it works. You're doing grand!'

He laughed then, a deep, sexy laugh, and I forgot all about twisting the pole before pulling it up from the mud.

It stuck.

I wobbled, gasped, and tugged again, harder, as the boat drifted relentlessly downstream.

'Let go!' Finn called.

I had a second to make the decision: to hold on and keep tugging, or bid the pole goodbye.

'Let go!' Finn yelled again, up on his knees now.

I gave one last tug, but the pole held fast in the mud.

I let go.

~ ~ ~

Later, as we returned the punt – complete with both pole and paddle – I reflected how kind he'd been.

Colin would have had a hissy fit, probably made a sarcastic joke about women drivers, and sulked about the humiliation of finding himself adrift on the river.

With Finn, however, it had been different.

'Are you okay?' had been his first words, even before reaching for the emergency paddle.

I'd been fine, of course, just mortified at allowing my mind to wander from the task at hand. But grateful, too, that the episode hadn't ended with a splash in the River Cam.

Finn had paddled us slowly back upstream, but by the time we reached the stranded pole, it had been retrieved by a group of six Japanese schoolgirls in a punt travelling the other way. Despite the language barrier, he'd thanked them effusively, bowing several times, a huge grin on his face throughout. They had responded with much giggling and nudging, then six phones had been produced for selfies with their new Irish friend.

Now, back on terra firma, I waited in the shade of a weeping willow tree while Finn collected his credit card from the rental booth.

'How are you doing?' he asked, as he joined me under the tree. 'No muscles pulled?'

I rubbed my shoulder. 'Not many.' I'd feel it tomorrow, in any case.

'Sorry to get you all soggy.' He gestured to the right side of my shirt, which had got wetter every time I'd heaved the dripping pole high enough to drop it in the river.

I felt my neck flush. The cotton shirt was clinging to me. Good job it was my own, and not a designer item on loan from Amelia.

'I'm fine.' I shrugged like it didn't matter. 'At least I'm not wet through from falling in.'

Finn didn't answer, just crossed his hands in front to pull his grey sweater off in one smooth move. For a split second, I caught sight of his bare torso as his T-shirt rode up too. Those few square inches of skin made me blush properly.

'I don't need that,' I muttered, as he draped the jumper around my shoulders. But the wool was soft, and smelt of lavender. Fabric conditioner, I told myself sternly.

'I know.' He shrugged. 'But I didn't get the chance to jump in and save you, so this is the closest to heroics I can get.'

He reached out to adjust the jumper at the same moment I looked up at his face.

'Okay, then.' My mouth was suddenly dry. 'Thanks.'

He held my gaze a second longer, then leaned forward to brush his lips gently against mine.

It was years since I'd been kissed by anyone except Colin, and even longer since I'd felt the flutter which ran from my toes to my ears, and back again. Just as I thought I might lean in, Finn drew back and gave my shoulders a gentle squeeze.

'You're welcome, Maggie Moone.'

I was walking home from Mrs Worthing's house, in need of a treat. My second kitchen client was proving not only demanding, but indecisive, too. She'd rejected Sudbury Yellow as the new paint colour, flirted with Dorset Cream, and was now expressing a strong preference for Tallow. I didn't much care either way, but each time she changed her mind (after I'd purchased the paint), her already tight budget shrank.

There was also no sign that she planned to do any of the decluttering Grace had recommended. The old lady's kitchen counters housed so many mugs, chopping boards, and baking dishes, you could barely see a horizontal surface. Why she needed two kettles, I'm not sure. But since I was hardly the queen of minimalism myself, I wasn't going to tackle her about it.

Nor had I slept well the previous night. I'd been mulling over my punting trip with Finn and the vivid image of him removing his sweater. The Shipping Forecast was almost finished before my thoughts slipped into dreams.

So, with my energy low, I crossed the street to the bakery. Brian had deemed the weather good enough to reinstate his outside tables, and their big yellow umbrellas gave the place a jaunty, welcoming air.

As I pushed open the bakery door, the sun glanced off it, and I failed to see a woman coming out. We almost collided as she attempted to squeeze past me, and her takeaway cup of coffee slipped to the ground.

'Sorry!' I tried to pick it up. The lid was askew, and some of her coffee sloshed over the pavement. 'That was so clumsy of me. Didn't see you.'

'You're all right, don't worry,' she said, in an accent I couldn't place. Then the sun caught her glossy dark hair and I looked at her again.

'Have we met recently?' In the village, it was perfectly possible. Maybe she'd been at Kenneth's engagement party, for example.

She smiled and, with her free hand, pushed her cute pixie fringe out of her eyes. 'Sorry, I don't think—'

I took three more seconds to stare.

'I've got it. You're the dream catcher seller.' At this, she paused. 'From the wellness fair?' I continued. 'At the malt house?'

Now she tilted her head. 'Oh! Are you the moon lady? For Finn?'

'That's me.' I remembered my manners. 'Let me get you another coffee. I was going in. Obviously.' She hesitated, and I gestured to the table and chairs outside the bakery. 'I'll just be a jiffy.'

When I came back out of Brian's shop a few minutes later, she'd parked herself at the nearest table. This time, I introduced myself.

'I'm Robyn,' she replied. 'Nice to meet you.'

I gave her the fresh coffee and she accepted a date slice as well. As I sat down, I studied her. Her hair really was gorgeous, almost as if she'd come from an appointment at a salon. And the rest of her wasn't bad.

'So, you're friends with Finn?' Should I be jealous? Did I like him enough to be jealous?

'Sort of. He's mates with my brother.'

I found I liked her offhand tone.

'And you make crafts?'

The dream catcher was now adorning my bedroom window.

She shook her head. 'Not really. I mean, no, I was helping a friend at the fair. It was her stall. Maybe next year.'

Robyn stopped, looking embarrassed.

'Next year?' Having knocked her coffee flying, I was being attentive.

'Maybe. If I have some work ready.'

I smiled encouragingly.

'I'm trying to get used to calling myself an artist,' she said. 'Somehow it doesn't feel genuine when I'm painting bits and pieces for friends, and working the rest of the time for Mary Lou.'

I was pretty sure Mary Lou was the bouncy American entrepreneur who owned the nearly new shop in the village. It did a roaring trade in kids' clothes and toys, and was always buzzing with families.

'What kind of art do you make?' I asked.

'Well, I have my own projects, but I haven't sold any of those yet. For other people I mostly take a photo of something dear to them, and paint a nice watercolour of it.'

'Like, their kids, you mean?'

'Spot on. I'm doing one of me and my brother for my mum's birthday.'

'Well, that's really nice.'

I thought of my own mother and how I'd never do anything that special for her. Or anything at all, in league with my brother Matthew. When our family had erupted into a vicious battle of words shortly after his twenty-first birthday, I suspected things would never be the same again. When he'd later emigrated to Australia, I thought that was the worst week of my life. Little did I know.

Robyn hadn't noticed I was lost in thought. 'Or often it's a pet, or a house they love, or anything, really,' she added.

I sipped my tea. Maybe I could get a photo of the treehouse for her to paint. That way, even if Colin sold it to a stranger, I'd have a reminder.

Colin's grandfather had built the treehouse before I was born, when Colin was about two years old. The tree was a yew, with several central stems. So there was a large platform around the tree itself, with one corner of the treehouse attached. The rest of it was then supported by three of its own stilts. There were two tiny windows, an arched door, and a sloping, shingled roof. The only access was a rope ladder, and I'm sure it was hopelessly deficient in terms of safety.

We loved it.

It had been damaged in a ferocious storm in 1987, but I was only three then, and don't remember. Repairing the treehouse had been almost the last thing Colin's grandpa had done before he died.

Now, was I more distraught at the thought of losing it, or more furious with myself for not considering the possibility sooner? What kind of post-divorce fog had I been living in?

'Could you paint a treehouse, do you think?' I asked Robyn.

If I had to, I'd wait until Colin and Keiko were out, then sneak into their garden to take photos.

'I don't see why not. Want a business card?'

As she reached into her bag, I decided I trusted Finn. That meant, if she was his friend, she was my friend too. 'And what about your own art?'

'Oh.' She laughed. 'I mess about with all kinds of things. Often, I'll take a famous painting and try to copy it. I have four abandoned *Mona Lisa*s at home.

'Really?'

She nodded. 'It helps me de-stress. And it's a great way to practise. There are competitions, you know, for best forgery.'

I shook my head and laughed. 'You're pulling my leg.'

'Seriously.' She smiled. 'Some of us get a real kick out of it. As a student, it's a fantastic discipline. You really have to get inside the other artist's head.'

'So, what's the hardest thing to copy?' I asked, curious now. 'I once heard that hair is difficult for the people who make computer games.'

'Hair can be, yes,' she said. 'And smiles, obviously. Especially enigmatic French ones.' She paused, taking a long drink of coffee. 'I find skies really tough. Skies, and clouds... smoke, too.'

'Smoke?' I put my tea down as a whisper flitted into my subconscious and out again. Rattled, I looked over my shoulder, but we were all alone in the street.

Robyn seemed unaware of my discomfort. 'Yes. Some people paint for years, trying to copy someone else's sky.'

I clutched at the thought in my brain, but it wouldn't form. The cloud was too thick.

'Are you all right?' Robyn asked me.

'I'm fine. Sorry.' Still the image wouldn't come. 'You reminded me of something, that's all.'

We said goodbye soon after that, and I meandered home.

It was three in the morning when it came to me, as these things sometimes do.

The scene was a market town in the north of England, and an old man there who sold his paintings while he worked on the next one. The subjects were often industrial, and lots of them featured fog, or steam... or smoke. As teenagers, we only noticed because his stall was next to the fish and chip van. We called him Albie. And he was never without a brush in his hand.

# Chapter 11

'Are you sure?' I asked, realising that I was talking myself out of much-needed work. 'I mean, this is kind of beautiful already.'

Camilla sighed. 'It's just not my style. And *honestly*, we were going to rip it *all* out, but Hunter heard he might be transferred back to the States. We can't justify it, honey.'

We were standing in her kitchen, in one of the larger, older houses in Saffron Sweeting. It was a lovely light-filled room which opened onto a conservatory. The cabinets were high quality, the countertops were marble, and the appliances all glossy stainless steel.

Camilla had been a magazine editor in New York and was supposedly working on a decorating blog while the family was in England for her husband's job. I'd never read it, but wondered if every sentence contained italics, like the way she talked.

'But even if we *do* sell the house, I *cannot* live with that red one second longer.'

'Ah,' I said. 'I see.'

Seconds passed. This seemed like such a privileged request. But even to my unrefined eye, I could see the accent colour chosen by the previous owners had been a mistake. The kitchen island was a deep red – almost bloodlike – and a row of accent tiles ran along the top of the backsplash. Three pendant lights, also red, finished the look.

'Please say you can fix it. It's *driving* me around the bend.'

Camilla must have a pretty pampered existence, if a few red splashes in the kitchen had whipped her into such a state of anxiety.

'Well, yes,' I said finally. 'I can paint the island. And if I'm really careful,' I walked over to peer at the offending tiles, 'I can get these off, then we – I mean I – can patch up and repaint.'

'Awesome!' Her voice rose three notches. '*When* can you start? And how much?'

I swallowed. The night before, Amelia had been lecturing about this in the pub. She'd been giving Grace an ear-bashing about her prices.

'Darling,' she'd cooed, after Grace had relayed the story of a celebrity client who had chauffeured her down to Notting Hill to spec out a project, 'if they get excited about everything else, and start talking dates, and only ask the price as an afterthought, you've *got* to bump up your quote. Now phone back immediately. Ask for more.'

Grace had refused, but now, I was in the same boat. I planted a stiff smile on my face, and doubled my mental estimate. 'And I could start, er, on Friday?'

'Awesome.' Camilla didn't miss a beat. 'I'll write you a cheque.'

I was still dazed as I walked down her front path. Unless the tiles were a nightmare, this would be excellent money for modest work. Who knew that unloved kitchens were so lucrative?

The answer to my question was parked opposite Camilla's house.

'Colin?' I waited for a tractor to rumble by, then crossed the street to his van. 'What are you doing here?'

For a moment, I thought maybe he'd reconsidered my treehouse purchase and had driven over to Saffron Sweeting to discuss arrangements.

'I was going to ask you the same thing.' He pulled his clipboard out of the van and shut the door. Then he jerked his chin at the house. 'Did you just come from there?'

'Camilla's? Yes.'

'Small world,' he said drily, leafing through the papers he was holding. 'I came to give her a nudge about my estimate. Nice lady, isn't she?'

I wasn't sure I'd call Camilla *nice*. Forceful, yes, glamorous, certainly, but not overflowing with *nice*. She hadn't even offered me a cup of tea. Instead, I asked, 'What estimate?'

Colin shrugged, as if it were obvious. 'To do her kitchen. Big job. Nice job. Fifty grand's worth. Everything out, down to the brick.'

'She's changed her mind,' I blurted.

With hindsight, I should have kept quiet, but I was so shocked that he'd quoted her fifty thousand pounds to tear out a perfectly functional kitchen, I didn't have the sense.

'What?' His head snapped around.

Too late, I tried to backtrack. 'That is, I think maybe... she said...'

As had been the case right through our marriage, Colin didn't stick around to listen to me explain. He strode off up the path to Camilla's house, clipboard in hand.

I paused, as the realisation I'd pinched a juicy contract from under my ex-husband's nose sunk in. Then I fingered the three hundred pound deposit cheque in my pocket, its ink barely dry.

I'd better trot on over to the bank, and pay it in quick.

~~~

I drove over to Newmarket and waited in a long queue at the bank. Someone had rammed a bulldozer into the cash machine the week before, so even people who only wanted money were forced inside. I asked for the form they'd need to change my name, reckoning that would count as making a start. But my guilty conscience about Camilla's cheque was growing.

On the way home, I popped my head in at the estate agents to ask Amelia's advice.

'I've done something really stupid,' I said, a split second after she put her phone down. 'Camilla wants her kitchen tarted up and I gave her an inflated price, like you suggested, and she went for it. But then Colin turned up and I've really, really pissed him off.'

Having let this tumble out, I flopped down in one of Amelia's visitor chairs.

'Whoa.' She leaned back in her seat and steepled her fingers.

As was often the case, her huge cocktail ring glinted. I didn't know how she could stand that thing, getting in her way all day. My hands were the epitome of plainness: nails sometimes bitten, never manicured, bare of rings. I'd even been quite pleased to take them off after Colin and I split up. The wretched engagement ring was always snagging things, or trapping bits of soap under it.

Amelia studied me. 'What makes you think you've pissed Colin off?'

'He was going to do her kitchen, a complete teardown job. I may have, er, stolen his business.'

This time, Amelia cackled. 'Well, funnily enough, that was Camilla on the phone. I called her to see if there was any news on how long they'd be staying here.'

Amelia was relentless at staying in touch with previous clients. Her reasoning was, if they'd bought a house from her previously, they might let her sell it when they were finished with it. And with so many American families in Saffron Sweeting, turnover was often brisk. Their employers didn't blink at spending thousands of pounds to shunt entire families back and forth across the Atlantic.

'You just spoke to Camilla?'

'I did. And for once she was happy to take my call. She said it gave her the chance to get rid of a kitchen chap who was in a tizz about losing a job. Apparently, she thought a vein in his neck might pop.'

'Oh, my gosh,' I breathed. 'That was Colin. I was right, he's livid. What have I done?'

'What *have* you done?' Amelia asked. 'I'm not following. Slow down and tell me.'

So I told her everything that had happened, from Camilla phoning me, to my meeting with her, to Colin turning up outside her house.

'Maybe I should tell her I can't do it,' I suggested.

'You'll do no such thing.'

'I shouldn't have paid the cheque in. That was stupid, right?'

'Wrong!' Amelia got up from her desk. 'Look, according to Camilla, when she discussed the kitchen with your ex, she tried to knock him down on price, in return for getting the finished thing featured in her fancy magazine.'

'Magazine?'

'Yes, darling. She's on leave from *Cornice*, you know. It's huge.'

I'd never heard of the magazine, but that didn't matter. 'So Colin thought he was going to get publicity from the job? Crikey, that's even worse. He's going to hate me.'

'Oh, do get a grip on yourself, Maggie.' Amelia wasn't famed for her patience. She crossed her legs and started twirling her court shoe on the end of her foot. 'You had nothing to do with Camilla changing her mind. If they're moving back to New York, spending all that money here would be totally loopy.'

'But I feel awkward about getting the business, when Colin's losing out.'

'Excuse me?' Amelia's shoe fell off. 'Why should you feel awkward? He'd have no qualms about doing it to you. And Grace told me he's cashing in on a painting of yours?'

'My dad's.' I still hadn't tackled Colin about that. What kind of wimp was I? 'Well, I suppose...' But there was the issue of the treehouse. 'I don't want him to be cheesed off with me just now. I'm trying to buy something from him.'

'Are you? What?'

I wanted to tell her, but it was hard to explain why a thirty-three-year-old childless woman was desperate to purchase a structure designed for kids. I didn't want to tell her the history. I didn't want to explain about Matthew.

'Oh, it doesn't matter. It was stupid to get on the wrong side of him.'

Amelia sat down next to me. 'Look, of all people, I *do* understand it's no picnic after a divorce. Even getting your shoes on the right feet is a victory, some days.'

You wouldn't know it now, I thought. In that moment, I resented Amelia, for her boundless energy and chic confidence, for her shiny auburn hair and pointed shoes.

'I just want to go back to how things were,' I mumbled.

'What, to moping around in your dreary cottage with its dreary front door? Coming home from your dreary bookkeeping jobs each evening, with nothing more exciting on the agenda than the six o'clock news?'

'Stop it. You're being cruel.'

'No, I'm being truthful. You've been stuck in a rut since your divorce, Maggie, and you needed shaking up.'

I was silent. She had a point, darn her.

'And as for nabbing a bit of business from him, well, that's rather funny.' She turned to her whiteboard and jabbed a marker pen at the score that was written there: *Maggie: 3 out of 10*. 'I'm giving you an extra point.' She licked a finger and erased the first number. 'Find that list of things he hates, and take something off that you weren't very excited about doing.'

'That list was a barking mad idea,' I grumbled.

'Tosh! But I do like this new one. Pinching his clients is fabulous. It's far more fun than painting your house pink or whatever.'

I was getting a headache. But it was a better way to look at the situation with Camilla's kitchen: one more act of defiance against Colin. I couldn't manage Amelia's glossy locks and I certainly couldn't manage flawless fingernails. But I had my friends, I had my glossy magenta front door, and I had my list.

'I mean it, Maggie.' Amelia saw she'd got ink all over her fingers, and started wiping them on a contract on her desk. 'I admit that list was a silly bit of fun at first, but it's brought oodles of good stuff into your life. You're turning into a badass! Promise me you won't stop.'

## Chapter 12

'So how's it going with Finn?' Grace asked on the phone. In theory, we'd been discussing Camilla's grout colour.

'Well,' I said, 'for a casual fling, he's fun.' I told her about the punting. 'He honestly didn't seem to mind me losing the pole.'

'That's important,' Grace said. 'How they behave, when things go wrong.'

She was right. Why had nobody told me that, when I was twenty-two and on the brink of marrying Colin? Mentally, I ticked off on my fingers the times I'd made small mistakes and he'd got all stroppy. A burnt Christmas dinner. A tiny dent in my car. An insurance payment overlooked. The time we got lost, travelling to a funeral in Sunderland.

'True,' I said. 'But it's not like I'm planning to get serious with Finn.'

Every time I'd thought about that kiss under the willow tree, I'd pushed it from my mind. Showing everyone I'd moved on from my marriage was enough; I didn't need to go getting involved.

'You're not seeing him again, then?'

I couldn't help a small smile. 'Oh, I wouldn't quite say that.'

~~~

We started at an ice cream shop on Castle Hill, where Finn took an extraordinarily long time to choose. The weather had turned warm, so I'd grabbed the opportunity to go swimming at the Jesus Green Lido beforehand. As a result, I would have guzzled any of the gelato flavours, but Finn deliberated for ages.

'Is this a sport for you, or something?' I whispered, as he prowled from one end of the cabinet to the other, and back again. 'You're like a child who's never seen the stuff.'

He laughed. 'Don't you find anticipation is part of the pleasure?'

I looked sideways at him to see if his words were laden with extra meaning, but his delighted gaze was fixed on the flavours. He'd already had two samples on tiny wooden spoons, and was making eyes at the young assistant to score a third.

'Anyway,' he said, as we left the shop, 'choosing was complicated. I wanted mine to be compatible with yours.'

'How so?' I licked furiously, to avoid drips. I didn't want to get sticky and messy, even though I wasn't yet sure about the significance of a third date.

'Well, I couldn't have rum 'n' raisin, if you were getting mint choc chip,' he replied.

'Why not?'

'Because I might want to kiss you later, and the flavours wouldn't go.'

A tingle went through me. It might have been gelato-induced brain freeze, but I suspected not.

I paused in my lip smacking, unable to stop my smile. 'So, are we okay? Raspberry ripple... and caramel chocolate?'

'Let's see...' He bent towards me in a deft manoeuvre.

His lips were chilly, in direct contrast to the sudden heat inside me. It was a tantalisingly brief kiss, as we both risked squashing our ice creams into the other one's chest. Possibly, he read my expression as we pulled apart. Raspberry ripple was running down my cone and reluctantly, I turned my mouth to that instead.

We set off down the hill. With hindsight, I wasn't planning to give Finn quite so much detail of my life with Colin, but he was so laid back and easy to talk to, it just kind of came out.

My tongue started to run away with me when he'd mentioned the day we met, and asked what had prompted me to spend good money on a tattoo. 'Most people aren't that fond of needles. I should know.'

I paused, aware that if I'd reached my thirties without skin adornment, he was right to suppose something had happened. Cautiously, I explained that I was celebrating going back to my maiden name, even though I was a long way off changing it everywhere. But I didn't say a word about the rest of the list, now propped on my dressing table. Nor did I mention that Amelia was keeping score on the whiteboard in her office.

'How long have you been divorced?' Finn asked, as we approached Magdalene Bridge. His voice was light, but I suspected he was checking the terrain to see if I was still a tangled mess, like knitting after a kitten's been home alone.

'Only a year.' I was careful to keep any sigh from my voice. 'But we'd been apart almost four. It's fine, really.'

'What was he like? Your ex?'

What could I say that was brief, accurate, yet appropriate? 'Arrogant,' I began. 'But also insecure in many ways. He had strong opinions about how he wanted me to behave.'

Depending what mood he'd been in, Colin might even have mocked me for my choice of ice cream flavour.

And I had to wonder, if he was such a prat, what did it say about me, that I'd married him?

'So that's why you got a tattoo?'

I stopped dead on the bridge. 'What makes you think...?'

He grinned. 'It's not that hard to work out. With it being your maiden name, and all.'

'Oh.' Jeez, this guy was perceptive. It probably came in handy in his work. I began walking again.

'And I still haven't seen it,' Finn pointed out. 'Your tattoo, I mean.'

'Is that why you asked me out again?' I attempted light flirtation, for the first time in years. 'And once you get a look at the moon, you'll be gone? I'll bear that in mind.'

He laughed, but dropped the subject of my thigh.

As he finished his ice cream, I found myself telling him about the painting Colin was trying to sell.

'So, he stands to make a tidy packet from art that's barely his?' Finn asked.

'There isn't much doubt it's his, really. But I was cheesed off because he pulled the wool over my eyes.'

Nonetheless, my subconscious had been noodling on the idea of Robyn creating new art from people's photos. And somewhere in the back of my mind, the idea had begun to form, that something about the painting wasn't right.

'And it's valuable?' Finn asked.

I nodded. 'I keep saying it's not about the money... oh, now you'll decide I'm a greedy, bitter ex.'

I noted with surprise that I didn't want Finn to think badly of me.

'No,' he said. 'It's okay, I get it.'

At the Round Church, we turned along Trinity Street, one of my favourite streets in Cambridge. Sure enough, there was the statue of Henry VIII above the gate of Trinity College, trying to look dignified with the prank chair leg instead of his sword. I'd love to make Colin look that foolish one day.

Could Finn be my ally in that? Would he stick around long enough for Colin to see us together? I looked hesitantly at him, strolling beside me. 'You're the last person I thought I'd be telling all this to.'

'I'm enjoying hearing about it,' he replied, sending me a half smile.

'Enjoying?' I hadn't read the book on dating after divorce that Amelia had offered me, but I was pretty sure it didn't involve bellyaching to an attractive new man about your ex-husband.

'Well, all right, I'm not in fits of laughter, but I'd like to know you better.'

'I've said too much already.' I paused for a bike to weave between us. 'And wait, I bet your job is to chat to people and make them feel comfortable, before you jab a needle in their vein.'

He laughed – that deep, Irish laugh, which I was starting to enjoy. I especially liked it when he laughed in response to something I'd said.

'You got me,' he said. 'But since I'm needle-free today, maybe you could trust that I simply want to hear about you.'

He really was a fantastic listener. His blood donors must adore his attentiveness.

'So, anyway, it's not that I'm hard up.' I put the vision of last week's bank statement to one side. 'But my cottage needs a lot of work...'

'Right.'

'Getting set up on my own after I left Colin was expensive. I had to go out and buy all kinds of unexpected bits and pieces. Everything from ketchup to toilet bleach.'

'I know what you mean. It was the same when I moved here from Ireland. Light bulbs, towels, it all adds up.'

'Why did you move?' It was time to stop talking about myself.

I'd slowed my eating, now that the immediate danger of melting was past, and was nibbling on the crunchy cone. That was the part I liked best, if I was honest.

'Well, for my gran, really. She had a fall last year, and although she's mended pretty well, we were worried about her.'

'You moved from Ireland so you could be near your grandmother? Wow.'

'Not just that. It was time for a change.'

I waited, but he didn't continue. Instead, Finn turned our talk back to me.

He asked if I had children, and I told him Colin had wanted to wait, and then it became clear the marriage was in trouble. At least I hadn't added a child to the mix. If I ever had kids, there was no way their parents would be getting divorced.

Finn asked whether I liked my job – I said sometimes – and I learned he loved his, although he wouldn't have turned down the chance to go to medical school if funds had allowed.

'You really do ask a lot of questions,' I said on King's Parade, as he quizzed me on my childhood ambitions, favourite TV programme, and earliest Christmas memory.

'Astronaut, any baking show, and a chestnut exploding in the fireplace,' I revealed. 'Your turn.'

'Doctor, *Call the Midwife*, and my uncle putting his back out pretending to be a reindeer.'

'Seriously, *Call the Midwife*?' I knew my surprise was impolite, but he nodded.

'I have nothing to prove, Maggie Moone. When you're a guy working as a nurse, you learn to have a thick skin.'

'Why?' I asked, although I could guess.

'Ah, you know...'

'Carry on.'

'Well, at eighteen my dad clouted me and told me to pick something more manly. At twenty-one, a patient asked for the first time if I was gay. And it's continued from there. On a good day, people assume I'm a doctor. Which, when you think about it, is just as insulting, to both me and the female docs.'

'I'm sorry,' I murmured. But it gave me pause. Hadn't I read a headline last week about a brain surgeon knocked off a bike in London, and I'd immediately pictured a man? *She'd* been critically injured and I'd been crestfallen to realise I'd made quick assumptions, exactly like most other people.

'Doesn't matter.' Finn shrugged, and he really didn't look too bothered. 'As I said, you get used to it.'

We passed a gift shop, with a window display offering ideas for Father's Day. Mother's Day never bothered me, but I thought wistfully of my dad at this time of year.

'Tell me about your family,' I said. 'You said your dad hit you... is it safe to assume you're not close?'

Finn shook his head. 'No, but it wasn't just that. He was constantly lying to Mum, hiding his money from her.'

'Hiding it?'

'Yeah, gambling and the like. Once I heard my grandma challenge him on it... He claimed he was trying to make our fortune. But week after week, Ma had less and less to feed us all with. So, no, we're not close. I wouldn't trust him as far as I could throw him.'

'My ex-husband always claimed he was anti-gambling...' I trailed off.

Finn said nothing, but turned his head to me. I took that as a sign to continue.

'But now I think of it, he was always taking ludicrous risks with his business.'

'What kind of risks?'

I told Finn how I'd had to scramble for cash on several occasions, even selling some of his mum's jewellery once, so we had enough to pay his guys on a Friday. And right at the end of our marriage, I found out Colin had overseen a project to build a dozen new homes near Cambourne, using mortar that had too much sand in. It was a foolish, cost-cutting shortcut, leaving the houses at risk of cracking.

'I don't know whether I was more incensed that he'd done it, or more devastated that he denied it to me,' I said.

Finn was quiet.

'Sorry. I'm talking about him too much, aren't I?

Finn didn't reply straight away. 'It's not so much a question of how much you're talking about him, more a case of how much you're thinking about him.'

~~~

We'd reached the corner of Silver Street when Finn asked, 'Do you want to keep going?'

I hesitated. In his gentle Irish tones he'd effectively pointed out that, on a mild spring evening when I was strolling in the golden twilight with a handsome new man, my thoughts had wandered back to Colin. Would this be a tactful place to end our date?

'I love walking,' Finn added. 'But you might be tired.' He looked down at my sensible shoes; the stylish wedges had thankfully been tossed in a corner of my bedroom.

'My feet are okay.' I opted for honesty. 'But am I boring you?'

The seriousness of his expression was unexpected. 'Boring me, Maggie Moone? Never.'

I allowed myself an uncertain smile. Was he for real?

'I mean it,' he said, as we continued in the direction of the river. 'I've only just started asking questions.'

'I'm all questioned out. Any more talking, I'll need another ice cream.'

'Now that's a grand idea.' He pretended to consider the notion, and we laughed, before agreeing to amble over to The Granta for a drink and to rest our legs.

Then he said, 'But you're not off the hook in telling me about yourself. If you like watching those TV baking battles, that must mean you like to make cakes? Is a Victoria sandwich in my future, if I play my cards right?'

Now I really did cringe. 'Sorry, no. I'm useless.'

Colin had been the culinary enthusiast in our house, and I'd never bothered to learn. Last time I made vegetarian chilli, he almost broke a tooth.

Seeing Finn's sceptical face, I added, 'I'm not being modest. I'm a terrible cook. I do *eat* cake with enthusiasm, though, if that's any good.'

'You've broken my heart, Maggie Moone.' He clasped both hands over his chest.

'I make jam sometimes.' But usually only when stressed. I bit my lip. 'That's it, though.'

This earned me another of his hearty laughs. 'I'm pulling your leg. If *I'm* fighting gender stereotypes, I'm not going to hold *you* to an expectation of baking me cakes.'

At this, I smiled and caught his eye. Finn now knew at least three downsides to my personality and abilities, and he hadn't run away yet. As if reading my thoughts, he reached out and took my hand.

'Anyway, jam sounds grand. Maybe I can help you sometime? I'm a dab hand at stoning cherries.'

'That would be great.' He had warm hands, and a firm grip, no doubt an asset in his line of work. With difficulty, I brought myself back to our conversation. 'We can make the jam, then we'll buy a Victoria sponge to slather it on.'

'Genius.' Finn made the word sound more delicious than the cake. 'Will we have clotted cream, too?'

I exhaled. 'You bet.' With my free hand, I gestured to myself. 'Sorry... not a domestic goddess.'

Without me noticing, our steps had slowed, and now we stopped.

'You know, Maggie...' Finn's voice was soft. 'I guessed as much.' He moved a little closer. 'But has no one ever told you, you don't have to be a goddess to be beautiful?'

My stomach gave a little skip. He was so laid back, I'd been unsure whether he'd been flirting for the last hour or not. Now, though, it seemed possible he liked me.

And a moment later, as Finn leaned in for a long slow kiss, it started to look not only possible, but probable.

I understood, too, why he'd been so particular about choosing those ice cream flavours.

## Chapter 13

I spent a boring but necessary day sanding down the island in Camilla's kitchen, and began carefully chipping at the tiles. Another day was occupied by a bookkeeping client. But the treehouse, and the fear that Colin would sell his house with the garden structure as part of the package, nagged at me.

Since my conversation at the start of the month about buying it, I'd done some research and knew that moving it would indeed be a huge undertaking. The saving grace was that most of it was on its own supports, with only one corner and a platform relying on the main tree. So I thought it was *just* possible it could be uprooted from its current site, without causing crippling damage to the tree.

As for quite where I'd put it, and the planning permission I'd probably need to install the structure in my own garden, I'd worry about that later.

I didn't dare approach my ex-husband again, since presumably his nose was still out of joint about the lost opportunity of transforming Camilla's kitchen. But might I have better luck with his wife?

'Hello,' I said brightly, as Keiko opened their front door.

It used to be my front door, of course, but I was never sentimental about the house. An array of rustic planks nailed to a tree in their garden, on the other hand, was different.

'Maggie?' She was thinner than ever. I'd never seen such perfect porcelain skin on anyone, including the waxworks at Madame Tussauds. She didn't invite me in, but if the roles had been reversed, I wouldn't have ushered the first wife into my home, either.

'I brought you some jam.' I held out a jar from a batch I'd made on Valentine's Day to cheer myself up. And I tried to look as though it was the most natural thing in the world to drop by unannounced, with a gift she probably wouldn't eat.

'Thank you.' She took it and gave a ghost of a bow. Maybe everyone in South Korea, where she was originally from, tended towards politeness.

With a jolt, I realised I hadn't seen her since the awful gala dinner at Saffron Hall.

'Er – you know the awards ceremony... that was total rubbish, what that bloke said about me still, er, you know... loving Colin.'

I was squirming, but I was careful to look directly at Keiko. However, she didn't react.

'You know that, right?' I prodded. A public accusation of being in love with her husband had to be faced.

Keiko dropped her eyes. She didn't say anything for several seconds, but then she nodded. 'Yes, I know.' I exhaled. But just as I thought I was off the hook, she added, 'But also, Maggie...'

'What?'

'You haven't exactly started new, have you?'

I bristled. 'What do you mean?' This wasn't right, the second wife commenting on *my* new life. Or lack of it.

She looked at me with her lovely dark eyes. 'Well, are you dating?'

'Sort of.' I scuffed a foot, then heard Amelia's voice telling me to get a grip. After all, Finn had kissed me. That counted, didn't it? 'Yes.' I raised my chin. 'He's, er, a doctor.'

In my pocket, I crossed my fingers, hating myself for promoting Finn in order to sound impressive to Keiko. But she might tell Colin. That would be brilliant.

Keiko raised her delicate eyebrows. 'Did you change your name yet?'

'I'm working on it.' I twisted my crossed fingers some more. 'It takes a while.'

She didn't say anything, merely gave a slow nod.

'So, your house is for sale?' I'm useless at small talk, but I forced myself to try.

'Yes.' Keiko was still holding the door at an angle. Since she wasn't giving me much to work with, I decided to get to the point. 'I'd love to buy the treehouse. I told Colin I was interested, but I haven't heard from him.'

Her face was expressionless. 'The treehouse?'

I took a deep breath. Was she playing dumb? Or had Colin mentioned it, and they were curious about how badly I wanted it? And how much I was willing to pay?

'Yes, is that okay?' Feeling like a pushy car salesman, I tried to channel Amelia. What would she do? Act like the sale was already agreed, probably. 'Shall I pay you cash?' I reached for my purse, aware that showing her some banknotes might move the conversation along. 'How does two hundred sound?'

I actually had no idea of the going rate for a second-hand treehouse, which would be a headache to transport. Still, I reckoned, if she started to argue about the price, it was a sign we could reach a deal.

Motionless, Keiko watched me counting the twenty pound notes. But she said nothing. When I'd finished, I looked up at her, and found her eyes focused on the money.

'Keiko?' I was breathing through the top of my lungs. 'Two hundred? Okay?'

There was a long pause. 'No, Maggie.' Finally, she looked back at me, her hands twisting and turning the pot of jam. 'I am sorry. Not okay. Colin say treehouse is not for sale.'

This time she bowed to me for real, and then shut the front door without another word.

~ ~ ~

Peter gave me a much warmer reception. He was Nancy's boyfriend and co-owner of the Saffron Sweeting Antiques

Barn. She'd told him I might be calling in to ask about Dad's painting, and Colin's plan to sell it.

'Well, I'd love to help, Maggie,' he said. 'However, fine art isn't really my specialism. My partner Giles would be better, but he's in Cannes for a month or two.'

'So, you don't know what procedures an auction house would follow to make sure a painting is genuine?'

I'd assumed they would have experts, like I'd sometimes seen on television, giving an instantaneous thumbs up or thumbs down to curiosities parading past them.

'What era did you say, again? And it's British?'

I hadn't explained why I was asking these questions, but vaguely described the art that was troubling me. 'It was painted in 1956,' I said. 'Probably.'

I'd dug around online to find out more about *Chasing the Train*. If the painting was original, it was by Magnus Monkton, a celebrated artist who'd fallen in love with steam trains as a young boy and featured them in many of his works. At one point, he'd even had a commission from a minor royal.

'Well, yes, someone at the auction house would have in-depth knowledge of that era, and a good idea of what other works had sold for.'

'This one was presumed stolen.' I'd looked up the Harrogate heist of 1963. 'At least, that's what the internet said.'

'That could add to its value,' Peter said. 'Any whiff of a scandal, or intrigue, and collectors get more excited. At least, they do with antiques.' He gestured at his stock, which including spinning wheels, gramophones, carriage clocks, and jewellery.

'And what if the artist met an unfortunate end?' I asked. Poor Mr Monkton had fallen off a railway bridge in 1975, while working on his self-proclaimed magnum opus.

Peter nodded. 'The gavel heats up fast, if there's a story behind the piece.'

I was starting to understand why a modest canvas splodged with oil paint could be equivalent to a new roof.

'But, would they do forensic tests, or something, to check it wasn't a fake?'

'I'm not sure. They might, but maybe only if they were suspicious. It would depend how convincing the provenance was.'

'Provenance?' I knew the word, but not the context.

'Yes, like the painting's pedigree. Its history, its documentation, to confirm it's the real deal.'

'Oh.'

I hadn't thought of that. I should have realised, Colin couldn't just breeze into an auction house and offload a complete dud. If a reputable dealer had accepted *Chasing the Train*, then presumably there was paperwork to back it up.

Maybe I was suspicious because, deep down, I was jealous about the money. Maybe I was being a bitter ex-wife, and a bad loser. I should shrug it off and get on with my life.

I thanked Peter and said goodbye.

~ ~ ~

By the time I'd driven home, brewed a pot of tea, and scrambled some eggs for my supper, my mind was churning again. The painting didn't add up. Dad didn't have that kind of money. He loved railway bits and pieces, but never talked about buying or selling any of them. He never went to galleries, or auctions, and he never once breathed a word that anything in his house might be valuable.

Colin might have been able to persuade the auction house that *Chasing the Train* was the real deal.

But, provenance or no provenance, I wasn't convinced.

## Chapter 14

After the divorce, there were all kinds of things I had to get used to doing on my own. Some were difficult, a few were heart-wrenching, and most were just strange. It wasn't as if Colin and I had done everything together, anyway, as he worked unpredictable hours. But going on holiday the first time on my own had been a jolt. Colin loved Christmas, so hanging my lonely stocking on the mantelpiece in Saffron Sweeting the first year had caused a few tears. Eating in a restaurant at a table for one had been weird, but not unpleasant.

And then there was the everyday stuff. He'd owned a fancy toaster, so if we were having toast, he almost always made it. When I moved out, I had to buy a toaster, and using it the first few times felt like a rite of passage. But there were perks, too, and not only eating sausage rolls in bed if I felt like it. I noticed strange things, like being able to choose my own preferred route around a supermarket. And if I bought fresh bread, nobody sulked if they didn't get first dibs on the crust.

Colin had fled from the kitchen in protest on the rare occasions he came home and found me elbow-deep in pots and jars. So having Finn as my assistant jam maker was a pleasant change.

'I thought you said you weren't much of a cook?' He eyed the astonishing amount of jam-making gear I'd produced from the various cupboards in my cottage. 'This is incredible.'

'Well, making jam doesn't feel like cooking to me. It's science, it's chemistry.' Or alchemy, I added silently. 'But you're right, we don't have enough space.' I squeezed by him to get from the stove to the sink. 'We'll have to use the dining table.'

The cottage, like so many British homes, had been built in an era where nobody wanted open living. Kitchens were hidden away, as if cooking were a shameful activity.

'Just tell me what you want where.' Finn touched my waist lightly as I passed back again.

'Well, line up all those jars on the table, then we'll see.'

But that fleeting touch lingered even after he'd disappeared into the dining room. I was forced to admit I could think of at least one activity which would be far more exciting than making jam.

By now, I'd been to his flat, and he'd spent a couple of evenings at my cottage. But he hadn't stayed over. One night we'd missed a whole episode of *Sherlock* as we kissed and cuddled on the sofa. Eventually he'd whispered, 'I'm too fond of you, Maggie Moone, to rush you.'

Finn was a nice guy, but alarm bells were ringing at the possibility of things getting more serious. I liked him, but there was no way I was ready for a new relationship. Was I?

Talking into the safety of his neck, I'd confessed I'd never been with anyone other than Colin.

'It's nothing to be ashamed of,' he'd replied. 'In fact, in Ireland, many people would applaud you for it.'

'I don't suppose they'd applaud me for being divorced.'

'Maybe not, but I'm glad.'

Then he'd settled me into the crook of his arm and we'd stayed like that, not talking, just breathing in not-quite unison.

Now, in close proximity to him in the warm, sweetly scented kitchen, I willed my heart to stop thudding, and dragged my thoughts back to jam.

'How many more of these bloomin' things are there?' Finn asked, when forty minutes of hulling strawberries and chopping rhubarb had passed.

'Almost there.' My own fingers and wrists were aching too.

We continued in silence for a few minutes, before Finn broke my train of thought.

'Earth to Maggie?'

'What?' I looked up.

'You threw a bunch of rhubarb leaves in the jam pot, and the good bits in the compost.'

I glanced down. 'Oh, hell!' I fished out half a dozen offending leaves. 'Sorry, bit distracted.'

Finn looked sideways at me. 'Penny for them?'

I shrugged. 'Ack, it's nothing.' Then, seeing him wait: 'It's my anniversary, that's all.'

'Your wedding anniversary?'

I nodded. We'd had a church wedding, at St Mary's in Burwell. Colin was more religious than me and his friends had turned up in droves. My dad was proudly awkward, but I was barely speaking to Mum. Colin's dad was already dead, and his mother was packing to emigrate. I'm sure, at the time, I'd been happy, but now, my strongest memory of the day was how oppressively hot it was.

Finn picked up another strawberry. 'Did you, er, celebrate each year, then?'

'Not really. For the first few years, Colin got me roses. Then, I suppose about four years in, we were on holiday, so no roses in Greece... and after that, no, nothing special.'

The first year, I'd attempted to cook a nice meal, something involving aubergine. That had been a disaster, but at least at that point, we had still been affectionate towards each other.

I stared out of the kitchen window, the romesco sauce clear in my memory.

'Well...' Finn cleared his throat, reminding me where I was. 'It's natural you'd be, er, thinking about him, on your anniversary.'

I snapped my attention back to the present, and smiled. 'Sorry.'

After a moment I asked, 'How about you? Has there been anyone special?'

He gave a short chuckle which didn't sound funny. 'Special is a hard thing to define, Maggie Moone.'

Should I drop the topic? At his age, surely not all his girlfriends had been casual flings. 'Well, longer term, say.'

'You're not letting me off lightly, are you?'

I shook my head as I felt him glance my way. 'You know all about Colin.'

'Longer term?' he repeated. 'Yes, okay, I suppose you could call it that.'

'And? What was she like?'

'Married.'

I paused. 'What happened?'

'Despite what she said, her heart was already taken.' He shrugged. 'It took a while, but I came to my senses.'

Finn didn't say any more, but as we finished preparing the fruit, I did see him shoot me a couple of pensive glances. But by the time the jam mixture was bubbling on the stove, our mood had lightened.

'Next time, maybe we can just buy the damn stuff?' he suggested, as I chased a solitary fly around the kitchen, terrified it would fall into the pot and spoil the whole sticky batch.

With a satisfying smack, the fly met its end against the kitchen window. 'Well, I didn't tell you this before, but the vicar said if a couple can make jam together without coming to blows, they can survive anything.'

'Really?' Finn looked up from stirring the huge pot.

I shook my head. 'No. But maybe there's something in it.'

He laughed. 'You know I'm only here in the hope I can lick it off you later. I never intended to put mine on a scone or anything.'

Oh, that Irish flirting could turn a girl's head. Good thing I was determined to keep our time together light. And the sooner Colin caught sight of Finn and me out together, the better.

So I frowned back at him, pretending to be appalled. 'That sounds messy, and disgusting... and...'

'And?' Finn prompted.

I shrugged. 'And, clearly, a waste of good jam.'

~~~

Aside from the occasional thunderstorm, the June weather was glorious. The fields around Saffron Sweeting were ablaze with yellow rapeseed flowers, and it wouldn't be long before haymaking started. Even better, in a few weeks, there would be an abundance of local fruit available. I was already fantasising about stirring up apricot jam, redcurrant jelly, and gooseberry chutney.

Sitting in my tiny, overgrown back garden, where daylight now lingered past nine o'clock, I thought I heard the quavering song of a nightjar. And I couldn't help but think about the perfect summer nights like this when Matty and I had stayed in the treehouse past dusk, listening to the call of birds soften to gentler night-time noises.

This reminded me that Colin and Keiko could sell their house any day. I had to try again for the treehouse.

'Hi, it's Maggie,' I said, when Colin answered his phone.

He paused. 'What's up?'

'How are you?' I said, then regretted it.

Since the divorce, with all the obvious arguments removed from our interactions, we'd been getting on much better. But we weren't on the kind of terms where I'd ring for a chat. And if there were rumours circulating that I fancied him, I wasn't going to initiate cosy conversations.

'Fine.' His tone was blunt, and I remembered he might still be cheesed off about Camilla's kitchen.

'I saw Keiko the other day.' I tried to make it sound as though we'd bumped into each other at Waitrose. 'And I think she's happy to sell me the treehouse, she just wanted to run it by you first.' My fingers were crossed for this bit.

Another pause. 'Oh yeah?'

I waited: he wasn't the only one who could try silence as a conversational device.

Then, he said, 'How's it going with Camilla's project?'

'Er, good.' Damn, he *was* still annoyed about it.

'You're going ahead with the work, then?'

'Yep, some of the nasty tiles are off and it looks better already.'

Colin coughed, then muttered, 'Bloody brilliant.'

Too late, I realised I should have been more vague. 'Although, er, obviously it won't be anywhere near as stunning as it would if you'd—'

'You don't say.'

I wavered. Mentally, he'd pushed me around throughout our marriage and the habit of being the pushee was hard to break. I bit my lip. Don't apologise, I told myself. Don't apologise.

'Look.' My voice rose. 'It's not my fault Camilla changed her mind about your ridiculously expensive quote.'

'It—'

'And I'm sorry you won't be getting a glossy mention in a glossy magazine.' I wasn't sorry at all, actually. 'But I've got every right to take on any work I want to. And when I've finished, her kitchen's going to look super.' I hoped that was true.

'Well, if that's your definition of ethical business behaviour, stealing work from your own family...'

'We're not bloody family! We're divorced!' I spluttered. That was a dirty trick to play. *Did* he suspect I still had feelings for him?

What would Amelia do? How would she handle this? She'd go on the offensive. She'd lift her chin, flick her auburn locks back, and throw down a gauntlet.

I attempted a hair flick, even though Colin couldn't see it. 'And how dare you mention ethics, when you're about to make a bomb selling Dad's painting?'

There was a long silence. He hadn't known, of course, that I knew about *Chasing the Train*.

'It's not your dad's painting. It's mine. You signed everything in that house over to me.'

Yes, I thought, when I was an emotional wreck, incapable of finding clean knickers to wear, let alone recognising valuable art. At one point before Colin took over, I was spending whole weekends in Pickering, sitting in the middle of the lounge carpet, crying.

'But—'

'But what?'

I didn't have any comeback over the value of the painting, and he knew it. I didn't even care, really, about the stupid train picture. It was the feeling he'd made a fool of me. And, if I was honest, the sense that there'd been a whole dimension to Dad's life I hadn't appreciated.

'Well, maybe we should agree that you keep your nose out of my business, and I'll leave you alone with yours,' I said.

'Fine by me.'

I sighed. I hadn't intended to make him cross again. 'And, yes, so about the treehouse – I was wondering—'

'You can stop wondering. The answer's no.'

It meant nothing at all to him. 'Please, just—'

'No, Maggie. And you can stop bloody pestering. You're not having it.'

~~~

I stomped into my cottage and made a beeline for my list of things which Colin hated.

I'll show him, I thought, and flipped it over to make a new section titled *Places to Change My Name*.

By the time I'd listed bank, passport, doctor, dentist, driving license, TV license, insurance, council, utility companies, and credit cards, the wind had gone out of my sails. I sighed. Becoming Maggie Moone again was going to take forever.

Never mind. It was time. It was definitely time.

*Chapter 15*

I felt a shiver of excitement when I saw Finn waving to me across the expansive lawns of Saffron Hall the following Sunday. It wasn't, I told myself, the thrill of seeing him, but the quiet satisfaction of being almost certain Colin would be here. Public relations had always been a strength of his: with Kern Kitchens sponsoring this play, he'd attend, even if live theatre was on his list of annoyances. I'd almost fallen over with glee when I'd seen the poster in the post office window, advertising the outdoor performance.

The funny thing was, Finn hadn't been exactly keen either.

'For sure,' he'd said, when I'd first mentioned Pimm's and thespians on a temporary outdoor stage at our local stately home. Then: 'What's the play?'

His face had fallen when I'd told him. 'Did you not do Shakespeare to death at school, Maggie Moone?'

'Not really.' I knew we'd read Macbeth but beyond that, I couldn't remember anything else.

'I'll come, as long as I can eat loads and watch you instead of the actors,' Finn had suggested. 'And,' he played his trump card, 'if you finally show me that tattoo of yours.'

So, here we were: me with the tartan blanket and ginger lemonade, and him with the picnic. There'd been a downpour last night and the grass was damp, but so far the fluffy clouds above weren't threatening the performance.

A cheerful crowd had staked out spots on the lawn, which sloped down towards the stage, with the imposing peach-coloured brick of the Hall behind. It was indeed a genteel setting.

'Come and sit with us,' Amelia called as she spotted us scanning the audience. She was with a tall, fair-haired man, whose expression was hidden behind dark glasses. 'This is Scott,' she said, as Finn and I settled down. 'He claims he's here for the champagne, but I know he's secretly yearning for a frilly shirt.'

Scott sat up, drank an entire glass of the fizz Amelia handed him, then lay down again as if preparing for a nap. 'Don't mind me,' he said. 'Frightful bloody English caper.'

Excellent, I thought. My ex-husband didn't like theatre, Finn didn't like Shakespeare, and Amelia's companion planned to sleep through the performance. Never mind. The play wasn't the point of being here.

I sat up as straight as I could on the blanket, neck twisting as I tried to see who else was here. For once, I felt confident in a crowd. I'd tried hard with my appearance today. Grace had summoned all her talents to twist my hair into a loose knot, and earlier in the week I'd allowed Amelia to coax me into buying a dark blue jumpsuit with a halter neck.

'You look divine,' she'd said, as I'd twisted and turned in the changing room of a boutique in Newmarket. 'Very sexy. Shows off your shoulders.'

My shoulders, I had to agree, were one of my better features. Putting up shelves and painting ceilings had the additional benefit of toning one's triceps. But the jumpsuit wasn't exactly practical and I'd have to cut back on every kind of drinking, so I wasn't grappling with it in the loo all afternoon. So, no champagne for me, and probably not even a cup of tea either. And Finn didn't stand a chance of glimpsing my tattoo today. But I hadn't told him that.

'Look, Maggie.' Amelia was kneeling up like a meerkat, waving at people she knew, which was almost everyone. 'Isn't that your ex-husband?'

She knew it was. I looked, and there he was, settling with Keiko about fifty feet away in a pair of low deckchairs. I noticed several of the American families had the same: they obviously knew more than us about comfort, or wet grass, or both.

'Keiko, darling, halloo! Hello, Colin,' Amelia called. How *did* she keep up with so many people?

The next moment, I got my wish. Colin looked across, just as Finn draped his arm around my shoulder to lean in and tell me something. I didn't catch what he said, but I smiled and tilted my head towards him anyway.

A frisson ran through me. That would show Colin. *Still in love with him*, for goodness' sake. Here I was, looking my best, with a handsome Irish almost-doctor beside me. Oh, and Scott was a real hunk, too. Colin wouldn't necessarily guess he was with Amelia. I snuggled closer to Finn.

'I know he's more or less the enemy.' Amelia jerked her head in Colin's direction. 'But I hear business is booming. My friend Bunty Brissinghorn was singing his praises the other day. She's having oodles of work done.'

Trust Amelia to have friends with silly toffee-nosed names. But I was glad Colin had plenty of work: it erased any lingering guilt I had about my project for Camilla.

'Did you two bring any strawberries?' Scott asked, apparently not yet asleep. 'Meely forgot ours.'

'I didn't *forget* them,' Amelia retorted. 'They're at home for after. And don't call me that.' She poked him in the ribs.

'We've got loads,' Finn said. 'Help yourself.'

'Thank God,' Scott replied. 'Makes the afternoon a fraction more bearable.'

'*Actually*,' came a pointed voice from behind us, 'they're hoping to make it a bigger thing, if it goes well.'

I turned and saw it was Violet, from the post office. She was sitting on a dog's lead, which in turn was attached to an attractive black and white spaniel. The dog, meanwhile, was panting happily and drooling at the surrounding picnics.

'We might even have our own Saffron Sweeting Shakespeare Festival,' Violet added.

'Goodness,' said Kenneth, who was sharing her blanket, with his fiancée on his other side. 'Much Ado about Something, then.'

'Why don't you like Shakespeare, anyway?' I whispered to Finn.

He shrugged. 'Forced it down our throats at school, I suppose. Him and Oscar Wilde. And even with all those battles, there was too much talking. Not enough actual swords.'

'Well, this one's a comedy,' I replied. 'So don't hold your breath for bloodshed.'

The actors did a respectable job and the setting was idyllic, but I got the feeling we wouldn't be taking on the Regent's Park productions any time soon. The picnic, however, was delicious: Finn had brought mushroom quiche and ripe tomatoes, with a strawberry-packed Eton Mess to follow.

Despite the lovely food, the scenes passed slowly, and I found my eyes repeatedly pulled towards Keiko and Colin. She seemed to find it entertaining enough, but he looked bored stiff and I caught him looking my way, more than once. Good.

'Not exactly Glyndebourne, is it?' Amelia murmured to me in the interval, as we queued for the temporary toilets. I wasn't looking forward to negotiating my jumpsuit.

'I wouldn't know.' I wasn't the kind of person who spent hundreds of pounds on opera tickets. 'But I think it's lovely the village is trying.'

'Oh, it is.' She nodded. 'Sorry, didn't mean to be catty.'

It was rare to hear Amelia apologise for something, but she knew better than anyone how much the village had struggled in recent years, and how its improving fortunes were good for everyone.

I was going to ask her about Scott. He had that polished air about him which suggested he might be from a family which actually owned a place like this, but she spoke before I could.

'So how's Camilla's kitchen coming along? Did you know you've got green blotches in your hair?'

'Oops.' I grinned. 'Camilla's not too bad. And she recommended me to her neighbour. I'm fixing up their kids' playroom, in an attic.'

'Let me guess,' Amelia said drily. 'Sloping ceilings? Wet paint?'

Paint or not, I was having a ball. Grace had once again made a few suggestions, but I was making it happen, from installing toy cupboards, to painting the walls, to improving the lighting. Not only that, but demand for my handywoman service was growing. In the last week I'd put up a mirror, bled a houseful of radiators, and repaired a dovecote. The doves didn't seem to mind. Finding time for bookkeeping jobs was increasingly hard, and even Finn had joked about writing himself on the calendar in my kitchen.

'You should make it official.' Amelia tapped her foot as the queue for the loo inched forward.

'What?' My mind went to Finn. It was too soon for that kind of development, surely? We were only larking around.

'Your room fixes, handywork, all that. Get some business cards. A website, even.'

'Oh, I don't know...'

'You enjoy it, right? More than stuffy old bookkeeping?'

I made a face. That was a no-brainer.

'Well, I can put loads more work your way. My usual guy's making noises about being a stay-at-home dad. And I happen to know,' she dropped her voice, 'people *love* having a woman do their work. Apparently, you take your shoes off, tidy up better, and don't leave the toilet seat up.'

I laughed.

'Think about it.' Then she seized her turn for a vacant portaloo. 'Finally!' she called, scurrying towards the toilet door. 'To pee or not to pee, that is the question!'

With two minutes of the interval remaining, Amelia and I picked our way across the grass, back to our picnic blankets and the men. From behind, I watched her swaying, sexy walk and tried to imitate her, as I sashayed past Colin and Keiko with my head held high.

~~~

The second half was less engaging than the first and I wasn't the only one getting fidgety.

Finally, a few minutes from the end, Finn whispered to me, 'Is there something I should know?'

'About what?' I whispered back, wondering if I'd missed the best joke in the play.

'About your ex-husband,' he replied in a low tone.

'Like what?'

'Like, why you keep looking across at him with that expression on your face.'

'No I don't,' I whispered. Followed by, 'What expression?'

Finn waited for a punchline, and the audience's laughter. 'Like there's something going on.'

'There's nothing going on!' I shot back, a little too sharply.

I didn't help myself by going pink.

Finn didn't say any more, but he shifted away, and appeared to be engrossed in the play. I stared at the stage too, but I'm pretty sure neither of us enjoyed it.

As we applauded the performance and endured the tedious encores, I sensed his mood was heavy.

'Are you okay?' I asked, after Amelia and Scott left and we were folding up the picnic blanket. As I'd suspected, the moisture from the grass had seeped through.

'I'm fine.'

He paused to watch Violet's dog, ecstatic at being set loose. The spaniel was careering across the lawns, nose down like a bloodhound, no doubt hunting for morsels of sausage rolls and cake. His long plumy tail waved with joy.

Finn turned to me. 'I really like you, Maggie. That's all.'

I was surprised at the jolt I felt. What was it? Shame that yes, I had been sending calculating glances in Colin's direction? Something else?

'Well, I… like you too.' It sounded lame.

'I'd just like to know your ex really is *ex*,' Finn said, as we made our way across the lawn towards the exit.

'Of course he is,' I replied. 'Why would you think otherwise?' But my eyes flicked to where Colin and Keiko had been sitting.

'You mention him a lot.'

'Do I?'

Finn sighed. 'You know you do.'

He didn't reach for my hand.

# Chapter 16

I was pretty sure Finn was annoyed with me, but I wasn't sure how chastened I felt in return. As for Colin, he'd looked like he wished we'd been watching Macbeth, with me playing Lady Macduff.

All this I pondered, as I donned my protective goggles and started chipping at the remaining red tiles in Camilla's kitchen. It was tedious work, and every time my hammer struck the chisel, a jolt went up my arm, through my shoulder and neck, to poke at my throbbing head. Even so, I didn't dare hurry and risk damaging the tiles we wanted to keep. I forced myself to focus on the meticulous work, and not worry about Finn, or Colin, or the treehouse.

There was one question my mind refused to drop. The art auction was supposed to be next week, and I'd been checking the auctioneer's website to get a sense of the other lots. I'd even contemplated going over to Bury to watch. But last night, I'd found a notice that the sale was delayed, as there was uncertainty over the inclusion of a famous piece.

The coincidence niggled at me. I'd been given more time to find out about Dad's painting.

As the last piece of kitchen tile yielded, it occurred to me I could absent myself for a day or two.

~ ~ ~

Driving the last few miles through rolling Yorkshire countryside to Pickering, my heart quickened at what I might find. My anticipation was short-lived as I promptly got lost in the one-way system. However, after a few wrong turns, I pulled up outside Dad's little house.

The place was unrecognisable. The old brick had been painted white, and the wooden sash windows replaced with soulless uPVC. Even the panelled front door was gone, in favour of a modern design. Outside the house was a skip, complete with gangplank. As I stood, gawking, a young chap appeared with a wheelbarrow. He steered this up the plank, and its contents tumbled in with a cloud of dust. My heart sank at the unceremonious finality of it.

Fifteen minutes later, I'd not only convinced this juvenile builder to let me rummage in the skip, but I was the proud owner of an old black iron fireplace surround. At twenty pounds, surely this was a bargain.

He must have sensed I was a soft touch, because he then mentioned two sealed cardboard boxes he'd found in the garden shed. I bought those too, sight unseen, for another fiver. Keiko and Colin would have rolled their eyes at me acquiring yet more clutter, when I hadn't yet dealt with what I'd got.

It wasn't rational, of course, why this stuff was important. My Yorkshire memories were of my teens, not the more recent year I'd spent before Dad died.

By the time I decided to move here and help him navigate the ugliness of motor neurone disease, my marriage was already as stale as old biscuits. When I got back from Pickering, wrung out from hospitals and watching dad fade, it became clear Colin and I had nothing worth saving. His mortar-with-sand scam was the last straw.

'I don't suppose you know where I'd find any of his friends?' I asked the builder, as we squeezed the fireplace into my car. 'The old man who used to live here, I mean?'

'No idea. I don't hang out with oldies.' My teenage pal drew back, as though senility might be catching. Then, patting the pocket where he'd stashed his windfall: 'But you could try the bowling green. They swarm around there, on a Thursday.'

The only problem was that today was Wednesday. When I reached the bowling green, it was deserted, except for a groundsman. He was pushing an antique roller over grass which already looked pancake flat. I hailed him and made small talk, before getting to my point.

'Old Jeremy Moone, you say?' He kept on rolling, inches at a time, eyes glued to his task. 'Haven't heard his name in a while.'

'Well, his friends, really.' I wasn't expecting to communicate with ghosts, after all. 'Anyone who would remember him.'

'In that case, Bert the Bristle would be your best bet.'

'Bert who?' I didn't remember Dad ever talking about a friend called Bert.

The man didn't clarify. His focus was on the lawn. 'Wednesday's market day. You'll find him there.'

'He has a stall?'

'Aye.'

'What does he sell?'

The roller moved another three feet before the groundsman stopped to wipe his brow with his handkerchief.

'Junk, mostly. Some pottery, bric-a-brac. Not good stuff, like he used to. Not since his eyes got so bad.'

'Thanks.' I turned to go, knowing I had to make it to the market square before the traders started packing up. 'And what did he sell before?'

'Why, paintings, of course. He was pretty famous, around here. Bert was our local artist.'

~ ~ ~

Fortunately, the market was still in full swing when I reached the town centre. Stalls with striped awnings clustered around the war memorial, and I spotted an old fountain, with room for horses to drink. Shoppers bustled to and fro, many of the older women wearing headscarves.

Some trundled shopping trolleys behind them. Their body language suggested a determination to get a bargain, whether from the fish stall where plaice was the deal of the day, or at the vegetable stall where two cauliflowers could be snatched for a mere pound.

I bypassed the food offerings – although the van flogging bacon sandwiches was doing a roaring trade – in favour of the other vendors: greetings cards, suitcases, hardware. At the end of this quieter row, I found a motley assortment of bric-a-brac and a sad smattering of antiques.

Then, in the shadows, I spotted him.

'Hello. Are you Bert, by chance?'

He'd probably been at Dad's funeral, but I didn't remember him. Nor did he look anything like the Albie I'd remembered from my teenage years. But, then again, that was two decades ago.

The stallholder looked up from underneath his flat cap, peering through glasses as thick as bottles. He wore fingerless gloves and, as the flimsy canvas protection of his stall flapped in the stiff breeze, I could understand why.

'That's me, love.'

'I'm Maggie Moone.' I shifted from foot to foot as the breeze nipped me too. 'I'm here for... a trip down memory lane. My dad lived locally: Jeremy Moone?'

I watched, hoping to see recognition cross his face. Bert was roughly the age my father would have been now, his face a patchwork of wrinkles.

'Aye,' Bert said. 'Jiggy. He were a pal of mine.'

I smiled. I hadn't heard that nickname in years.

'You look chilly,' I said. 'Been out here all morning?'

Bert nodded.

'Well,' I said, 'as it turns out, I didn't have time for lunch. Can I bring you a bacon sandwich?'

Bert's eyes were bad, but there was nothing wrong with his nostrils. He sniffed in appreciation as I returned with our food, and waved me into the relative shelter of his stall to perch on a camping stool beside him.

'You seem like a nice lass,' he said.

At this, I adopted my most congenial expression. I probably resembled an apologetic puppy, but it was the best I could do. If he liked me, that was good.

'Have you sold much today?' I let my eyes roam over his offerings. Even before he'd called me a nice lass, I'd known I would buy something.

He made a sound that was half grunt, half snort.

'Folks don't value old stuff any more,' he said. 'Not like they used to.'

I nodded in deference to old treasures. We chewed for a few minutes, and when I'd finished my roll, I got up to examine the wares. He had a couple of clocks, and some vintage wristwatches. Spying an antique pocket watch, I held it up and was surprised to hear a solid tick.

'How much for this?'

Bert was still eating, but squinted at the watch. 'For Jiggy Moone's daughter? Tenner.'

I should have haggled, but it was a pretty thing and something about its steadfast ticking appealed to me. Maybe I should look for a clock for my mantelpiece, too.

'Okay.' My eyes ran over the rest of his stall, taking in railway nameplates, station signs, and what might have been a whistle. 'Hey, you've got some train bits. My dad was really into those.'

'Aye. He was.' Bert nodded. 'Give him a tenderplate to polish and he was happy for hours.' He appeared to think about this. 'I was keen on locomotives myself, at one time. Until they gave up on steam, I mean. It weren't the same, after that.'

Bert the Bristle, I thought. Bert loved to paint.

'Do you remember the painting he had? Above his fireplace?' I kept my tone casual. 'I thought you might, since you know about art.'

Bert stopped chewing. He put his head on one side, watching me.

'What?' I asked, uncomfortable.

'Are you taking the mickey, Miss Maggie?'

I hadn't been called Miss Maggie in years. But I shook my head. 'No. Why?'

Bert looked down at his bacon roll, before taking a bite and chewing slowly. Maybe he had false teeth: he was making that sandwich last ages.

Then he asked, 'Why did you say you're here?'

I swallowed. 'Like I said, I wanted... a reminder of old times.' I was sure, now, that Bert was the Albie I remembered.

Bert coughed. 'Can you prove you're Maggie Moone?'

'Er, yes.' Could I? 'I suppose so. I mean, I can tell you all I remember about my dad and... my school... and stuff?'

Damn, why hadn't I got on faster with changing my name back? I didn't have a new driving license yet, or cheque book, or anything useful to show him.

At this crucial point in our conversation, a middle-aged woman in a beret came to browse. I wanted to shoo her away, but sat on my hands instead.

Finally, when the woman had touched every item on Bert's stall before buying a signal lamp, he returned to his chair.

'Am I in trouble?' he asked.

'What?' My stomach lurched. Until then, I'd only had an inkling about *Chasing the Train*. 'Of course not.' I took a breath, then added, 'But, maybe you know about the painting?'

'Like what?'

'Oh... like, I was wondering, perhaps it wasn't quite... genuine?' Through those bottle lenses, his expression was unfathomable. 'I mean, I heard you liked to paint, Bert?'

Bert made a dismissive sound.

'You were quite the artist, I heard, before your eyes got bad.'

'I was never all that good.'

'I think you were.' I didn't know where this certainty came from. But at that moment, I would have bet my cottage on Bert being the true artist behind the painting Colin was selling. 'And I think, maybe, you liked to paint trains.'

The old stallholder made me wait until he'd finished his lunch before he spoke again.

'You've got the wrong end of the stick, lass.'

He was lying. He had to be.

'Fine. I'll stop beating about the bush and ask you straight.' My heart was racing now. 'Did you forge a copy of *Chasing the Train*?'

Bert took his glasses off, and looked me right in the eye. His own were watery blue, and although I couldn't tell how much of me he could see, somehow I was sure he was telling the truth.

'No,' he said. 'I didn't.'

# Chapter 17

It was a long day in Camilla's kitchen. I repaired the minor damage to the wall where the tiles had been, and painted two cautious coats of primer on the island. I couldn't afford for anything to flake or peel: this job had to be perfect.

Paint fumes didn't usually bother me, but something wasn't right today. By lunchtime my throat felt scratchy and by four o'clock I also had a throbbing headache. I cleaned up diligently, worried that Camilla would flip out if she came home to any mess. By the time I finished, I was exhausted.

As I put my things in my car for the short drive home, Finn phoned.

'Maggie Moone!' This was his usual greeting. I hadn't heard from him since the previous weekend and our Shakespeare tiff. But he sounded normal.

'Hi,' I said cautiously.

'I had to change shifts to cover someone who's ill. Now I have two days off. Can I take you out?'

I sighed. 'I feel a bit rubbish.' I was startled how his voice gave me a boost. I hadn't admitted I'd been bothered about last weekend. 'I'm pretty sure I'm coming down with something.'

'What kind of something?' His medical mind wanted details.

'Just a crappy head, crappy throat, feel like crap,' I said, ladylike as always. 'Want to go home and go to bed, actually.' I attempted to sit on the rear bumper of my car.

There was a pause. Then he said, 'I'm coming over.'

'Uh, I dunno...' I'd be terrible company. 'I mean, I'm really tired and there's no food in the house.'

'Doesn't matter. I'll make soup.'

'Soup?' I shut the boot of my car.

~ ~ ~

What a difference an hour made. My initial fear that Finn thought going to bed included him had evaporated. Within the span of sixty minutes he'd arrived, brewed me a steaming dose of Lemsip, and shooed me upstairs to put my pyjamas on. 'And then into bed with you, Maggie Moone,' he'd commanded.

I did as I was told, tuning my bedroom radio to the soothing sounds of Radio 4. During my dad's long illness, he'd often asked for that station, and together we'd listened at all hours of the day and night. It didn't matter how highbrow or irrelevant the programme was: it passed the time and saved us voicing our fears about his prognosis. For some reason, he especially liked the Shipping Forecast, read each night before the national anthem and the station closedown.

Before long, I found I looked forward to the gentle harmonies of *Sailing By*, and then the contradictory thrill of gale warnings for boats, while we were tucked up inside. As his health declined, it became the one reliable thing in our routine. When I'd returned to Saffron Sweeting, my grief for Dad raw and my marriage in tatters, the nightly Shipping Forecast saved me from vodka and pills.

Soon, an incredible aroma began to drift up the stairs. Shortly after, Finn appeared, carrying a tray.

'What on earth are you listening to?'

My regular forecast was broadcast in the middle of the night, but there was an earlier one too. I was hardly ever in bed for that.

'Just the radio,' I said, as the announcer warned of cyclonic winds in FitzRoy.

'I hope you like toast with your soup.' He landed the tray on the bed.

'You really *did* make soup.' I wasn't sure whether to trust the mirage before me.

'Careful, it's hot.' He paused, looking like he might pick up the spoon and feed me like a baby, but then he settled on the spare half of the bed.

I wriggled into an upright position and reached for the bowl. 'It smells wonderful.'

'Chicken and leek,' he confirmed, watching me.

I took a few cautious sips – it was indeed piping hot – and felt the comforting warmth spread through my body. 'That's amazing.' I paused for a nibble of toast. 'Where did you learn...?'

He shrugged. 'You make jam, I make soup.'

I took another mouthful. 'I love it. How many recipes do you know?'

Now he grinned. 'One. Chicken and leek.'

'Oh.' Feeling a little better, I smiled back. 'Well, okay. Why mess with perfection?'

~~~

I woke at dawn the next morning, aware I'd slept for many hours. As I rolled over, I realised Finn was asleep beside me. He was fully dressed, on top of the duvet, stretched as if trying to reach his toes to the foot of the bed and his fingers to the top. Colin had tended to sleep in a tightly curled ball, fists near his face. From Finn, I got the impression he had nothing to hide.

The curtains weren't quite closed and the morning light glinted off the dream catcher I'd hung there. I never imagined, that day at the malt house, that I'd be waking up beside the man who gave it to me.

On my bedside table was a glass of water I hadn't put there. I reached for it, trying not to disturb the duvet, but as I lay down again, Finn opened his eyes.

'Maggie Moone.' He sounded surprised to see me.

'Hello.' By now I'd wriggled until the duvet was pulled up to my nose.

'How are you feeling?'

I paused. 'Better, I think.' And shy.

'Grand.'

'Thank you for the soup.' That didn't cover what I was trying to say. 'And for coming over.'

He reached out an arm and placed it on the lump of duvet corresponding to mine. 'You look gorgeous in the morning.'

'I do not. I need a long bath and a tonne of toothpaste.'

'And I *almost* saw your moon tattoo last night.' Finn smiled lazily.

I tugged down the shorts of my pyjamas. 'I thought you were a gentleman.'

'Relax. I didn't see anything you'd mind. Yet.'

'You're obsessed with that tattoo.'

'No... but I'm quickly becoming obsessed with you.'

I definitely needed some toothpaste. I bit my lip and looked away.

He seemed to sense my unease. 'Are you cross that I stayed?'

I shook my head. 'It's just a bit strange, that's all.'

'Yeah, I know.'

'Before you woke up, I was thinking—' I swallowed.

He rubbed my arm, then prompted, 'What?'

'Well, if I'd known sooner there were men like you in the world, I wouldn't have stayed married so long.'

That's done it, I thought. He'll get up and leave now.

He didn't. His eyes darkened, and he wriggled closer so he could slide his arm around me properly. After a couple of breaths, he said, 'There is the small matter of your story, though.'

'My what?'

'Your life story. We've spent the night together, so you're obliged to tell me all of it. Start to finish. Or, start to now, at least.'

I gave a sleepy laugh. 'No way. You already know about the exploding Christmas chestnut. The rest of it's too boring.'

'No it isn't.'

'I'm under the weather. Can't talk today.'

'All right, Maggie Moone.' He shifted me into a different position in the crook of his elbow, and settled us back down again. 'All right, maybe not today. But soon.'

I'd had three phone calls offering work in the last two days, all from people I didn't know, with American accents. Presumably, Camilla had told more friends about me. One of the calls was from someone called Betsy, and when I relayed this to Grace, she almost jumped with excitement.

'Oh, you *must* do that job. She's *lovely*.'

I hadn't been planning on turning down the work, but this was nice to hear.

'And their house is like something out of a period drama. It's amazing,' Grace said. 'When I die, I've told James to creep into their grounds and scatter my ashes.'

'You can't be serious.' I was freaked out, both at the notion of planning one's death before age forty, and also at being blown to the winds on private property.

'No, not really.' Grace had laughed. 'But you'll see, it's gorgeous.'

~~~

Remembering this conversation, I left my car in the village and walked the last part mile to Ted and Betsy's mansion. Damsons, although not yet ripe, clustered on the trees which gave the lane its name. As for their house, it was indeed stunning. Crunching up the driveway, I decided the depth of gravel on the approach to your house must correlate with how rich you are.

As I waited at the massive front door, I pondered what they could want. People like this had personal assistants, butlers, and probably entire concierge teams to deal with dripping taps and loose door handles. I hoped Camilla hadn't inflated my skills and reputation in her referral.

'She's here!' The door flew open and I was wrapped in a female bear hug. At least, I assumed it was female, from the stature of the bear and the appealing floral perfume. Then she let me go.

'I'm Betsy.' The immaculately dressed blonde woman beamed at me. 'We met last year at the pub quiz, do you remember?'

Ah, this explained the bear hug. If we'd met once at a social event, we were practically sorority sisters. This was in direct contrast to the English, where you lived next door to someone for eight years before you graduated to saying good morning.

'Hello.' I tried an awkward wave.

'Ted, she's here!' Betsy turned to bellow again, at a volume which didn't match her size. 'Meet us outside!'

She threw an arm around my shoulders, then propelled me off the front step and across the courtyard.

'You're wondering why you're here,' she said, as we came to a halt outside an outbuilding, which might once have been a stable block. 'You're wondering what these loud, rich Americans want with you and your toolkit and why they haven't hired some fancy designer from London. Or Grace,' she added as an afterthought.

Was I that easy to read? 'Er, well—'

'Our builder's in disgrace.' Betsy flung open the door and led me inside. The space was dingy and smelt damp. 'He came over to do a quote, and the next thing we knew, he was in bed with my personal chef. Except, they weren't actually in bed, they were in the kitchen.'

'Where my food is cooked,' said a male voice, and I turned to see a man – Ted, presumably – taking up the space behind us. 'All the same, Betsy,' he added. 'Did you have to tell her that?' He held out a hand to shake mine. 'I'm Ted. This is my wife, with the complete lack of verbal filter.'

Few things are as sad to me as a couple who take digs at each other in front of strangers – or, worse, friends. Colin had done that enough times over the years. But I was relieved to find Ted was smiling broadly, his arm around his wife. She leaned into him, unperturbed.

'So...' Betsy gestured at the large room around us. 'We want to turn it into a sort of studio. My sister's coming to visit in the fall, and we want her to have her own space.'

'She's a musician,' Ted added.

'Right, yes, a composer, and I'm *thrilled* she's coming, but...'

'...But we don't want her symphony-in-progress screeching through the house at all hours.'

'She doesn't screech, Ted.'

'She does.'

I decided I liked them both.

'Oh, all right.' Betsy tutted. 'She does screech a bit sometimes.' She walked over to the far wall and placed a hand on it. 'So, Maggie, we want to do this old tack room up a bit.'

'But only a bit,' Ted said. 'Helen heard we were planning work for her arrival, and got bent out of shape. She can be a bit touchy about that sort of thing.'

I didn't follow which sort of thing, but Betsy saw my expression. 'Touchy about money.'

'Okay...' I was glad my cash-flow problems were my own. 'So...?'

'So, can we do a quick spruce up, make it nicer, without appearing like we spent a boatload of cash? Shabby chic, or something?'

I wasn't sure of the definition of shabby chic, but by now I knew the most cost-effective ways of cheering up a room. And this was hardly the type of project which would antagonise Colin. Only last week, I'd noticed he'd started a kitchen extension, at a big house near Amelia's.

'Well,' I began, 'you might have a problem with damp. That's the biggest issue. Is there any heating?' I looked around.

'Does this thing count?' Ted heaved a few boxes to one side, revealing an ancient-looking gas fire. 'I doubt it works.'

'We can find out,' I said. 'Although not today.' I'd phone Vincent, he could test it.

They both nodded.

'Then, paint,' I suggested. 'Lots and lots of paint. Walls, ceiling... floor if you like. It'll make a huge difference for not much money. The natural light's really good.'

Or it would be, once I'd shimmied up a ladder and given those high windows a good scrub. The tack room had no view, but it would feel airy.

'And Helen can pick out furniture when she gets here,' Betsy said. 'We'll get second-hand, if she insists.' She said *second-hand* as though it were a foreign word. 'Or antique, if I get my way.'

'So, can you help us, Maggie?' This was Ted.

'Yes, of course.' I decided I'd love to work for them. I'd charge a fair price, too: no need to inflate my estimate, just because they could afford it. 'It'll make a nice change from kitchens. Shall I work out some costs, and let you know?'

'Sounds good.' Ted nodded.

'And will you stay for dinner?' Betsy asked. 'Ted's heading out to play squash; I'll be home alone otherwise.'

'Careful,' said Ted, 'she wants to experiment on you.' But he winked.

'I'm learning British dishes.' Betsy pretended to be offended. 'I've got an Aga cookbook and I haven't had a disaster yet.'

'Well... what are you making?' As my cold subsided, my appetite was back with a vengeance. But I hoped she didn't suggest something vile, like eel pie.

'Toad in the hole,' Betsy said proudly. 'What do you say, Maggie?'

I smiled, and mentally reduced my estimate by a few more pounds. 'I'd be honoured.'

~~~

'I know it probably isn't much like Ireland.' I tried to keep the apology from my voice. 'But I kind of like it.'

Finn and I were standing at the edge of the sand dunes, looking out across the vast expanse of Holkham Beach. Despite it being June, we were bundled up in jackets against the stiff breeze whipping in from the sea. Summer in Norfolk was a relative term.

'You're right.' He turned to me, his hair a crazy windswept mess. 'Not much like Ballycurrane. But I love it.'

Partly in apology for the Shakespeare play, and partly as a thank you for the chicken soup, I'd suggested to Finn that he choose our next date. I'd half expected him to opt for bingo, but to my surprise, his eyes had taken on a dreamy look.

'I miss the sea,' he'd said.

As I looked up at him now, I was suddenly lost for words, which was odd because we'd talked non-stop in the car on the way here. I knew he'd broken his arm jumping from his bedroom window at age eight. That it took him three goes to pass his driving test. That his favourite Womble was Wellington. He knew that I once queued for four hours to see Aled Jones, that I was scared of sharks, and that I used to take my coffee black until I read that psychopaths were more likely to prefer it that way.

'It's good to get away,' he murmured, reaching to brush a piece of hair from my own face. I'd tied it back, but some rebellious strands were flying around. 'Helps with perspective, you know?'

'Perspective?' How was I supposed to think, with his fingers grazing my temple? 'Like what?'

'Like whether you'd be okay with me kissing you.' He put his arms around me, reducing the wind's bite.

I glanced up and down the beach. Apart from a man in the distance, walking a black dog, it was deserted.

'I'd be okay with that.' I lifted my face.

'Good,' he whispered, and brought his mouth down to mine, gently at first, but then with growing intensity.

I reached up and put my arms around his neck, surprised how natural it felt to tilt my head back and lean in. The wind seemed to drop, and all I noticed was the delicious saltiness of his lips on mine, and his chest pressed against me.

It was some time before I pulled back.

'It's a pretty wild day for kissing.' My voice was strangely husky.

'I was thinking pretty wild, too.' He let out a long breath.

We were standing on firm sand, but I felt myself slipping nonetheless.

'Finn...' I snuggled into his arms. 'Does it bother you that I'm divorced?'

'Only if it bothers you.'

Why, oh why, had I brought up my marriage again? Despite what Finn said, I knew he was uneasy about my feelings for Colin. If he'd previously lost his heart to a married woman, it was fair enough.

He leaned back a little, to look at me. 'I'm a lapsed Catholic, Maggie.'

'Oh.' I was embarrassed at overlooking that angle. 'No, I meant more... I met Colin when I was about seven. We grew up together. I don't know how any of this... works.'

'Works?' His eyebrows went up.

'You know. The... relationship thing. The rules of... dating someone.'

Finn smiled and shook his head. 'There are no rules. Beyond honesty and respect, I mean. We just... well, we work it out as we go along.'

'Oh.'

'But no,' he added, 'if you don't care, then I don't give a fig that you're divorced. Although – what was your married name?'

'Kern.'

'Ahh, well that's okay then. I do so much prefer Maggie Moone.' He gave a slow, sexy smile.

Funny, I thought. I'm starting to prefer Maggie Moone, too.

Finn stepped back, letting go of me. 'I don't know about you,' he stamped his feet on the sand, 'but I could use a walk.'

~ ~ ~

And so we walked. The tide was out and the beach stretched for miles. Apart from a couple of other dog walkers, we had the place to ourselves, with only the gulls overhead and wailing wind for company.

I tried not to think about Colin, who hated English beaches for just this reason. He'd complained about the weather, the sand blowing everywhere, the squally grey sea, and even the other families. He'd claimed they were there because they couldn't afford to go abroad. For Colin, a beach holiday was only tolerable if it was in Greece, or, better still, the Caribbean. Funny, though. For all his talk that next year we'd go to Barbados, we never had.

'It feels like there's twice the oxygen, compared to Cambridge,' Finn said.

'That's because it's blowing into our lungs without us having to inhale.'

'True.' Finn took gulps of Norfolk air. 'But it's so exhilarating.'

'You'll sleep well tonight,' I said, then bit my lip as he looked at me. 'From the sea air, I mean.'

'For sure, Maggie Moone, for sure.'

After what felt like a mile at least, we turned, the wind at our backs now.

'I don't mean to be a killjoy,' he said, 'but isn't it a little brisk for a picnic?'

We'd stopped at Waitrose in Swaffham, optimistically buying sandwiches, pork pies, treacle tarts, and even a small bottle of red wine. Now, a Norfolk pub, a roaring fire and a bucket of garlicky mussels seemed a much better plan.

I kept walking, my head down so he couldn't see my face. 'Don't take this the wrong way,' I said, 'but I have a surprise.'

My mind could picture only one scenario, and it didn't involve pork pies.

'Oh yeah?'

I pointed to the row of beach huts, a few hundred yards away. They were huddled on the dunes, a long line of sentries, like the last defense for England against the force of the sea. I reached into my pocket and produced a long, silver key, tied on a striped blue and white ribbon.

'Shelter from the storm.' I wondered if Finn was too young to know the song. The age gap between us hadn't been a problem so far, despite my initial concerns.

He looked at the beach huts, then out to sea for several seconds, before looking down at me. 'Really?'

I smiled, more certain of this than of anything else in my world. 'Yes.'

He kissed me again, deep and long and sweet. Then he raised his head and touched his fingers to my temple. 'Lead the way, then, Maggie Moone.'

~~~

The beach hut belonged to a friend of Amelia's. Many of her connections were wealthy, famous, or both. It wouldn't have surprised me to find that a Lord or Baron owned the rustic structure. This beach, after all, was on aristocratic land.

While Finn jogged back to the car for the food, I unlocked the beach hut, holding my breath at what I might find. It was indeed basic. No Laura Ashley stripes or pink bunting here. No electricity, of course, just a small gas stove and a kerosene lamp. Some low cupboards along one wall, a wicker sofa with deep cushions on the other. And blankets. Soft, snuggly blankets, probably blended from cashmere or alpaca. All the same navy, all with the same crest in the corner.

I heard a cough from outside and returned to the door. From the top of the steps I saw Finn looking up from below. He didn't speak: just stood there, hesitant.

Then, so softly the wind almost whipped his words away, 'Do you want me to come up?'

He wasn't talking about the picnic any more.

I gave a tiny nod.

He closed his eyes briefly. 'I don't have to, you know. We can,' he gestured to the steps, 'sit here and eat.'

'No.' I swallowed hard. 'Come up. Come up here, Finn.'

He took the steps two at a time, dropping the picnic onto the front porch, then backing me carefully into the shadows of the beach hut.

~ ~ ~

Afterwards, we sat, wrapped in a nest of blankets, looking out at the sea. The tide had turned and, in the far distance, the waves were starting to roll in across the expanse of sand.

'You're awfully quiet,' Finn said.

'Sorry.' I snuggled against him, my back to his chest, his chin resting on my shoulder.

'Regrets, Maggie Moone?'

I shook my head. 'No, it's not that.'

'But you're... thinking about him?'

'No. Yes. But not like you mean.'

Of course I was thinking about Colin, but only because what I'd just experienced with Finn had been so different from the last years of my marriage. If I was honest, maybe even the whole of my marriage. Sex with Colin had been transactional: give and take, a trade for affection, cuddles, companionship. With Finn, I'd felt a connection, a compatibility, a feeling of being in precisely the right place. Even if that place turned out to be a draughty beach hut in North Norfolk.

'If you must know,' I tried to keep my voice light, 'the part I regret is wasting so much time with Colin.'

I breathed twice before Finn answered.

'Maggie, let me tell you a secret.' He dropped his lips to kiss my head. 'It's never too late to stop wasting time.'

'I gotta say, every time I think I've seen the ultimate eccentric English activity, y'all surprise me with another one.'

It was my first day at work in Ted and Betsy's stable and she'd brought me a cup of tea. She was a fast learner: she'd worked out that no manual labour can take place on British soil without a mug of Typhoo to wet the whistle.

'Why?' I asked. 'What have you been up to?'

I half expected her to say bingo. Finn was still threatening to take me and had even showed me the hall where his gran played every week. He'd mentioned it again, on our way back from the beach.

'Ted wants to be the next Bill Bryson. Last week, he was determined to see the summer solstice at Stonehenge. We spent about ten hours in traffic, then had to sleep rough, nose to toe with the strangest people.'

I'd never been to a pagan festival in Wiltshire, but it did indeed sound esoteric. And far worse than bingo.

'And, forgive me,' she added, 'but it's a load of boring stones, really.'

'True.' I sipped my tea. Stonehenge could indeed be underwhelming. 'What else has Ted been finding?'

'Well,' she said, 'in May, there was the cheese rolling competition. And more recently, a boisterous crew racing event, called the bumps.'

I nodded. 'The Cambridge colleges? Yes, they love their rowing races here.'

'Last fall – I mean, autumn – we got tangled up with a load of runners, trying to re-create *Chariots of Fire*. You never know what you'll come across next.'

I balanced my hot mug in one hand and my tape measure in the other. 'Next year, you should try the Eel Festival.'

'Ugh, how disgusting.' Her face said it all.

'Or how about the World Pea Shooting Championships?'

'You're kidding me. Pea shooting?'

'Nope. It's soon. Out near Ely, somewhere.'

They certainly had unusual ideas of entertainment, out in the Fens.

'Are the peas the target, then?' Betsy asked.

'No, the ammunition.' I slurped some more tea and prepared to get to work. 'As long as they blow the peas with their mouth, competitors can come up with any method they like.'

'Right...' Betsy sounded unconvinced. 'Well, please, whatever you do, don't tell Ted.'

Unlike the eels, I thought a battle of peas sounded fun. I'd considered suggesting to Finn that we go, but we'd opted instead for a traditional funfair. The Ferris wheel, after all, qualified as something high. So that took care of number two on my list of things Colin hated.

There wasn't any harm, I told myself, in using the list for dating inspiration. It wasn't like I was slavishly ticking everything off, like a science experiment. It wasn't like I was sending my ex-husband postcards, every time I did something that would wind him up.

It wasn't like I was keeping the list a secret from Finn on purpose.

~~~

I honestly couldn't believe I'd let Amelia talk me into hosting my own birthday party. When I'd protested I'm a terrible hostess, she'd assured me that ample alcohol was the sole secret to a successful bash. When I'd mentioned the dreary state of the cottage, she'd pointed out at least I didn't have nice furnishings which could get ruined. Then Grace had joined in, as though they were on a two-woman mission to see me plough through the list.

'You could rent a karaoke machine,' Grace had suggested. 'For Queen and Abba songs.'

I'd pulled a face. 'Not sure that's fair on the neighbours.'

'Well, invite them, dummy.'

I *had* invited them, although we'd agreed karaoke would be too painful for all concerned. But the Queen angle did have something going for it. Amelia had hit on the solution.

'Make it fancy dress, darling.' She'd flung out one arm theatrically. 'Everyone can dress up as a Queen song.'

Grace and I had gaped, but the more I thought about the idea, the better it sounded.

~~~

So, I raced home from Betsy's at lunchtime on Friday, my mind buzzing with party details, like buying a new plastic dustbin, and ice, so there was a chance of getting the drinks cool by 7pm.

I eyed my cottage critically as I approached. The magenta front door gleamed, and new lavender bushes stood like sentries on each side of the path, now scrubbed free of lichen. But that was as far as I'd got. The fireplace I'd bought in Yorkshire was leaning against the living room wall, hoping one day to be installed properly. I'd intended to pull up my carpets and see what was underneath, and strip all the gloomy wallpaper so I could paint. But every time I started one of these tasks, my energy had fizzled, especially when it involved moving one of the cardboard boxes containing either my stuff from the Burwell house, or the mysteries from Dad's shed.

I was also worried I'd invited too many people.

'Do you think we'll have enough food?' I asked Bella. Although normally occupied with flapjacks, she'd kindly accepted my low-budget catering challenge. Now, she was bringing platter after platter from her car.

'Don't worry,' she replied, helping me set up a trestle table disguised with a sheet. 'Once people get yakking, they won't eat as much. You're okay for drink, yes?'

I nodded. Why did everyone mention the alcohol? You'd think the residents of Saffron Sweeting spent the whole time legless. Even so, I'd taken the precaution of including *bring a bottle* on the invitation.

'Good. People drink more when it's humid. So count on the booze disappearing fast.' She nodded at the sky, where grey clouds were forming into towers.

'You are coming back, aren't you?' I asked, as I paid Bella for the food.

My new cheque book in the name of Maggie Moone had finally arrived, and I got a thrill every time I used it.

'Yes please.' She pocketed the money. 'Your Queen theme is the talk of the village.'

~~~

First to arrive was Finn.

'I wasn't sure,' he said, 'if you'd be a laid-back hostess with champagne in one hand, or madly stressed, polishing the toilet bowl.'

'I'm somewhere in between.'

I did have a tension headache, but I put that down to the air pressure as much as anything.

'Happy birthday, Maggie.' He pulled me in for a hug.

'Not until tomorrow, actually.'

We were holding the party a day early, as Amelia had red-hot tickets for a choir concert at King's.

'We'll celebrate properly tomorrow then. Just us.'

Those two words – *just us* – carried their weight in meaning a dozen times over. My birthday was already looking significantly better than last year, when I'd watched television alone, then eaten chocolate truffles in bed.

'Er, where's your costume?' I was afraid he'd forgotten, or that he might think dressing up was juvenile. Colin certainly wouldn't have been into it.

'Here.' He pulled a large bag from behind his back and held it so I could peek in.

'It's... a hat.'

'Aha!' With a flourish, he extracted a formal top hat. Attached to the brim was a working barometer, ominously reading *stormy*. Finn settled the hat on his head and beamed. He resembled a handsome steampunk character, but I was puzzled.

'No, sorry,' I said, after a moment.

'"Under Pressure"!' He held onto the brim as he watched light dawn on my face and swooped in for a quick kiss. 'And what about you?'

I took him upstairs to show him the slinky ice blue dress lying on my bed.

'Amelia helped me with it,' I said. 'It's not one of their well-known songs.'

'Sexy dress. Put it on.'

The way he said this made butterflies rise in my chest. But I dutifully changed into the dress. It was cut on the bias, with snaking strips of shimmering beads.

'It's not me at all, really.'

'I like it.' His hands were roaming now, as well as his eyes. 'Hello, what's this?'

He'd found the back of the dress, where Amelia had helped me pin a long, white fur tail. She'd promised me it was fake.

'Rowr,' he growled, kissing me.

I kissed him back. 'You can't get it, can you?'

He stepped away, pulling out his phone, which had a crack across the screen. 'I dropped it yesterday. If it still works, can I cheat?'

I nodded and he began tapping and scrolling. Just as I thought he'd given up, he gave a low whistle. 'Clever one, Maggie Moone.'

I grinned. 'You've got it?'

He nodded. '"A Winter's Tale".'

~ ~ ~

After that, we barely had time to kick off a Queen soundtrack on Spotify, and throw more drinks in the iced-water dustbin, before guests began arriving.

'I should have waited to make a grand entrance, but I was too excited, darling!' Amelia strode into the cottage in stiletto heels, black cocktail dress, and a tiara which looked genuine. The plastic machine gun slung over her shoulder, thankfully, was not.

'"Killer Queen",' Finn said. 'Very appropriate, if you don't mind me saying.'

'You remember my friend Scott?' Amelia introduced her companion.

'I didn't have much time for a costume.' Scott gestured to the stick of rock jutting from his shirt pocket. 'Sorry.'

'No, no,' I said. '"We Will Rock You", very good.'

'Or "Brighton Rock",' said Finn. 'Two for the price of one.'

'I told him he should do the one about being in love with his car.' Amelia gave a sly grin and poked Scott in the chest.

A look passed between them then, and it was if they held a whole conversation in a few short seconds. I don't believe in telepathy, but these two appeared to share an exclusive wavelength. It sent a shiver of regret and envy down my spine.

Other people began to stream into my cottage. Within minutes, the place was filled with shrieks of laughter as people tried to decipher each other's costumes.

Violet, from the post office, arrived with her son, who turned out to be Peter. She had several lengths of ropes coiled around her. 'I'm "Tie Your Mother Down",' she said with uncharacteristic levity. Peter himself, in slippers, cardigan, and a copy of the *Sunday Telegraph* tucked under one arm, admitted to 'Lazing on a Sunday Afternoon'.

'We couldn't resist!' Grace and Bella arrived together, along with Bella's friend Sophie, plus Robyn. All four wore T-shirts and black leggings, and had padded themselves below the waist.

'Not sure.' It was time I got a drink in my hand, like everyone else. 'The one about bicycles?'

'Nope: "Fat Bottomed Girls"!' they cackled, in unison.

'Well,' Sophie added, 'once I heard Bella was doing the food, we wanted to be comfortable.'

And so it continued. Grace's husband was 'White Man'. Nancy had raided someone's Halloween dressing up box to be 'Cool Cat', and dutifully chased 'Great King Rat' up and down the lane outside. The rodent in question turned out to be Bella's boyfriend, Leo. Considerable applause went to Ted and Betsy. He was wearing a box painted to look like an old wireless set, while she appeared to be dressed as Zsa Zsa Gabor.

'What the heck are they?' I whispered to Amelia, not wanting to be rude to my guests and clients.

'"Radio Ga Ga"!' she chortled back. 'Bloody priceless!'

But the unofficial winner, for creativity if nothing else, was Fergus from the pub. He arrived dressed top to toe in denim, a watermelon tucked under one arm, with a placid borrowed sheepdog on a lead.

'First one to guess gets free beer for a week,' he said, causing the party to grind to a halt while hopeful suggestions were made.

In the end, it was Kenneth, the librarian, who got it. 'Doing the cryptic crossword helps. That, and I was something of a rock star myself, in the seventies.'

'For heaven's sake, tell us, will you,' called Sophie. 'Then us thickies can carry on with the party.'

Kenneth looked at Fergus, who nodded his permission. '"My Melancholy Blues", of course.'

Some of the guests began to groan, while others looked perplexed.

'Melon – collie.' Grace cringed. 'That's terrible.'

Someone turned up the music, and from there the party took off. Several people told me how pretty the front door looked, and one guest, whom I'd never met before, wanted to hire me to replace her banisters. Most of the food disappeared, with murmurs of approval for Bella's mini pork pies and dainty cheese sandwiches.

'So, are you and Scott an item?' I asked Amelia, after she'd worked the room twice and distributed about a dozen business cards. She had other people's tucked into her tiara.

'Lord, no!' She waggled her fingers as if batting away an imaginary fly. 'He does make me laugh, though.'

I looked across at where Scott was winning an acrimonious debate with Violet about Brexit. Robyn was trying to keep the peace. 'Hmm, hilarious, yes, I can see that.'

At ten o'clock, that wonderful hour when I was drunk enough to let my hair down but still sober enough to notice other people's enjoyment, Finn sidled up beside me, slipping his hand around my silky waist.

'I think,' he let his lips brush my ear, 'this is the best party I've ever been to.'

It wasn't until I felt his breath on my neck that I realised I was having an amazing time, too.

'And I do like your dress. Any chance you'll wear it again?'

'With or without the tail?' The dress wasn't really me, but I was enjoying the flattery.

'I don't care. As long as I get to take it off you.'

A few people tried to dance, but the sitting room was too tiny. Despite every window in the cottage being open, it was oppressively hot. In the kitchen, someone had produced a guitar and was strumming chords which sounded like 'Bohemian Rhapsody'. Others, realising the alcohol was stored outside, began to spill onto the back patio. The last time I saw the collie dog, she was sitting halfway up the stairs, surveying us all like we were sheep she'd round up later.

Shortly after midnight, when the last few revellers left, I realised I hadn't seen Finn for an hour or so. Had he left without saying goodbye? The thought chilled me, even through my warm boozy glow. And that's when I knew that he meant more to me than I'd admitted.

I reached behind me to unpin the tail and found I'd already lost it. Hopefully it would turn up tomorrow. I locked the back door, as a single fork of lightning split the night sky. Then I plodded upstairs.

Finn was sprawled face down on my bed, with one arm bent near his face. Fully clothed and fast asleep, he looked adorable.

He wasn't alone, though.

At the foot of the bed, entirely at home on my threadbare rug, was the borrowed sheepdog, curled up next to the abandoned watermelon. In the dim light, the dog opened one eye, thumped her tail, and then settled down again with a snuffle.

I unzipped the slinky blue dress, brushed my teeth, and slipped into bed next to Finn. He mumbled something, turned over, and flung one arm over me.

'Crazy Little Thing Called Love', I thought, and then I fell asleep.

# Chapter 20

At six the next morning, I was woken by a cold wet nose in my face. Through the fog of an oncoming hangover, I realised this was the dog, not Finn.

'It was a huge mistake,' I told her, as I staggered downstairs and opened the back door, 'to let you stay over. Don't go getting ideas.'

As I waited, I wondered if stray dogs were a specialty in Saffron Sweeting. Grace claimed she didn't like it that Violet's spaniel kept showing up at her place at random times, but we could all see through her. The dog had arrived one night several years ago, and settled in. Much like this collie.

'I'm not falling for it. You're not staying,' I said, as she trotted back into the kitchen, waving her tail. 'Even if you are an item on Colin's hate list.' Then I relented and got out a bowl, which I filled with water and placed on the floor. 'I'm going back to bed, but when I wake up, you're going back to Fergus.'

The collie sniffed the water but didn't touch it. She sat down, staring at the bowl.

'What?' I ran myself a glass of water from the tap, awake enough to know this might lessen my headache later. 'You drink it, like this.' I demonstrated by draining my own glass.

The dog wagged her tail once, then looked at her bowl again.

I was still thirsty; I opened the fridge for a pint of milk. Behind me, I heard an immediate swoosh of tail on the kitchen floor. I turned, to find a pair of soppy brown eyes.

'Really?' I said. 'Expensive tastes?'

No answer, just more swooshing. I sloshed a little milk into the bowl on the floor, and plodded back upstairs to bed.

~ ~ ~

By ten, Finn and I were both awake, although moving cautiously and talking quietly. I ignored the party debris, but made a half-decent breakfast of scrambled eggs for us. From outside there was a rumble of thunder, way in the distance.

'I have to go.' He kissed the top of my head.

'I know. No problem.' It wasn't that unusual for him to work overtime on a Saturday.

Three minutes later, he was back. 'My mate said he'd pick me up, but my phone's died.'

'Call him from mine.' I cradled my coffee mug in both hands. 'It's upstairs.'

I considered making an extra piece of toast. I couldn't remember how much I'd eaten last night, but I was famished this morning.

As I heard footsteps overhead, I called, 'You might have to dig around a bit – try the dressing table.' Like many people, my idea of tidying for a party consisted of sweeping daily life into a pile, and hiding it in my bedroom.

There was a long silence from upstairs, but by that stage I was slathering honey on toast and didn't think anything of it.

Then Finn came down, a large piece of yellow paper in his hand.

'I'm some kind of dare?' His face was white.

'What?' My brain was fuggy.

'You made... some sort of list.' He stared down again at the yellow sheet, the reflection from it making him look jaundiced. 'You've been ticking things off. I'm number four.'

Too late, I realised what he'd found. 'Where was it?' I said, stupidly, irrelevantly. Then I remembered the pile on my dressing table. On top of my phone. 'It's not what it looks like,' I added, and immediately kicked myself.

Finn dropped the paper onto the kitchen counter. 'So this isn't a list of ways to piss off your ex-husband?'

I opened my mouth to deny it, then remembered the swirly heading in Amelia's bold handwriting. It was there in black ink.

'And you've been working your way through them, haven't you? The day I met you – the tattoo? I sat through live theatre. We just did a whole evening in honour of Queen. Are you sending Colin photos? You're *totally* not over him, are you?'

'Finn—' I stepped towards him, but he moved back, palms raised.

'I even went on that flipping Ferris wheel – that was your something high, was it?'

'Of course not. Please,' I said. 'It's nothing—'

'Nothing? It pretty much spells out our whole relationship. It's all here! Your list said you had to shag someone medical, right? Preferably on a beach?'

'No! Look, most of it's coincidence. The beach was your idea, remember? *You* wanted to go to the beach.'

Finn glared at me, his jaw clenched. 'Right. Sure I did. And the key to the beach hut? Those nice soft blankets? How convenient was that? Number seven, all taken care of.'

I glanced down at the list, although I didn't need to, as I knew it pretty much by heart. He was right. It did look like a chronicle of our relationship. Oh God, I'd even ticked some of the items off.

'It started out as a joke,' I said lamely. 'You have to believe me...'

'Were you going to dump me today? Were the Queen songs the finale? Congratulations, well done.'

'Finn—' I started to cry.

He shook his head, backing out of my kitchen. 'I really liked you, Maggie. And you were playing with me, all along.'

'Please!' I begged. 'I wasn't. It doesn't mean anything.'

'Well, it meant something to me.'

It was already a lost cause. It had been a lost cause from the moment he'd laid eyes on the list. But matters weren't helped when he then tripped over the collie, who'd positioned herself in the doorway.

'Jesus,' he said, 'you've even got yourself a dog.' He reached down and gave her a swift pat, before stepping over the lounging canine. 'Watch out, mutt. She's heartless.'

And then he slammed my magenta front door behind him.

## Chapter 21

I started to follow Finn, but got as far as the stairs when my legs gave out. I crumpled onto the second step and dropped my head to my knees. How could I have been so stupid? Why was I slavishly pursuing a list of things to irritate Colin, instead of getting on with my life? Why hadn't I come up with my own ideas for spending time with Finn? Why hadn't I destroyed that list, especially when the personification of number four became so special to me?

Because he *was* special. In a few short weeks, I felt like I'd known him for years. He was like a best friend. He laughed at me, teased me, yes, but he also encouraged me, believed in me, and trusted me. And I hadn't treated that trust as the precious gift it was.

A cold wet nose interrupted my sniffling. The collie dog was there again, eyes inquiring.

'I suppose you're after that toast,' I said, remembering the uneaten morsels in the kitchen.

She wagged her tail.

'And don't look so pleased with yourself. You didn't help matters, Miss Number Six. Don't think I'm going to fall into your arms on the rebound.'

In the bathroom, I splashed cold water on my face, and noticed the tail lost from my dress last night, draped over the bath. I grabbed my phone from the bedroom and called Finn before I remembered his own was broken. Not that he'd necessarily answer my call in any case.

'Come on, collie.' I came back downstairs and looped the fake tail through her collar as a makeshift lead. 'You're going back where you came from.'

The pub wasn't open when we got there, so the dog and I sat morosely on the edge of the pavement and waited until Fergus unlocked the doors.

'Maggie!' He stepped outside. 'I'm surprised to see you out and about.'

'I'm returning your melon-collie. She was bad luck, as it turned out.'

'Ah, Trixie.' Fergus bent down to fondle her ears. 'I was worried about you.' Then he looked at me. 'Sorry. Sore head this morning. Wasn't sure where I'd left her.'

'Fortunately for you, she was with me.'

But I knew it wasn't fair to blame the dog, or Fergus, for the sixth list item being right there, when Finn found the sheet of paper.

The pub landlord studied me. 'You don't look so perky yourself, if you don't mind me saying.'

'Not at all,' I replied. 'I feel like hell. What have you got to cure both hangover and heartbreak?'

He raised his eyebrows. 'Like that, is it?'

I nodded, tears welling again. 'I've really mucked things up, Fergus.'

'Come on in, pet.'

I declined his first suggestion of a tomato juice with raw egg, but then we agreed Irish coffee was an acceptable pick-me-up.

'Irish,' I repeated, as Fergus ground the beans and fiddled with the filter paper. 'That's ironic.'

'Ingrid'll be down in a minute. She'll do you a bacon sandwich. Not much a bacon sandwich can't fix.'

He was wrong about that, but I was too distraught to tell him. I sat at the bar for a few minutes, sipping my scalding coffee and trying not to cry. What a bloody idiot, I thought.

Then I pulled out my phone, checked for messages from Finn – there were none, of course – before texting Amelia: 'Need your help.'

It was several minutes before a reply came back. 'Super party, darling. What's up?'

I typed again. 'Need new list. Ways to win back Finn.'

There was a much shorter pause, followed by, 'Where R U?' Then, 'Be there in 20.'

But barely ten minutes had passed when we heard a booming rumble. At first, I assumed the storm was breaking, but the sheepdog raised her head and growled.

A couple of minutes after that, the door of the pub burst open. A man in a tweed jacket and deerstalker hat came rushing in. 'There's been an explosion,' he cried. 'Phone 999!'

'Where?' Fergus reached for the phone, dialling and talking at the same time. 'What happened?'

'No idea,' the man said, puce-faced. 'But there's smoke behind the church. Over towards Damson Lane.'

~~~

In Saffron Sweeting, any kind of emergency is big news. People still talk about the November storm when the vicarage was struck by lightning, and the spring day a tractor got stuck in the ford and had to be pulled out – eventually – by a combine harvester.

I followed the gent in the deerstalker out of the pub. We paused on the pavement, wondering where the blast had come from. As we stood there, we were joined by a window cleaner, and a woman with a beagle on a lead.

Within seconds, Violet emerged from the post office and locked the door. She was tying her headscarf as though it were a tin helmet.

'What are you doing, just standing there?' she cried. 'This isn't how we won the war! Man the pumps!'

The window cleaner looked at me. None of us had any idea which pumps Violet was talking about. After all, it had been eighty years since Saffron Sweeting had needed to defend itself against anything. Also, I knew for a fact the old fire engine house had been converted into a chic single-storey pad for Amelia.

Still, I stepped forward and the window cleaner picked up his bucket of water too. The beagle, sensing a mission, strained on the end of his lead, yapping and ready for the off.

As we paused at the corner by the duck pond, I saw there was indeed smoke belching into the sky beyond the church. And at least a dozen other villagers were heading that way as well. Two were in their pyjamas, while others carried blankets. One woman, the receptionist from the doctor's surgery, gripped a first aid kit. Another man strode along with a huge mug of tea, whether for himself or potential victims, I couldn't be sure.

Our collective pace quickened and by the time a fire engine stormed past us, we were practically trotting up the road. An ambulance whizzed past and the first smoke entered my nostrils, a sickening dread formed.

As we turned into Damson Lane, the buzzing of speculation about both the cause and effect of the boom grew more anxious.

'Can you see where it is?' asked a short woman, puffing to keep up. 'Is it someone's house?'

'I think so,' the window cleaner told her, trying to judge where the smoke was coming from. It was a couple of hundred yards ahead of us, more or less where Betsy and Ted lived.

We rounded a bend.

'It's that posh house, isn't it?' said the man with the tea. 'The one where the Americans live?'

My hand went to my mouth. It *was* the one where Betsy and Ted lived.

A small crowd had gathered in the road outside. The ambulance blocked the gate, and up the driveway I glimpsed the fire engine.

Behind us, the sky was charcoal grey too, but nobody paid any attention to that, or the distant rumble of thunder that warned a storm was rolling in. This was far more enthralling.

'Can you see? Can you see?' cried the short woman.

'No.' I looked desperately at Kenneth, who was the tallest in our little group.

'I don't think it's the house.' He craned his neck. 'Or at least, not the front of it.'

I was there, only yesterday, I thought. I'd left when Vincent arrived. My mind raced through the work I'd done... and the chemicals I'd been using. Were Betsy and Ted okay?

I pushed my way closer to the front of the crowd, where the Saffron Sweeting vicar was trying to persuade people to make space for more emergency vehicles.

'Everyone!' He implored his flock: 'Please ... keep calm and step back.'

But the flock was thronging around the gate, having none of it. Violet offered her first aid skills, and even the window cleaner, who'd sloshed most of his bucket's contents in the lane, was jostling to be allowed closer. Where was that sheepdog when we needed her? She'd get this lot rounded up.

Excitement grew as a man came down the driveway towards us. He looked stunned.

'It's Greene!' called someone from the crowd. 'Greene, mate, are you all right?'

As he reached us, I recognised Ted and Betsy's gardener. Another time, I'd have been amused by his name, but not today.

Greene's hands were shaking. 'I was pruning,' he repeated a couple of times, removing a flat cap and tussling his thinning hair. 'Pruning, I was.'

'What happened?' someone asked, for about the hundredth time.

Greene shrugged. 'Stables went up. Just like that.'

The little crowd gasped. I put my knuckles to my mouth. The stables. Oh, no, please no.

'Why? How?' These were collective questions, uttered by several villagers. We knew where and when, after all. How long before they asked *who*?

Greene shook his head. 'Dunno. Nasty business. Looks like gas.'

'Gas!' The crowd seized this information, repeating the short but deadly word amongst themselves. Then they extended the story. 'A gas leak!'

I wanted to elbow through the throng to talk to the gardener, but I couldn't move. I felt like I'd been caught by the explosion myself. My ears rang, my eyes wouldn't focus, and there was a taste like metal in my mouth.

Finally, Violet had the decency to ask the most important question of all. 'Mr Greene, tell us, was anyone hurt?'

I closed my eyes, dreading the answer. It seemed an eternity before the gardener spoke, and even then, it did nothing to soothe me.

'No idea. Sorry. But the cars were there.'

'Vicar,' I blurted, 'I need to get through. I was working in the stables, you see.' I dropped my voice. 'With tools, and paint stripper, and... stuff. I need to...'

'Oh dear.' The vicar looked stricken. 'Oh dear.'

I was about to duck past him, when someone else stepped forward.

'Don't let her through.'

'Colin?' I could barely get his name out. Smoke, fear, and shock were mingling in my lungs. 'What are you doing here?'

'Working.' He jerked his head in the general direction of the village and I remembered he did indeed have a client in the middle of a kitchen extension.

I turned back to the vicar. 'I'm going up to the house. I might be able to help.'

'Help?' This was Colin. 'Don't you think you've done enough? Don't let her through, vicar. She probably caused it.'

I gasped. Even though this fear had been jabbing at the back of my brain, hearing it voiced was another thing entirely.

'Now, now, let's not be hasty.' The vicar raised both hands in a centuries-old gesture of conciliatory benevolence. 'We don't know what—'

'It's obvious.' Colin's lip curled. 'She was working at the house, she didn't know what she was doing. That bloke told us there was gas involved.' He looked at me. 'You were way out of your depth, Maggie. I told you to stop playing at fixing other people's houses and leave it to the pros. And now you've destroyed someone's home.'

I couldn't speak. My stomach heaved and I clamped my lips together.

'Let's just hope no one was killed.' Colin was relentless.

'Lord have mercy,' said the vicar, which I suppose was his job. He reached out to pat my arm, but I wasn't listening. I bent double, wanting to vomit, but all my body produced was shaking and some noisy gulps.

From my doubled-over position, I saw the swirling blue lights of a police car. The uniformed legs which emerged first were female. I straightened up.

'All right.' She donned a fluorescent tabard and adopted a no-nonsense expression. 'Let's all move back, thank you very much.'

The muttering crowd obliged, respecting the Old Bill far more than the vicar. I stepped to one side, darting glances up the driveway.

Another car purred up the lane, forcing its way through the onlookers. Someone announced it as the bomb squad, while another diagnosed MI5. But as it jerked to a halt behind the police car, it was Amelia who emerged. She was dressed in black silk pyjamas, with leopard print slippers.

'What the bloody hell's going on?' she asked, not in the least embarrassed by her outfit.

'Maggie blew up half the village,' Colin said.

'Balderdash,' said Amelia. And before anyone could stop her, she strode off up the driveway towards the house.

'Hey!' called the policewoman, and rattled something into her walkie-talkie.

'Officer,' called Colin, realising he'd lost the limelight, 'I'd like to make a statement about what happened here.'

'There'll be time for that, sir.' The policewoman waved her walkie-talkie at the throng. 'Now clear a path, please.'

Colin wasn't to be dissuaded. 'This woman is responsible.' He pointed at me and my knees sagged. 'She was doing building work at the property without necessary planning permission or insurance.'

The crowd gasped and turned to me, the policewoman included. 'Is that correct, madam?'

The vicar was wringing his hands.

'I... I wasn't doing anything wrong,' I said, but my head swam.

'Ask her about the gas,' Colin said. 'What was it? Boiler? Hot water?'

Initially I think he was bluffing, trying to stir up trouble. But the look on my face told him he'd hit a bullseye.

'No... I didn't... it wasn't...' I was about to mention that Vincent had handled that, but remembered his warning that if Colin found out, it could cost him his job. I shut my mouth and backed towards the hedge.

'Are you on the Gas Safe Register, Maggie?' My ex-husband's eyes were glittering.

The policewoman now looked extremely interested.

'No,' I said miserably. He knew damn well I wasn't. 'But I—'

'You do know it's *illegal* for an unregistered person to work on domestic gas appliances?' Colin wore an expression of triumph.

The crowd gasped and through my despairing haze, I heard the rumour start to ripple.

Colin shook his head to emphasise disgust. 'You could be prosecuted. Done for manslaughter. After this, you won't even be able to get work unblocking a toilet.'

The police officer pulled out her notebook. 'What's your name, madam?'

The onlookers, already simmering, broke out in a babble as an ambulance came from the house and whizzed past us, siren blaring.

My vision went dark. It swooped in from the periphery, until I couldn't see, and my hearing went fuzzy. I felt myself sway, then stagger. Someone – the vicar, perhaps – reached out an arm to try to help me, but it wasn't enough. I clutched at the hedge, which tore off in my hands. Then I hit the ground, and everything went black.

## Chapter 22

I woke, lying on my sofa, with a splitting headache. Outside, it was getting dark and I could hear the steady splosh of rain.

'Maggie? Are you awake?' Grace got up from a chair near the fireplace and peered at me.

I wriggled to sit up, which sent a dagger of pain through my right temple. I reached up and found a wad of dressing. My hands were all scratched, too. 'What happened?' I asked again.

'What do you remember?'

I tried to swallow, but my throat was dry and my mouth tasted foul. Grace pressed a glass of water to my lips, then picked up her phone and sent a text.

'I remember killing Ted and Betsy and that I'm going to jail.'

'Woah. Slow down.' She looked shocked. 'Right. I'll put the kettle on.'

Within a few minutes, Nancy arrived, with Amelia hot on her heels. The former looked grim. The latter, I noticed, had changed out of her black pyjamas.

'What time is it?' I asked, but they ignored me, conferring instead with Grace. Yet more tea was made, with much whispering and huddling. I heard them say *head* at least three times.

'How are you holding up?' Nancy asked finally.

I shook my head gingerly. If I spoke, I might burst into tears.

Grace refused to tell me anything until I'd drunk some tea. Amelia was uncharacteristically quiet, first looking disdainfully around at the dangling wallpaper I'd started to strip, then sighing and reaching for her phone. The cottage was a mess, but that hardly mattered now.

I took two sips of hot Earl Grey, then said, 'Please tell me. It's better I know.'

The three of them exchanged glances.

'The vicar told me you fell in the hedge,' Grace said. 'Then you fell out of the hedge, and hit your head. They stitched you up at the Sweeting doctor's surgery, though, and gave you some kind of strong painkiller.'

'Sedative,' Amelia corrected, not looking up from her phone.

Grace carried on. 'Then they sent you home and told us to look out for signs of concussion.'

'I didn't mean *me*,' I said, although this did explain why my skull felt like the Battle of Trafalgar. 'I meant Betsy. And Ted. Are they—?' I couldn't say it. All I could do was grip my mug.

'Are they what?' Grace looked at me.

'Dead.' I bit my lip, hard, but felt nothing, probably due to the medication.

'Good grief, no!' Amelia dropped her phone to her lap. 'Darling, of course they're not dead!' She leaned forward. 'You *have* had a bump on the bonce.'

Nancy added, 'No one was badly hurt, Maggie.'

'Thank God.' I lolled back on the sofa and felt the weight inside my chest shift, if not exactly lift.

'That is, not counting Betsy's toe,' said Amelia.

I sat up again. 'Her toe?'

Amelia shrugged. 'She jumped a mile high – fair enough – and dropped a vase on her foot.'

Nancy interjected. 'We heard she broke a toe, but basically, she's fine.' Then, to Amelia: 'Stop torturing Maggie.'

At this point, I recalled Amelia's concert tickets. Assuming it was still Saturday, she was missing it. I was about to apologise, when I remembered my more serious crime.

'But the explosion...' I said. 'That's where I was working. If something went wrong, I'm ultimately responsible.'

'Well...' Amelia threw Nancy a look. 'We don't know that. We won't know anything for a few days.'

'But that's what everyone's saying, right?' I looked from one to the other, guessing the village must be abuzz. 'I'm a pariah.'

'Of course you're not a pariah.' Nancy sounded unconvincing.

'Goodness, no, darling,' Amelia agreed. 'But, er, it does appear the stable block was destroyed in the blast. Terribly tiresome.'

I put my hand over my mouth. Then, through my fingers, I said, 'I'm finished. I was barely getting started, and I'm finished.'

Amelia left a long pause before she said, 'So, darling, just in case, we were wondering,' she plastered a bright smile on her face, 'if you've thought about hiring a lawyer?'

'You think I need one?' Surely taking such a step was admitting my own guilt? But then of course, I *was* guilty, so who was I kidding?

Amelia clicked her tongue a few times, trying to look as though she was mulling the point over. Then she sighed. 'Yes. 'Fraid so.' At the panic on my face, she added, 'Obviously, it's a silly storm in a teacup, but...'

Nancy was trying to put her own cup down and found there was nowhere in my messy living room to land it. 'But, Ted and Betsy are American,' she said, 'and part of their house blew up. We'd better assume they're gonna litigate.'

I let out a whimper, then dropped my pounding head back to the cushions behind it.

'Don't think about that,' Grace said soothingly. 'Get some rest and try not to worry.'

That was like telling a runaway train to slow down and admire the scenery. Aside from the horror of picturing anyone being caught up in the blast, I had no liability insurance, no coverage of any kind. They could sue me for millions. There might be criminal proceedings.

'I'll probably go to prison.' I closed my eyes.

'Shall I phone Finn?' Grace was still trying to be helpful.

I jerked my eyes open again, in time to see Amelia shaking her head furiously and making *shut up* gestures.

'That's the other thing.' I stared into the remains of my tea and knew that no amount of Earl Grey could fix this. 'I didn't just wreck someone's house. I've wrecked it with Finn, too.'

~ ~ ~

I laid low for twenty-four hours. It rained pretty much the entire time, with occasional thunder and lightning thrown in for good measure. I emptied the buckets in my attic twice, and prayed the roof wouldn't get any worse.

Meanwhile, I took double doses of the painkiller the doctor had prescribed, and chased them down with cooking sherry. Since the party, I couldn't find any other alcohol in my cottage.

And I ate the jam I'd made, straight from the jar with the biggest spoon which would fit. With every sweet, sticky mouthful, I told myself he'd phone soon.

He didn't.

I lasted until Monday lunchtime before my pride admitted defeat and my heart won the argument. Then, I started calling. And texting. And calling. And texting.

Nothing.

The day after that, I went to his flat, but he wasn't home.

'He works shifts, dear,' called an elderly neighbour.

'Yes, thank you.' I tried to be polite, despite my disappointment. 'If you see him, please say Maggie was here?'

I left a few more messages, and camped on his doorstep one evening with a takeaway pizza, hoping he'd come home. He didn't.

Next, I braved the melee of the nearly new shop where Robyn worked. It was usually a seething mass of toddlers, but the little coffee area gave me an excuse to pop in.

'I don't suppose you've seen Finn?' I asked, as she made my double espresso.

She gave me a sharp look, possibly taking in the dressing over my stitches. But then she shook her head. 'Not recently, no.'

I waited, hoping she might say something else. But no other information was forthcoming. 'Well, if you do happen to see him,' I took a deep breath, 'could you say Maggie misses him terribly?'

This time, her look had tinges of sympathy, before she dropped her eyes and reached for the cocoa shaker.

And after that, in my twitchy caffeinated state I didn't know what else to do, except go home and make jam.

Lots of jam.

~ ~ ~

By the end of the week, as my thumping headache eased, I expected the pain in my heart would subside too. When it didn't, I resolved to give Finn's place one more try, then retreat with the shreds of my dignity. What was the worst that could happen? If he told me to *feck off* in that adorable accent, it would be worth it, just to see him.

Ringing the bell at his flat, I arranged my face into apologetic hope. As the door opened, I held out the giant Yorkie bar of the kind I knew he liked.

But the chocolate wavered in mid-air. The Irish eyes staring back at me were two generations older, and female.

'Oh!' I recognised Finn's grandmother, the bingo ninja. 'Sorry.'

She glanced down at the Yorkie. 'Finn's not here.'

I dropped my hands. She didn't live here, did she? He'd never mentioned it, and there'd been no sign of her, the couple of times I'd visited. It was a one-bedroomed flat, I was sure.

Apparently, Grandma McCarthy read some of my thoughts. 'He's gone to Limerick. I'm only here to feed the cat.'

'Will he,' I could hardly bear to say it, 'be back?'

I truly didn't want to pursue him to Ireland, like some desperate cliché. Not least because I wasn't sure he'd have anything to do with me, and I didn't want my first visit to that country to end in rain-soaked heartbreak.

Finn's grandmother sniffed. 'Of course he'll be back. Unless he gets it together again with Maureen O'Flannery.'

My face must have hit the floor. She gave what can only be described as a cackle and poked me in the arm. 'I'm messing with you, Maggie O'Moone.'

'Moone,' I said feebly. 'Just Moone.'

'His sister's not well. He's gone to help out.'

'Oh.' That sounded better, although now I knew about Maureen O'Flannery, I wouldn't sleep tonight.

'And he's none too pleased with you, I might add.'

'I know.' I stared down at the chocolate bar. 'I came to tell him how sorry I am.'

There was a stony silence. This was about as much fun as getting my stitches taken out.

'Could you... I mean, if you speak to him, maybe you could... say I stopped by?'

'I could.' She tipped her head to one side. 'If you make it worth my while.'

I looked at her blankly. What did she want? Was this a hint to rig her bingo numbers? Or was there some other Irish custom I wasn't aware of?

She gave a thin-lipped smile and jerked her head towards the chocolate. 'Sweet tooth. Runs in the family.'

'Oh. Of course.' I handed the Yorkie bar over. 'Absolutely.'

'You're a smart girl, Maggie O'Moone.'

'So you'll... tell him, then?'

But it was too late. Grandma McCarthy had turned away, already peeling back the wrapper, and closed the door gently in my face.

# Chapter 23

Well, I thought, having had one door shut in my face, another one couldn't hurt. The following Monday, I knocked at Vincent's house. His home gave the appearance of being unoccupied, and I was turning to go when I saw him coming along the street, wheeling a baby in a pram. A young girl skipped at his side.

'Hello, Maggie.' His eyes were wary.

'Vincent... hi... I really need to talk to you.'

He looked at me from under heavy eyebrows, then jerked his head. 'Come on in.'

I followed him into the semi-detached house. Toys were everywhere, together with a clothes airer of washing.

Vincent bent to his small daughter. 'Princess, go up and take off your uniform, okay?'

The little girl took herself off and I turned to him, not sitting down and not expecting to be asked.

'You heard about the explosion?'

'Uh-huh.' He was wearing his habitual work overalls and thrust his hands deep into the pockets, shoulders hunched.

'Colin thinks it was me. Working on the gas.'

'It wasn't the gas,' he said immediately.

I opened my mouth to remind him that stable blocks don't spontaneously combust, but I recognised professional pride when I heard it.

'The point is, Vincent, I'm being investigated. I could be prosecuted for unregistered gas work.'

He was silent.

'And I know I promised to keep the arrangement between the two of us, but I'm in big trouble.'

I'd been on the internet and spent hours on the website of the Health and Safety Executive. They were awfully keen on prosecutions.

Vincent sat down on a sagging leather settee, while I hovered in front of the television.

'I know it's a lot to ask.' I let the words hang there.

After a minute, he gave a sigh and dropped his head. But before he could speak, the front door banged.

'Hello, have we got company?' His wife, her hair scraped back in a ponytail, put her head around the living room door. She was wearing some kind of protective smock, with *Cleaning Angels* emblazoned across the front. I hadn't seen her for quite some time.

'You remember Maggie, love? Colin's wife?'

'Ex-wife,' I muttered.

Vincent's wife stepped into the room and nodded hello. But her manner was cool.

'I was... explaining to Vincent that I need to tell the HSE he was working with me,' I said. 'There was... an accident... and they'll think it was my fault.'

'Well, it wasn't Vincent's fault,' she shot back. 'Was it, Vince?'

'No, no.' I saw I'd made a false start. 'I mean, it's not a question of fault, just that I wasn't working there alone.'

'This is the explosion, right?' She looked at her husband. 'Don't people know you were there?'

He shook his head. 'Maggie and I were keeping it quiet. From Colin, you know.'

'Why?'

Vincent looked awkward. 'He's a bit... uppity about her muscling in on his clients.'

I wanted to say I wasn't muscling anywhere, but didn't.

'Col threatened to cut me off with no work, if I helped her.'

'But you did help her?' His wife folded her arms.

He shrugged. 'Few extra quid for me, love. What Colin didn't know didn't hurt him.' Vincent stood and went over to his wife, putting his arm around her. 'You know what a bully he can be.'

'Fine,' she said. 'I'll put the supper on.' But she didn't leave the room.

'I'm sorry,' I tried again. 'But I'm going to have to tell them. I'm in serious trouble, otherwise, if they believe I was working without a license, and caused an accident.'

'Now, look, Maggie.' She jabbed a finger at me and I took a step back. 'I'm sorry there was an... incident. But it wasn't Vincent's fault. So there's no point telling anyone he was on the job.'

'But—'

'I don't think you see,' she said, as if talking to one of her children. 'Vincent needs the work Colin puts his way. We've got a family to feed.' Her eyes went to the toys littering the room. 'And then there's his insurance,' she continued. 'The last thing we need is the premium going up, if they think he had a part in something like this.'

I swallowed. 'I really am very sorry.' This was awful: I was worried about my own fledgling business, and I only had to put food on the table for myself. I closed my eyes for a moment, then pressed on. 'But, I'm not a registered gas engineer. I'll need to tell the authorities there was a professional there.'

Dammit, I thought. Vincent was trained and qualified. If something had gone wrong with his work, I couldn't take the blame for that.

I turned to him. My stomach twisted, but I had to try to protect myself. 'Vincent, you don't believe you made a mistake, do you?'

He gave a dismissive snort. In the pause that followed, the possibility crept into my mind that maybe, just maybe, the explosion wasn't due to gas.

'Then there's nothing to fear. As for Colin, you said yourself he's a bully. We have to stand up to him.'

His wife tutted, but I kept my eyes on Vincent. 'Help me do the right thing here.'

Seconds went by, and if anything, his bushy eyebrows drew closer together.

'Daddy! I'm stuck on my homework!' The little girl stomped into the room and stopped when she saw us all. Then she remembered her question. 'I need to define *prediction* and *integrity*.'

She couldn't quite pronounce the R's.

Vincent's wife bit her lip. She glared at me, then looked away. Behind my back, I dug my nails into my palm.

Vincent reached down and scooped the little girl into his arms. 'Integrity means, princess, that you tell the truth and do the right thing.'

Over the top of her pigtails, he caught my eye, and nodded.

~ ~ ~

'Now what?' I watched Grace attack a buttery yellow Victoria sponge.

Brian had won a prize for it, a few years back, and from the towering slice in front of her, he hadn't lost his touch.

On my own plate was a generous slice of Bakewell tart, with its firm pastry providing a base for a layer of jam, then frangipane, with an almond topping. Normally, it's one of my favourite cakes, but today, I couldn't even summon up the interest to critique the jam.

We were sitting outside the Sweeting Bakery, taking advantage of the first dry spell in days. I was shaded behind dark glasses, not because of the sunshine – there was barely any – but because I was kidding myself it would lessen the chance of villagers recognising me and nudging each other.

'No sign of Finn?' Grace frowned.

'Not according to his grandmother.' I prodded my slice of tart. 'She claims he's in Ireland.'

'And you believe her?'

I shrugged; I had no contradictory evidence. 'Do you think I should go after him?' I hadn't discounted that idea, even though it wasn't quite my style.

'Do you have an address?'

'Er, no.'

Instead of pointing out I was deluded, Grace gave a sympathetic smile. 'I flew across the Atlantic on a whim, once. To see someone, I mean.'

My eyes widened. 'Really? What happened?'

'He wasn't there.' She shook her head wistfully. 'Expensive waste of time.'

'So you wouldn't recommend it?'

'Not if you can avoid it.'

A combine harvester, probably lost, manoeuvred up the street towards the village hall. My efforts to find Finn were equally clumsy.

I sighed. 'I wish I'd realised sooner... how much I like him.'

*Like* didn't come close to it, but Grace understood.

She squeezed my hand. 'Have you phoned him?'

'Yeah.' I had left more voicemails and texts. I'd even emailed, praying Finn wasn't so furious with me that he'd forward my heartfelt note to friends, who'd then ensure it went viral.

But it was worth the risk. Without Finn, I was starting to understand that the hollow lethargy I'd felt when my marriage ended was the loss of familiarity, comfort, and routine. It had little to do, I now understood, with losing Colin.

But with Finn gone, I'd lost a soulmate. I wanted to tell him stuff, show him things, discuss everything from minutiae to world events. I ached to hold him and be held. Without him, I was out of equilibrium. My centre of gravity wasn't right. I was like that wobbly slice of Victoria sponge, but without the jam and cream to hold me together.

'And the worst thing is,' I said to Grace, 'he has every right to refuse to talk to me. That list was insulting.'

She sighed. 'I'm so sorry. We didn't expect you to fall for Finn. It was only meant to be a bit of fun, to shake you up a bit. And to stick two fingers up behind Colin's back.'

'I know. In any case, it was a lot more fun to stick two fingers up to his face. Until he sunk me, good and proper.'

'You're not sunk,' Grace said. 'I'm sure you'll hear something about the cause of the explosion soon.'

A cuckoo's call floated over the trees, but that didn't help me much.

I hung my head. 'Whatever the cause, I'll still feel responsible. Betsy and Ted won't return my calls, and half the village thinks I'm some kind of corporate criminal.' To my utter shame, a piece in the *Cambridge Evening News* had reported thirty-four-year-old Margaret Kern was helping authorities with their enquiries. 'In their eyes, that basically means I'm guilty,' I said, regretting every time I had assumed the same thing.

Not only that, but the newspaper piece had prompted an irate phone call from Colin, pointing out he had a business to run in the name of Kern Kitchens and why the hell was I continuing to use my married name? I'd changed back to Moone in a few places, but hadn't finished the others.

'It'll blow over.' Grace sounded like she was trying to convince herself, too. 'People were thrilled with the work you did. Even the ones who just liked having a female handyman.'

'I dunno,' I said. 'I don't think I can carry on, not after this. Not with Colin out to get me.'

Grace furrowed her brow. 'Still, the whole point of the list was to establish a life for yourself without worrying about what Colin would think. If you give up on your business, then...'

'Then what?'

'Well, isn't that kind of letting him win?'

I chased some Bakewell tart crumbs around my plate, not wanting to meet her eye, not wanting to admit she was probably right.

But my instincts were telling me, Colin might already have won.

## Chapter 24

The bakery meeting with Grace left me sure that people were pointing and gossiping. I wasn't imagining the dramatic dip in requests for handywoman services, and one client cancelled our appointment with a lame excuse at short notice. Either people had concluded I was directly responsible for blowing up Ted and Betsy's house, or they feared I'd bring bad luck.

I couldn't sit at home and do nothing, but my stamina was non-existent. So, I made half-hearted attempts to tackle the boxes from Dad's house, which I'd bought sight-unseen in Yorkshire.

The first contained mostly railway timetables, but near the top were some photos of my father when he was young. I pulled one out that showed him and a couple of friends, and stuck it on my fridge. Then I kicked the boxes back where they came from, my energy depleted.

My friends tried to help. Nancy sent me back to the Antiques Barn to help her boyfriend Peter. I unblocked the gutters and cleaned out the drains: both of them nasty, smelly jobs. But Peter was kind and paid me partly in cash, partly in a square mantel clock. 'It's reproduction,' he warned, as my eyes lit up. 'And it chimes.'

Good, I thought: my cottage might feel more homely if I broke the lonely silence.

Grace apologised that she couldn't find me any paid work, but we did spend a couple of happy days stripping the floorboards in her some-day nursery. I wanted to tease her for the snail's pace of her cottage renovations, but I wasn't in a position to criticise. At least her place hadn't gone up in smoke. Still, she was three years older than me, so she might want to finish the nursery sooner rather than later.

Amelia was the most effective at keeping me busy, dispatching me to unblock toilets, set rat traps, and even free a jackdaw from a house she was trying to sell.

'It was bloody awful,' she chortled. 'Walked into the lounge with potential buyers and found soot everywhere. Stupid bird fell down the chimney and panicked.'

I laughed, and cleaned up the mess, but I had a lot of empathy for the jackdaw. I felt about as welcome at the moment in the little community of Saffron Sweeting.

So, I took to going for walks around the village an hour or so before it got dark. The businesses were all closed by then, and most people were home watching television. As long as I avoided the pub, I usually only had a few hedgehogs and the odd wily fox for company.

~~~

About ten days after the explosion, I was out for my evening jaunt, albeit earlier than usual. I was passing one of the fancier houses in the village when a plank came crashing down. I jumped, shoulders around my ears, as if that would save me from a chunk of tree through the skull. Fortunately, there was a thick hedge separating the pavement from the garden, and the offending piece of wood landed mostly in the privet.

'Now look what you've done!' A shrill child's voice rang out from somewhere above my head. I looked up.

'Oops,' said another voice, which I was now able to identify as coming from a tree. 'Er, sorry, miss.'

'Call me Maggie.' I fished the wood out of the hedge and held it aloft, offering it to the tree. 'Is this yours?'

Although the plank weighed several pounds, a grubby hand on the end of an even grubbier arm came snaking out of the tree, grabbed it, and withdrew.

I looked around, but there was no one in sight on this side of the hedge. Nor was there any adult supervision on the other side, as far as I could tell.

'She's still there,' came a whisper from high up.

'Shhh,' was the answer from similar altitude.

'Should I not be here?' I couldn't resist teasing them. Whatever they were up to in that large ash tree, I'd probably done worse at their age.

There was silence, then a giggle. I remembered that urge when I was young, to giggle even when I was in trouble. It didn't go down well with my teachers.

I took an educated guess and addressed the tree. 'Either you're trying to kill me, or you're building something.' No answer, but I thought the leaves rustled. 'And I'm not sure you're trying to kill me, because you haven't tried again.'

There was a commotion behind the leaves before a young male head poked out. 'We're not trying to kill you! No way!' Behind the streaks of dirt on his face, he looked stricken.

'Good. I didn't think you were.' I smiled. 'So you're building something?'

The leaves rustled again and the girl's face appeared. Her jet black hair and almond-shaped eyes matched her brother's. 'We're building a treehouse!'

My heart gave a little judder.

'*I'm* building a treehouse,' he corrected her. 'Amy's just helping.'

It reminded me of how Matthew used to put me in my place, too. He had better luck, though.

'No, *we're* building it.' Amy was clearly younger, but also feistier. What she lacked in strength to manoeuvre planks of wood, she probably made up for in determination. Then she looked at me. 'I'm going to be a civil engineer.'

'Good for you.' At her age, I'd assumed astronaut jobs were easy to come by. Maybe I'd been aware of the term *engineer*, but not the different types. Maybe that was why

I'd drifted into a back office job helping Colin. Hopefully, she'd do better. 'How's it going?'

The young lad – what was he, twelve, maybe? – looked away and wrinkled his nose. His sister looked at him, as if wanting permission to speak. None came. She sniffed, but it was a sniff of irritation, not sorrow. 'Not too good.'

'What's the trouble?' My neck was starting to get sore from this conversation.

Again, Amy glanced at her pouting sibling. 'The planks won't stick.'

'Stick?' Clearly, she was early in her engineering career. I tried to keep my face straight.

'For the walls,' her brother said. 'Our uncle started it...'

'But then he had to go away,' Amy added.

'...And now we're stuck,' finished her brother.

'I see.' I pretended to think about this. 'That's a shame.'

'Mum said, if it's not done during the school holidays, we'd better forget about it.' The little voice was so sad. 'But she isn't here at the moment to help us, and Grandpa never comes outside.'

'Well, that's a pity,' I said. 'Maybe someone else can help you?'

'Like who?' The forlorn tone tugged at my heart.

I looked at my watch, as though my time were extremely precious. But what else was I going to do on a fine summer's evening?

'Well, like me.' I shrugged, trying not to look as excited by their project as they were. 'If your parents agree, that is.'

~~~

Alas, there were no parents to be found, at least not that evening. I learned later that their mother was working in Osaka, and the father was no longer in the picture.

Instead, the children took me into the house and down a dark hallway. The boy, whose name was Tim, knocked on a door at the far end.

Upon entering, I found a room that was half study, half Victorian conservatory. The entire back wall and part of the sloping roof had been replaced with glass. The ornate ironwork and complex pane designs suggested it was decades old.

This airy space was crammed with plants. Huge ones in massive pots stretched to the lofty glass ceiling. Smaller ones crowded laboratory benches. Some were tropical, some not. On the walls hung a combination of massive plant charts, and a collection of leaf specimens pinned in custom frames. The room smelled like a rainforest.

'Yes?' The voice came from the foliage and pulled me back to business.

'Grandpa, we have a lady with us,' said Amy.

'Yes?' repeated the voice, and then an elderly man emerged from behind a towering orchid.

I guessed he was from China, or that region. His hair was snow white and he wore chunky, dark-rimmed glasses. His wrinkled face was dotted with age spots.

'He's actually our great grandfather, but he doesn't answer to that,' Tim whispered.

'Hello.' I stepped forward to offer the diminutive gentleman my hand. 'I'm Maggie.'

For such a humid room, his grip was dry. And extremely firm. 'Derek Wong.'

I started to say I was pleased to meet him, but he'd released my hand. With a sprightly sidestep, he was already tending to a nearby fern.

'Maggie says she can help build our treehouse.' Tim's voice was cautious.

'Is that so?' Mr Wong reached for a brass plant mister. 'And you tell me this why?'

I cleared my throat. 'Er, I'd like your permission, sir.'

He didn't look at me, adjusting the mister's nozzle and then aiming two sharp sprays at the feathery leaves.

'To, er, be on your property and work with the kids?' This jungle version of a headmaster's study had rattled me.

'You charge me how much?' With his free hand, he rubbed his fingers together in the monetary gesture.

'Oh, no. You don't have to pay me. That's not the idea.' It was a treehouse, after all.

'Please, Grandpa?' Unlike her brother, who was standing quietly, Amy couldn't keep her feet still. 'Can she help us?'

The old man leaned in close to a flower that looked like a yellow thistle. 'I show them plants. I teach them herbal medicine. The flora of their ancestors.' Then he gestured around the cavernous room. 'Roots, leaves, seeds. No good. No interest.'

I paused. 'They, er, like trees, though.' I swallowed, hoping I wasn't about to get hay fever from the exotic pollens assailing my nostrils. 'That's a start, right?'

Grandpa Wong stared at me for such a long time, I thought I could hear his plants growing. Then he broke into a toothy grin. 'You know how to build treehouse?'

'I do, sir.' Well, more or less. More than these kids, surely.

'And my children, they will be safe?'

'Yes, sir.' Had he heard about the explosion? I waited, studying the nearest ficus.

The kids, too, were silent, but I sensed their agitation.

Their great grandfather cleaned a pair of vintage pruning scissors, then held them up to his face and looked at me through the handles.

'So be it.' To the children, he said, 'Go build your house in the sky.'

~ ~ ~

It wouldn't win any prizes, but as far as I could tell, Tim and Amy's uncle had made a reasonable start on their treehouse before his company transferred him from Cambridge to Singapore. Rather him than me: I hated extreme heat.

There was indeed a decent platform, constructed around the sturdy ash tree, about a third of the way up the trunk. That was good: less risk from wind. The uncle had left a small gap for the tree to grow, which suggested he'd known what he was doing. Even though I'd never built a treehouse myself, I'd spent many enthralled hours watching videos online.

'Did your uncle drill into the tree for these supports?' I asked Tim. He nodded. 'Good.'

I nipped up their ladder to check the stability and evenness of the platform. There were diagonal braces, too, and three wall supports in place.

'Well, it seems sturdy enough. But I bet you haven't got a power drill, have you?' Two heads shook in unison. 'No problem. I live five minutes away. I'll nip home and get mine.'

When I got back, resplendent in tough boots and gloves, I handed them both spare safety goggles. But there was something else on my mind.

'Before she went to Japan, did your mum happen to talk to anyone at the council about your treehouse plans?'

Although I was still determined to buy my old treehouse from Colin, research had revealed that these days, planning permission was needed before constructing one.

Tim shrugged. 'No idea.'

I pondered this. Despite being close to the street, the tree in question didn't actually overlook any neighbours, who would be the main source of a complaint. And it wasn't as if they were spending thousands of pounds constructing it. They might get away with it.

'Well, technically,' I said, 'you're supposed to have permission.'

Tim scowled, while Amy looked like she might cry.

'But if we keep it small, you might get away with it. We'd better keep the noise down, though.'

Even if we were officially breaking the rules, I consoled myself that the kids building the treehouse with me present was infinitely less dangerous than them tackling it alone. And if they were stuck here for their summer holidays with an eccentric great grandfather, a project like this would do them good.

The three of us weren't strong enough to assemble the walls on the ground and lift them into place, so we did it the hard way, screwing individual planks to the walls. The treehouse wouldn't be as robust as the one I was pining for, but it would be good enough for fair-weather play.

'Where did this wood come from, in any case?' I asked, as we searched the pile for sturdy, regular pieces for the walls.

'It's the old garden shed,' Tim said. 'Grandpa wanted a better one.'

Mr Wong no doubt had heaps of horticultural supplies for his green-leafed prodigies.

'The new one's even bigger,' Amy added, as I tried to lift a ten-foot plank on my own.

I gave up on that and kicked another, hoping it was sound. The last thing these kids needed was dry rot.

Eventually, with a mixture of sweat (mine), blood (also mine), and tears (Amy), we managed to get two ramshackle walls in place.

'It doesn't look like much,' I said. 'But it's firm enough. You can always improve on it, later.'

By this point, Amy was beside herself with excitement. She had elaborate ideas for the final structure, including solar lanterns. Tim, meanwhile, was hoping to install a water cannon. What Grandpa Wong would make of that, I didn't like to speculate.

'Okay. That's enough for tonight.' It was getting late for drilling, especially if we didn't want the neighbours to get shirty. Plus, the light was fading, and I was struggling to find all the coach screws we'd dropped in the grass.

'You will come back, won't you?' Tim asked.

I hesitated. This project didn't fit my hopes of keeping a low profile in Saffron Sweeting, even if we were trying to be discreet.

'I'd just... rather the whole village didn't know I'm helping you,' I said.

'Why?' Amy's question was foreseeable.

I sighed. 'Er... I'm not very popular around here at the moment. I made a mistake and... damaged something.'

'A treehouse?' Tim looked up at our work, as if it might collapse any second.

I shook my head. 'No, not a treehouse. But people are gossiping about me and I don't want them starting on you.'

The kids looked at each other, their frowns matching. Lucky things, if they hadn't yet learned what gossip felt like.

'So does this mean, you can't come back and help?' Tim asked.

I paused. I was dying to assist them with the next stages, but I was desperate to hide from village tittle-tattle too.

'Look, I'd love to help—'

Amy caught my hand. 'Please, Maggie.'

That was the moment I realised I still wanted kids of my own.

'Let me think about it,' I said.

Tim didn't meet my eye. 'So we might have to do the rest of it ourselves?'

During our evening together, he'd learned that building a garden shed in a tree wasn't as easy as it looked.

'We've done the hardest part,' I lied. 'Two more walls, and a roof, it'll be fine.'

He didn't look convinced. And I wasn't about to let him loose with my drill, either.

'But at the very least, I'll bring you some roof membrane.'

'Thank you!' This was Amy, who was clearly chief visionary officer for the project. Tim had the burden of making it happen. She nudged him.

'Thanks, Maggie,' he added.

I nodded, trying not to show what a good time I'd had.

Then I took myself off home for a hot bath, where I picked splinters out of my hands with tweezers. I lay in the soapy water for ages, daydreaming about a different treehouse, and remembering the brother who'd shared it with me.

## Chapter 25

I woke, covered in sweat, shortly before five in the morning. The dream had been a chaotic swirl of an exploding tree, and the only way I could save the kids was if I could find a painting strong enough to serve as a stretcher to carry them out of danger. But every time I grabbed a piece of artwork and tried to load either Tim or Amy onto it, the picture changed and they fell off.

I showered, then drank coffee standing at my kitchen sink. As I made my second cup, I couldn't shake the feeling that I hadn't learned the truth about Dad's painting. Reaching to the fridge for milk, I glimpsed the photo I'd stuck on the door, of my father with those other two kids. One of them was wearing glasses, and even in the old, grainy picture, you could tell they were as thick as bottles.

I poured the milk into my coffee, and stirred. Then I stirred again, and stirred some more, as a theory began to form.

It wasn't yet six: if I left straight away and put my foot down on the A1, I could be in Yorkshire by ten.

~~~

'Hello, Bert,' I said, as soon as he'd finished a transaction for a candle snuffer. The market was busier than last time; perhaps the favourable weather had started to bring out the tourists. 'Remember me?'

He lifted his chin, but didn't speak for several seconds. Then he said, 'Hello, lass.'

'I brought you a cup of tea.' I handed him one of the paper cups I'd purchased.

'Thank you.'

I forced myself to wait while he took a few sips. He wasn't stupid. From behind those thick glasses, I was sure he was watching me, waiting for me to speak.

'So, I don't think you were straight with me, Bert.' No reaction. I carried on. 'When we talked about *Chasing the Train*. I asked you if you painted it. And you said no.'

'Aye. That were true.'

'I believe you. But I think I asked you the wrong question.'

His head inclined a fraction.

'I think...' I took a deep breath. 'Just because *you* didn't paint it, doesn't mean it's genuine.'

Bert stared at me for several seconds. 'You really are Jiggy's daughter, aren't you.'

'I told you I was.'

'I wasn't asking.' He shook his head. 'I wasn't sure, last time. Thought you might be a meddler.'

This time, I'd come prepared. I dug into my bag, looking for the old photo of me and Dad. But as I tried to show him, Bert waved it off.

'Nah, lass, you can put that away. I see it now, you're his, sharp as a pin.'

My lack of sleep and several hours of driving were catching up with me. I was dying for a nap and a bacon sandwich, not necessarily in that order. I summoned my last ounces of patience.

'Bert, last time you said, *you* were never that good.'

He nodded.

'But somebody else *was*, weren't they?' Along with the photo of me and Dad, I'd brought another one, much older. I showed it to him. 'Somebody you knew well, someone you'd grown up with – someone who had very similar talents as you.' I paused. '*She* was a good enough artist to make a convincing copy of *Chasing the Train*.'

There was a long silence. I waited, fierce in my certainty, but needing to hear it from him.

Bert took the photo and looked at it for a long time. He held the frame of his glasses steady with one hand and stretched his other arm as far as he could, to help his focus. He turned it over, saw the caption, *Jerry and the twins*. Then he turned it back again, studying the three grainy faces again.

Despite it being summer, the wind in Pickering carried a nip that morning. Possibly, that explained the glint of a tear in the corner of his eye.

'Bert?' I said gently. 'It wasn't you, was it? It was your twin.'

Finally, he handed back the photo. And he smiled at me then: a sad, proud, honest smile.

'Clever girl.'

~ ~ ~

Within twenty-four hours, I was perched on a stool at the tiny Saffron Sweeting beauty salon, with Grace and Amelia hanging on my every word. I didn't normally go there, but I couldn't wait to tell them the news. They were both getting pedicures, so that's where I found them.

'Your refusal to be in society didn't last long,' Amelia said drily. 'Don't tell me you've decided shellac nails will cure your grump?'

In my line of work, fancy nails would last three minutes. I was bursting with news, but glanced at the owner of the salon, who was bent over Amelia's feet.

'Don't worry about Holly.' Amelia saw my doubt. 'She'll take our secrets to the grave.'

Holly, who'd barely said a word since I arrived, smiled and reached for another towel.

So, I told them how I'd been back to Pickering and had confirmation the painting Colin was selling wasn't genuine.

'No way!' Grace gave a surprised kick and splashed water over the floor.

'So this old geezer, who's practically blind, is an art forger?' Amelia asked.

I shook my head. 'No. It wasn't him, it was his twin sister. She's dead now. But yes, it's fake. One hundred per cent knock-off.'

Amelia threw her phone on the little table beside her. This meant I had her attention. 'Oh, fabulous, I love a good scandal!'

'But how? Why?' Grace was continuing to paddle her feet.

'According to Albie – I mean, Bert – she did it just to prove she could. The original had been stolen and not recovered; it was all over the Yorkshire papers. Dad joked that he wouldn't ask questions, if someone knocked on his door with it one dark night.'

'And this twin sister took it into her head to paint a copy? For your dad?' This was Amelia.

I nodded. 'Seems that way. Bert hinted she and Dad were sweethearts. He said she signed the real artist's name on it, gave it to Dad... and then they all forgot about it.'

Or maybe Dad didn't forget about it. He kept it all his life, and even after he married my mum, it hung in his study. There was probably more behind his decision to move back to Pickering than I'd realised.

'I don't understand,' Grace said. 'How on earth hasn't the auction house spotted it's a fake?'

Amelia chuckled. 'Sounds like she really *was* good.'

'That's been puzzling me, too,' I said. I couldn't stop chewing on that point, all the way back from Yorkshire. 'Maybe there's been a mistake? Peter said paintings are usually sold with provenance, to back them up. Something got mixed up, perhaps, or someone at the auctioneers is inexperienced, or...'

'Or Colin's pulling a fast one, more likely,' Amelia finished.

'Wow.' Grace drummed her knuckles. 'This is more thrilling than *Broadchurch*.'

'Careful, darling,' Amelia gestured at Grace's fingernails, which were drying. 'So, Maggie, your slimy ex-husband stands to make a bucketload of dosh by flogging a fake painting?'

'It looks that way,' I said. 'If you believe Bert.'

'Do we believe Bert?' Grace dropped her voice.

Holly didn't react, which was good, because her nail clippers looked vicious. If I needed any help prising old nails out of the wood for Tim and Amy's treehouse, I'd know who to call.

I shrugged. 'I don't see why not.'

'And even if Bert is telling porkies,' Amelia added, 'it makes an interesting twist in the tale, doesn't it?'

'Does it?' I said. 'We already knew Colin's a piece of work.'

'Oh Maggie,' Amelia tutted. 'You are dim.'

'What do you mean?' I yawned. The road back from Yorkshire had been slow, and the jolt of Bert's revelation was wearing off.

'Let's assume what Bert says is true.' Amelia leaned forward, fixing me with her clever brown eyes. 'The question for you now is, what are you going to do about it?'

For the first time in ages, I slept well that night. Probably, the long drive had worn me out.

Nonetheless, the dawn chorus roused me at a time when no human should be awake. My eyes were barely open before my brain started churning from one topic to the next.

First, there was Bert, and his incredible revelation that his twin sister had painted *Chasing the Train*. Colin was selling a fake. Did he know this? Did he suspect? Why hadn't the auction house figured it out?

I was grimly aware that Colin had only got his hands on the painting because I'd allowed him to. If I'd been stronger about clearing out Dad's house, my ex-husband would never have got involved. By not facing up to that task, I'd set off a chain of events.

But regretting my inability to purge clutter wasn't helping now. More important was Amelia's question: what *was* I going to do about it?

Thinking about Colin reminded me of the gas explosion. It was the waiting that was getting to me. Was this why people arrived at police stations to confess to crimes? Was the burden of guilt, of looking over one's shoulder, enough to drive people into the arms of the law? I was beginning to understand it might be.

Then, as I stretched my arms above my head, I found the muscles in my back were still painful from helping Amy and Tim with their treehouse. The combination of physical work and problem-solving had brought me alive. The pleasure on their young faces, as their little house took shape amongst the leaves, was the icing on the cake.

This brought me back to *my* treehouse and the hours I'd spent there with my brother. I wanted it more than ever. And yet there it was, nailed to an eighty-year-old tree in the back garden of my antagonistic ex-husband. What on earth could I do about that? Colin hated me. The treehouse was his.

I lay in bed for a few more minutes, before the frenzy of my brain threatened to drive me nuts. I simply had to get up and do something. But what? I'd got no work in the village, and in any case, my aching back was begging for a day off. So what, then?

~~~

The shop where Robyn worked was due to close at five o'clock, so I was stationed at a table with a coffee made by her colleague by half past four. Then, I pretended to read the newspaper, but in reality didn't take in a word of the latest Brexit kerfuffle. I don't know if Robyn even knew I was there, as she was busy in the clothing section today, trying to stop twin boys yanking everything off the rack.

I kept a close watch and, to my relief, at ten to five, the last customer left. Robyn began cashing up and I waited to catch her eye.

'Hello,' I said, when she looked up.

Recognition crossed her face. 'I haven't seen Finn.'

'I'm not here about Finn.' I shook my head, although I *had* been hoping she'd have some news of him. Truth be told, I was longing to curl up beside him on my sofa and tell him all that was happening. He'd be able to make sense of it, surely. But if he didn't want anything to do with me, moping around after him wasn't the answer.

Robyn had folded her arms.

'I was hoping to talk to *you*.' I kept my voice low, in case her boss didn't welcome personal visits. 'Er, about art?'

'Oh yes?' Her face flickered interest.

'Umm, about a commission, maybe?'

Immediately, I chastised myself. What was becoming of me? I had no money to hire her. No wonder I was making enemies all over the place, letting my tongue run away with me. Not to mention blowing things up.

I regrouped. 'That is... well, not so much a commission, as... er, some advice?'

'Advice?' Robyn's voice was dry. She clearly didn't trust me, and I didn't blame her.

'About art,' I clarified. 'The art world, art sales, er, forgeries... that kind of thing.'

'Really?' She laughed.

'Just a quick chat.' I swallowed. 'Really quick.'

Robyn glanced at the clock on the wall, then came out from behind the counter and flipped the sign on the shop door to read *Closed*.

'I'll pay you,' I blurted. 'For your time? Twenty minutes, say?' I added this last part because I feared she'd name an hourly rate of hundreds of pounds, and with no work on the horizon, I needed to be careful. Especially after paying for two lots of petrol to Yorkshire, the hotel there, and my impulse buy of the fireplace from the skip.

Robyn unpinned her name badge and put it in a drawer. 'So, not about Finn? About art?'

I nodded. 'We can go for a drink, if you'd like.'

Her expression lifted, then she shook her head. 'I have to let Mungo out. Violet's gone to a memorial service.'

I didn't know who Mungo was, but this was a pain. 'How about I come with you? Then I'll buy you a drink after, if you want.'

Finally, Robyn smiled. She produced a tote bag from behind the counter. 'Well, now you're talking.'

~ ~ ~

As we crossed the high street from the nearly new shop to the flat above the post office where Violet lived, it occurred to me if Robyn wanted a drink later, I should suggest a pub outside the village. I didn't want to show my face at The Plough. Nobody had been outright mean to me since the explosion, but the whispers continued. More than one villager had crossed the road when they'd seen me coming.

Mungo turned out to be Violet's spaniel, and I remembered the enthusiastic tail from the Shakespeare play. He was a beautiful dog, his black ears almost as glossy as Robyn's hair.

'He only needs a quick walk,' Robyn said. 'Violet warned me to keep him on the lead, though.'

'Fine.'

We set off towards the duck pond, Mungo straining at first to show the way, then in his hopes to bully the ducks.

Robyn kept telling the dog to slow down, but it wasn't until we turned the corner onto the road which led past Amelia's house that his enthusiasm abated.

'So, what was it you wanted to know about art?'

Much as I wanted to talk about Finn, I knew I'd better stick to my stated purpose. I liked Robyn, but could tell she hadn't made up her mind about me.

'Thank you for letting me talk to you. I had a quick chat with Peter, but he says he's not an expert.'

'I'm hardly an expert. I'm even struggling to land a Saturday internship at a gallery.'

'Oh. Sorry.' I'd blundered by implying that knowing one end of a paintbrush from another, or visiting a few galleries, qualified one as an omniscient expert. 'But, well, the thing is, I know absolutely nothing, and I wondered how things work.'

'What kind of things?'

'Well, for example, auctions. Like, when a painting is sold, what happens?'

The pavement had ended and Robyn pulled Mungo towards the safety of the grass verge. His nose was down, no doubt enjoying the aroma of pheasants, squirrels, and more.

'Gosh, Maggie, that isn't my area. I don't know.'

'Oh.' At this rate, the conversation was destined to be disappointing.

'I mean, I've never worked in an auction house, or anything.'

I waited for a car to pass. 'Well, do you know how they check a painting is genuine? Say, not a forgery?'

'They'll look at the provenance. Receipts, previous auction brochures, and the like.'

There was that *provenance* word again. How on earth had Colin found something to show the painting had pedigree?

By this point, Robyn was looking at me strangely. 'This isn't some random conversation, is it?' she asked.

I paused. She was onto me. 'Not really, no.'

'Are you trying to sell a forgery?'

'No! Not me. But I think someone I know is. And, well, to be honest, I'm not sure what to do about it.'

'Well, you have to report it, obviously.'

The certainty with which Robyn spoke surprised me. 'I do?'

'Yes, of course. Why wouldn't you?' We'd passed Amelia's house and turned up a quiet leafy lane, startling a pair of wood pigeons. 'When's it being sold?'

I explained what I knew of the auction date. 'It was supposed to be sooner, but there was doubt over whether a piece by someone called Cuneo would be included. So there was a delay.'

In the interim, I'd done more research on twentieth-century railway artists. I knew now that Terence Cuneo's work had probably influenced Monkton.

'Okay.'

'So, what happens if it's sold, and they later find out it's not genuine?'

'I'm pretty sure the auctioneer has to cough up. It depends, though, what information about the piece they guaranteed. Usually, that's only the stuff in bold in their catalogue.'

'You mean—?'

'Potentially, they'd refund the buyer. It's complicated, though. Is it a big auction house?'

I shook my head.

'Well, that's bad news then. It could really harm a smaller outfit. Wipe out their profits from the whole auction, or worse. And it'd be a PR nightmare, obviously. They might hush it up and take the financial hit.'

That sounded pretty bad. From what I could tell, Brissinghorn & Beem did appear to be a small player.

Robyn shot me a sharp look. 'Scandals like this are really damaging for the art world.'

Mungo knew we were near the river. He was panting and tugging on his leash again, hoping for a swim. This reminded me, I should go too. Not in the village stream, of course. But forty minutes of front crawl might help soothe my dread of being sued for the explosion.

'Yes, well,' I began. 'It's a bit complicated. The person selling it – he's going to make a lot from the sale.'

'And swindle the poor buyer, and stir up all kinds of grief for the auctioneer, too.'

The thing was, just because Colin was making strife for me didn't mean I was comfortable landing him in equivalent trouble.

'And, well, he kind of hates me already.'

My new confidante raised her eyebrows. 'So, you've not got much to lose then, have you?'

'It's not that simple.'

But Robyn laughed. 'I think you'll find it is.'

*Chapter 27*

I was coming out of the post office, jubilant that I'd sent off my passport form applying for my new identity as Maggie Moone. This was last on my list of places to change my name, and the taste of satisfaction was sweet.

It soured, though, when the person on their way into the post office turned out to be Betsy.

It had to happen sooner or later, of course. You can't live in a village the size of Saffron Sweeting without bumping into people, including those you'd rather fling yourself into the nearest ditch to avoid. For a split second, I did indeed look for a ditch, but since we were in the middle of the high street, I was out of luck.

'Oh!' Betsy stopped dead, then took a step back.

She looked as thrilled to see me as I was to see her, only my reaction included guilt and embarrassment, whereas I think hers was revulsion.

'I'm so sorry,' was the first thing out of my mouth. If I'd taken any legal advice, they would probably have told me not to speak to her at all, let alone apologise. But I didn't think about that. Seeing her made me choke at what I'd done.

In return, Betsy went pale. 'I'm not allowed to talk to you.' Clearly, she'd had the sense to consult a lawyer.

'Okay,' I said, then, immediately: 'How's your foot?'

She looked down. 'It's fine.'

Thank goodness. I'd been having nightmares that she was maimed.

'And the stable?' I don't know why I asked this: the whole village knew it was reduced to a heap, like the crumbs you shake out of your toaster once a year.

'Not fine.'

'I really am—' I began, but she shook her head.

'Look, Maggie, you'll be getting a letter from our attorney.'

'Okay.' This was fast becoming my standard response for meaning the opposite.

She stepped around me and pushed open the door of the post office. 'It's nothing personal.'

'Of course not.' I swallowed hard and let her go on her way.

After all, if someone had blown up part of my house, I'd sue them too, wouldn't I?

As soon as I was alone on the street, I took a few steps, but stopped next to the pillar box to steady myself. I was shaking from the encounter, my knees and stomach both reminding me I could have killed someone. And now, here it was, the certain knowledge I was going to be prosecuted, or whatever happened during legal action.

I wanted to go home and howl into a pillow, but I was due at the library for a paperwork blitz. I thought about cancelling, but with my handywoman income slashed, I couldn't afford to. Anyway, at least Kenneth was willing to work with me, unlike half the village. When I arrived, my legs were still wobbly and I had an inkling I was going to cry.

'You look like you lost a tenner and found sixpence,' Kenneth remarked, as I made straight for the little kitchen to put the kettle on.

'Morning,' I mumbled in return.

'Feed me!' called the library parrot, whose name was Stanley.

Well, I thought, at least someone's talking to me.

'Seriously, buttercup,' Kenneth said, as I brought two cups of tea to the front desk, 'what's the matter?'

That was all it took, those few kind words from a gruff individual, and my eyes filled.

'I just saw Betsy.'

He nodded. No one in the village needed reminding of why that would be significant. The explosion had been the Saffron Sweeting equivalent of the Profumo Affair.

'I feel like a leper,' I said. 'And, once they sue me, I'm going to be a bankrupt leper.'

Kenneth took his glasses off and polished them. This was his habit when thinking, and sometimes it could go on for almost a minute. Today, he broke his own polishing record.

'Have the police, or the health and safety people, established you're liable?'

I shrugged. 'I don't know. No one's telling me anything.'

I hadn't been questioned yet, although I assumed it was coming. I carried the dread in my stomach everywhere.

'Vincent swears he didn't make a mistake with the gas,' I continued. 'But Betsy says I'll be hearing from their lawyer.'

Kenneth replaced his glasses and patted my arm. 'There's a famous quote, you know, Maggie dear.'

'Is there?' I wasn't in the mood for citations.

'Mmm. Sherlock Holmes. It's something like ruling out the impossible. And then whatever remains, even if it's improbable, must be the truth.'

'I don't follow.' I knew he was trying to be helpful, but this literary musing was hardly practical.

'Well, dear, if it wasn't the gas, it must have been something else.'

I fumbled for a tissue. 'But what?'

'Indeed.' Kenneth paused as the kettle whistled at top volume. 'What, indeed?'

~ ~ ~

There's nothing quite as cruel as having time on your hands, enabling you to stew in your own worries. For the rest of the weekend I mooched around, knowing I should come up with a plan, yet failing to do anything constructive. I couldn't even fall back on the paperwork to change my name, as most of it was finally done.

The weather was unsettled, too, with sunshine and clouds taking turns to illuminate the village, then cast it in shadow. On Sunday afternoon the heavens opened, just in time for the annual cricket match against Bottisham.

'Come on, pip squeak, you need a project.' Amelia arrived on Sunday evening, with Grace in tow.

'You sound like Mary Poppins,' I grumbled.

'Well, really, Maggie, look at this place.' Amelia nudged the nearest skirting board with her toe, as if she suspected it would crumble over her gladiator sandals.

'You might feel better if you finished this wallpaper,' Grace added more kindly.

'What's the point? I'm probably going to have to sell the cottage. I mean, when they sue me, I'll need cash, right?'

'Sell it?' At this, Amelia's eyes lit up. 'Well, all the more reason to spiff it up!'

I looked at Grace, who shrugged. 'She's right. Of course.'

Amelia wandered into the kitchen, where most of the counters were still covered in jam jars I'd filled after the explosion. 'Oh lord, Maggie, it's a blooming jam factory in here!'

I tried to defend myself. 'Well, I can't eat the bloody stuff all in one sitting, can I?'

Amelia came back from the kitchen with a jar in each hand. 'If you need money, darling, you could start by selling it.'

'Right, what, join the WI and ask for a stall at their market? I'll be dead welcome there at the moment.'

Saffron Sweeting was officially run by the village council, but everyone knew the Women's Institute wielded the real power. Their monthly market was where alliances were formed, negotiations took place, and treason was punished. All under the guise of selling a few sponge cakes and homemade tarts. The jokers called it *Game of Scones*, for good reason. I would sooner string up a noose at the duck pond, then put my own head in it, than go anywhere near the WI brigade.

'She's right,' Grace said. 'They're terrifying.' Then she snapped her fingers. 'But you could sell your jam from here, Mags.'

'Here?' Amelia and I chorused. My front room was not a delicatessen in the making.

'Well, not *here* here,' Grace amended. 'From the front garden. You know, put out a table and an honesty box.'

Only a fortnight ago, I'd discussed this concept with Nancy, who'd assured me the English didn't have a monopoly on this summer custom for offloading excess eggs, vegetables, and sometimes cut flowers. The offerings usually sat on ramshackle tables at front gates, accompanied by a biscuit tin to collect the money. The whole thing, of course, relied on people not stealing, but more often than not, it worked okay.

'I haven't got room for a table,' I said. 'The hedge is in the way.'

'Well, cut it back.' Grace glanced at Amelia, who nodded approval.

'You'd feel better, darling. Work off some of that depressive brooding.'

'I'm not depressed.'

'Of course you're not.' Amelia smiled blithely. 'Still, why don't you give it a try?'

~ ~ ~

At eight the next morning, I tore down the front hedge. The fresh air *did* lift my spirits, and it only took me two trips to bring all the debris to the recycling centre. I told myself I was in a hurry to clear up the clippings before it rained again, but in truth, the sky was cloudless.

Coming back into the cottage to make tea, I noticed the light streaming through the front windows. I had no idea the hedge was blocking so much sunshine. But what could I use for a table to sell the jam? I didn't have any spare furniture that was suitable. As I waited for the kettle to boil, my eye fell on the dreary kitchen cupboards.

One cabinet was awkwardly placed, so I pulled it down and tore off the door. Then I turned it sideways, and had the structure I needed. Next, I nipped to Homebase to buy materials for a little pitched roof. The old cabinet was sturdy, but I gave it a coat of paint: lucky magenta for the walls, and green for the roof. I painted the inside white, so that the jam jars would show clearly.

Admittedly, the garden looked a little bare without the hedge, but the free space enabled me to drive a couple of sturdy poles into the soft earth. From there, it was easy to attach the jam house, although I admit I fiddled around with the spirit level for a while, until I was satisfied it was level.

As I walked back into the kitchen to round up the jam to sell, I saw what a mess I'd made by tearing down the cabinet, and how much better the room would look without its gloomy curtains. So, they came down too, and then it was only reasonable to tear up the Flotex carpet. After that, I patched the wall, and the next logical step was to give the room a lick of paint, using the remainder of the white from the jam house.

~ ~ ~

Once my pent-up energy was released, it was like a dam had broken. As soon as I started on practical projects, I found I couldn't stop. For over forty-eight hours I worked feverishly, taking only short naps. Every time I closed my eyes, I found I was buzzing with enthusiasm for further improvements.

By Thursday afternoon, my cottage was transformed.

The front door no longer opened into seventies gloom: the ugly wallpaper was gone, with the walls painted a simple pale linen. I'd stripped and sanded the floorboards, and hung a new light. The fireplace was still a work-in-progress, but that was okay. The kitchen, obviously, looked fresh and clean. The stairs, also free of carpet, wound steeply up, their risers newly painted.

The good thing about having such tiny rooms, was that I could paint each in a few hours. Eventually I hoped to get new carpet upstairs, but in the meantime I could ask Grace to help me find inexpensive rugs.

Most surprising of all, my new surroundings gave me the momentum to finish sorting not only the first box of stuff from Dad's house, but four of my own which I hadn't touched since I moved here from Burwell. I'd never felt this decisive or confident about getting rid of things: in little more than an hour, most of it was on the back seat of my car, ready to drop off at a charity shop.

I paused for a quick cup of tea, and the thought occurred to me that Amy might like some of my castoffs to furnish her treehouse. There was a serviceable quilt, for example, and a tea set which was old-fashioned, but pretty enough. The kids had explicitly asked for more help. So how about now?

With boxes on the back seat and wood sticking out of the boot, my car looked like it belonged in the rag and bone trade. Hoping the local gossips wouldn't spot it outside Tim and Amy's house, I rang their front door bell. After a long delay, during which I feared another interview with Great Grandfather Wong, it was opened by Tim.

My shoulders relaxed. 'I brought you some bits and pieces.'

'Cool! We tried to do more, but we're stuck again. Did you bring your drill?' He turned and hollered for his sister. 'Amy! She's here!'

Tim tugged off his jumper, which looked like part of his school uniform, and threw it somewhere behind him. 'Grandpa said you wouldn't come back.'

'Well.' I noticed warm anticipation at the task ahead. 'Bad luck, here I am.'

## Chapter 28

Thanks to the long summer twilight, we made phenomenal progress on the treehouse walls. The punishing part, however, was the constant shimmying up and down the ladder. Initially I stationed Tim in the tree to pass things up, but there was no getting around the climbing that was needed when things were forgotten or, as was more often the case, dropped.

And then we started the roof, which should simply have been a case of tacking membrane to the joists, followed by a layer of planking. In fact, it was a nightmare: I ended up tied to the tree with a safety rope, leaning out precariously as I drove nail after nail through the shiplap.

'I hope you're not planning to live up here,' I said, knowing the end result couldn't possibly be watertight. The whole thing didn't actually look too bad, but I had a new appreciation for the beautiful treehouse Colin's grandfather had constructed in Burwell, forty years ago.

'Okay, that's it.' Yet another clout nail slipped through my gloved fingers, never again to be found in the long grass. 'Break time.'

Amy disappeared inside the house and came back with three ice pops. We settled at the base of the tree, me in the middle and the kids on either side, resting our backs against the trunk.

'We really didn't think you'd come back, Maggie,' she said.

'Sorry to disappoint.' I sucked on my frozen treat.

'Yes, why *are* you helping us?' Tim asked.

'I like trees, I suppose.'

Poor kids, if their mother was overseas and their chlorophyll-obsessed great grandfather was filling the role of guardian. I'd heard that parents these days could be stifling, but that clearly wasn't the case here. 'And you two, you sort of remind me of me, and my brother,' I added.

'You have a brother?' Amy looked up with interest. 'Where does he live?'

I paused. This was a conversation I tended to avoid. But they were kids, it wasn't like opening up to an adult. 'I... *had* a brother.' Was she too young for this topic? I hoped not. 'He, er, he died. He was living in Australia until... well, until.'

'Wow,' said Tim.

Amy put her head on my shoulder. 'That's sad.'

'Yes,' I agreed. 'It's really sad.'

A few moments passed, then Tim asked matter-of-factly, 'He didn't fall out of a treehouse, did he?'

I couldn't help but laugh, the pain of remembering Matty dulled by the two young bookends beside me. 'No, Tim, he didn't.'

We never actually discovered how Matthew died. He'd been at a late-night beach party, with new friends, and a young man I was pretty sure was his boyfriend. The autopsy report stated Matty drowned, and mentioned alcohol and other substances in his blood. The boyfriend – no doubt influenced by a disastrous Skype call the previous Christmas, when my brother tried to introduce him to my parents – cut off all contact. One day, I might travel to Brisbane and track him down, but in the meantime, I hoped Matty's death had been an accident. And I prayed it had been quick.

'Okay,' I said to my young companions. 'Tea break over. Back up that tree.'

~~~

Around nine o'clock, I announced we should call it a day. My marathon week of physical projects was finally catching up with me.

'I've loved working with you, but you can manage the rest on your own.'

Amy was brimming with excitement. Despite the late hour, she was fidgeting like crazy, and every sentence started, 'When the treehouse is finished...'

Tim, though not as vocal, wore a look of immense pride, and kept looking up as if to check our work was still there. I didn't know if he was old enough to have a mobile phone, but if he did, I suspected photos of the new structure would be shared before I'd even started my car engine.

My own phone was out of battery – again – but that wasn't a problem, as there was nobody I wanted to speak to. My friends were local and knew they could come to the cottage if they felt like giving me a pep talk. Finn clearly wasn't going to get in touch. And I certainly didn't want to hear from the Health and Safety Executive, or lawyers, or Colin, for that matter.

'Give my regards to your great grandfather.' I put the last of my tools in my bag.

'I'll tell him I did it all,' Amy said. 'Then maybe he'll let me take woodwork at school.'

'Grandpa says she should do needlework next term instead.' Tim rolled his eyes. 'She never shuts up about it.'

'That's rough. I took needlework. I grew out of the skirt before I finished it.'

'See,' said Amy. 'Wood isn't like that. I'll never grow out of our treehouse.' She paused. 'Not for years and years. Even when I'm old like you, Maggie, I'll still love it.'

I tried to be offended by this, but I *did* feel old. My back was killing me and my triceps weren't happy either. But at least the kids were content. At this moment they were my biggest fans in this village.

I drove the short distance home, momentarily confused by the lack of hedge outside my cottage. There was the jam house standing proudly on its poles, but it didn't look like I'd sold a single jar yet. Having worked like stink to build it, I was plagued with doubt that nobody would want any. After all, if I couldn't be trusted with blowing things up, how good could my kitchen skills be? Would people think my jam was dodgy, too?

The light was fading fast and the streetlights gave only a dim glow as I pushed open the gate on its perennially squeaky hinges. I wasn't even sure why I had a gate, and made a mental note to get rid of it.

I was unlocking my front door when I saw the envelope stuck on it.

Oh jeez, I thought. Was this it: a court summons? Hand delivered, so I couldn't claim it was lost in the mail?

I paused on the doorstep, envelope in hand. Somehow, if I took it inside, that would make it official. But I was bone tired, and I couldn't stand there all night holding it and hoping a passing fox would snatch it from my hand. So I shuffled into the cottage, noticing the smell of fresh paint and how much nicer the living room looked with most of the messy boxes gone. Naturally, I then put the kettle on, as no bad news must be read without an accompanying cup of tea. Then I checked the fridge – woefully unexciting – and the biscuit tin, where I at last found a handful of chocolate digestives.

The envelope stared at me from the kitchen counter, and I'd eaten at least three of the biscuits before I noticed my name was handwritten. In turquoise pen. On closer inspection, it didn't look very official at all.

Now, I didn't want rid of the envelope. I wanted to know what was inside it, very much. So much, that I tore into it with chocolatey fingers, smearing Cadbury's all over the back.

*Dear Maggie,* I read. *Sorry for the note but your phone seems to be switched off. Please would you come for a cup of coffee tomorrow morning? About ten, if you're free? Yours, Betsy and Ted.*

Admittedly, I didn't know anything about legal action and the typical proceedings of a case. I'd avoided finding out, in fact. And I certainly didn't know how the Americans liked to conduct litigation. But a cup of coffee? On the property I'd been responsible for blowing up? I didn't need to be a law student to know that wasn't likely. At all.

## Chapter 29

Counting sheep didn't help me that night. Nor did the gentle rhythms of the Shipping Forecast: I was as wide awake for the Southeast Iceland weather as I'd been for Viking. My bed was too hot, then too cold, too rumpled, and too scratchy. I stared at the ceiling, the wall, and the edge of my pillow, all of which glimmered a faint silver thanks to the moon and my inadequate curtains.

Around four, I did drift off, but by eight I was up and showered, too nervous to stomach anything except three strong cups of tea.

Realising that some moral support would be invaluable, I phoned Amelia first.

'Sorry, darling,' she said. 'I'd love to help, but there's a property auction I simply can't miss.'

Nancy was my next choice – after all, she spoke American, that would be a help – but of course she was off to work.

That left Grace, who protested that she hated arguments, but finally agreed to meet me in the high street a little before ten. She was wearing a navy dress, and I wished I'd thought to put on something more formal. As it was, I was in a striped shirt and my smarter jeans: the best I could do at short notice.

'We should have allowed time for a croissant or something, to boost our energy.' Grace cast a longing look towards the bakery.

Her answer to almost any crisis was an injection of calories, the more the better.

'Maybe after.' I shook my head. 'I'd throw it up, if I had anything now.'

'Come on, then.' She linked an arm through mine, a gesture I thought only happened in boarding school books by Enid Blyton. 'Let's face the music.'

As we passed the library, we bumped into Kenneth who had just come out and locked the door.

'Ah, *there* you are,' he said, as if expecting to see us.

'Who, me?' Grace was jittery too.

'No, young Maggie.' He was wearing a tweed cap and gave the brim a nudge as he nodded to me. 'Morning, love.'

'Where are you off to, then?' The library was closed on Fridays in any case, but I couldn't think where he might be going.

'Same place as you, I expect.' He fell into step beside us.

'Really?' Grace voiced what I was thinking too. 'We're not sure whether we're going for Darjeeling, crumpets, or the firing squad.'

But Kenneth nodded and tapped the side of his nose. 'Wait and see.'

I hadn't been up Damson Lane since the day of the explosion. This morning the short distance had expanded, and the normal two-minute stroll felt like a five-mile hike. Grace tightened her grip again as we turned through Ted and Betsy's gates.

'I can't bear to look,' I muttered, meaning the stable block. I held up a hand to shield my eyes, as if worried there would be a solar glare bouncing off the remains.

'There isn't much to see,' Grace said. 'Just some construction fencing.'

Kenneth nodded. 'Don't distress yourself, Maggie. It's not a moon crater.'

'I can't do this,' I said, as Kenneth rang the front door bell. But it was too late: in the blink of an eye, Ted swung the door open.

'You made it!' he said, as though we'd crossed the Arctic tundra.

'Safe and sound,' Grace replied.

Unlike the stable block, I thought. Before I could make a bolt for it, Grace stepped over the threshold, tugging me behind her. Kenneth came last, as rear guard.

'Great, come on in, then.' Ted stepped back to make more room, although their hall was so large it wasn't necessary. 'Through here,' he added.

I shuffled my way into their beautiful living room, which had tall windows overlooking the back lawn. Fortunately, there was no view of the stable block – or what had been the stable block – from here.

'Thanks for coming, Maggie,' Ted said, and I forced myself to look at him. He was wearing jeans and a T-shirt, and didn't appear as if he wanted to strangle me.

I managed the smallest of smiles before Grace coaxed me to sit on a squishy linen sofa, which would have taken up my entire front room. She'd helped Betsy choose this furniture, but I wasn't interested in designer details right now. Grace sat beside me and Kenneth chose an armchair. Before us was an expansive coffee table, set with an array of cups, saucers, and a plate of cheese scones.

Betsy arrived, half hidden behind a teapot and coffee pot.

'Sorry, had to wait for it to finish brewing.' With Kenneth's help, she landed her heavy cargo.

I stole a glance at her, too: she was in long chino shorts, paired with a lilac short-sleeved sweater. Hardly the sort of thing you'd wear to tear someone off a strip. But what did I know? Maybe this breezy air was their way of disarming me, before they stuck a knife in my jugular.

Then there was the rigmarole of who wanted tea, or coffee, and who took milk or cream or sugar and would we have a scone with it?

I declined all the refreshments, knowing my hands were shaking so much I'd be at risk of adding a smashed cup to my offences. After what seemed like an eternity, the five of us were settled. The only sound was the ticking of a carriage clock on the mantelpiece.

'Is, er, anyone else coming?' Grace looked around.

I was wondering the same thing, half expecting a lawyer – or two – to emerge from behind the bookcase.

'No.' Betsy smiled, looking for all the world like she was hosting a coffee morning. 'Just us.' With that, she signalled with her eyebrows to her husband.

'Okay, awesome, well, thanks for coming.' Ted cleared his throat and in the pause that followed, something in me snapped.

'I'm so terribly sorry,' I blurted, against any logical advice to shut up and listen. 'I want you to know how truly appalled I am at what happened. And I'll take full responsibility in, er, making amends.' I said all this in one breath, paused to gulp extra air, then finished lamely. 'I really am sorry.'

There was silence. Grace patted me on the knee, Ted took a long sip of coffee, and Kenneth coughed.

'Oh, Ted,' Betsy said, 'we have to put Maggie out of her misery.' She gave me an apologetic smile and I assumed they were about to serve me with papers, or however this legal checkmate worked.

'Right.' Ted put his cup down. 'Yeah, sorry, let's fill you in.'

I held my breath as he reached for reading glasses, then pulled out a folder of papers which had been stuffed down the side of his chair.

'We've got a report here.' He leafed through the file. 'From the, er...'

'Fire Department,' Betsy offered.

Ted nodded. 'Cambridgeshire Fire and Rescue, in conjunction with the... let's see... the Health and Safety Executive.'

Please, I thought, would you *please* get on with it.

'They've sent preliminary findings,' said Ted.

'Although we don't expect them to change substantially,' Betsy couldn't resist chipping in. 'Which is why we wanted to talk to you.'

Ted cleared his throat again: he was finding this awkward too. The knowledge allowed me to breathe a little.

'They, er, sent us a forensic report along with this summary and, let's see, preliminary lab analysis.' Ted hadn't actually put his glasses on, but was holding them at an angle to help him read the text on each page of doom.

'Okay.' Grace was as keen as me for him to spit it out.

Happily, Betsy spat. 'We know there have been some terrible rumours in the village, Maggie, about what happened, and that you were to blame.'

I swallowed and nodded. Studying their plush carpet was easier than saying something.

'But we got this awesome news,' Betsy continued. 'It wasn't your fault.'

'What?' said Grace, as my head jerked up.

I darted my eyes from Betsy to Ted and back again. I couldn't read his face – he was still leafing through papers – but Betsy was smiling.

'It wasn't your fault, Maggie,' Betsy repeated.

My stomach did at least three somersaults but I wasn't sure my ears could be believed. For some reason, I looked at Kenneth, who nodded encouragement before biting into his second cheese scone. Had he known something in advance?

'So, you mean, like, the gas was faulty or something?' For all Grace's loyal friendship, she'd been anxious that my work had caused the blast.

Ted had fanned out several papers but now he stacked them back together on his lap. 'It wasn't gas.'

My mind raced. What was it, then? Paint stripper? What else did I have in the stables? Nothing, surely which would cause a boom big enough to be heard from the pub.

'Or at least, we call it gas in America, but you Brits don't.' Betsy laughed, and Kenneth gave a little harrumph of approval.

'I don't understand.' Grace caught my eye.

I agreed with her. This whole conversation was bizarre. And how was Kenneth in on their inside jokes?

Ted took a breath. 'It was petrol.'

'Petrol?' Grace and I spoke in unison.

My jaw dropped, but she continued. 'You mean, petrol from a car?'

'Yes,' said Betsy, at the same time as Ted said, 'No.'

'Please.' I was grateful I didn't have a cup to drop. 'Will somebody just *tell* me?'

'Okay,' said Ted slowly. 'It *was* petrol, but not *in* a car.'

'Where, then?' asked Grace.

'It was stored in the basement,' said Betsy, as though she'd revealed the punchline to a great mystery.

'Which basement?' Grace tried to answer her own question. 'The stables? There was a basement?'

For the first time, Kenneth sat forward in his chair, before glancing at Ted and Betsy. 'May I?'

'Please do,' they chorused.

Kenneth took his time, wiping imaginary crumbs from his mouth and draining his tea before replacing the cup precisely in its saucer.

'Well, young Maggie,' he began, 'I know you think I'm terribly old, but I wasn't alive for this. But I remembered something Violet had said, something her mother told her about the war.'

When people of Kenneth's age mentioned *the war*, they generally meant World War II.

'And that was enough to get me cogitating. Based on that, I did some digging. Not *actual* digging, you understand, but digging in the archives.'

I clenched my fingers and vowed not to interrupt him.

'And Violet helped me, of course. She's got a remarkable memory, that lady.'

Beside me on the sofa, Grace shifted. She was longing to wring it out of him, too. Kenneth, however, was enjoying his role as narrator.

'It really is quite bizarre,' Betsy said.

'So, during the war... you are aware petrol was strictly rationed?'

Was he finally starting to get to the point? I nodded with all the patience I could muster.

'Well, it was no joke, you see. Even if one had access to a car, not being able to get around was awfully tedious. Having a few drops of petrol available when needed gave one immense freedom and power.'

Nope, I'd been wrong, he wasn't getting to the point at all. We were getting a philosophy lecture on freedom of movement.

Grace glanced at me, then looked at Kenneth. 'I'm sorry to interrupt,' she said, 'but poor Maggie's in agony here.'

'Oh, forgive me!' Kenneth shook himself. 'Of course you are, buttercup.' He took another breath and picked up the pace. 'So, petrol was rationed and it cramped everyone's style terribly. A black market developed for it – along with all sorts of other things, as you know. And anyone who could get hold of some, well, they tended to hang onto it.'

'Hang onto it?' Grace prompted.

'Yes, dear. Stored it. In bottles, or cans, or whatever they could lay their hands on. They hid it in garden sheds, and outbuildings, and—'

'Stable blocks?' I whispered.

'There was a cellar, you see,' Betsy said.

'We didn't know about it,' Ted added. 'Sometime between then and now, it had been boarded up.'

'A cellar?' Grace repeated. 'A cellar of petrol cans? Oh, my—' She turned to me, eyes shining. 'Maggie! Petrol! In the cellar!'

I looked at her, then at Kenneth. I made hesitant eye contact with Ted, who shrugged apologetically, then Betsy, who saw my tears forming and jumped up to give me a hug.

'It wasn't your fault, babe,' she said into my ear. 'You couldn't have known.'

Grace was more collected than I was. 'How did you work this out?'

Kenneth pursed his lips. 'As I said, Violet got me thinking. Then it was a matter of combing the archives – we found the original architectural drawings of the house, showing cellars in the stable block. And we've got records of the local newspaper in the library, too. They were trickier, but eventually I dug up a wartime report that someone at Damson House had been questioned about black market dealings.

'The black market!' Betsy repeated. 'It sounds so exciting!'

'The scoundrel in question drew attention for transactions involving sugar and bacon.' Kenneth looked disapproving at the label attributed by Betsy. 'Although I wasn't able to find anything about petrol.'

'No, well, not if he hid it all,' Grace said.

'So, Kenneth kindly tipped off the forensics folk,' Ted said. 'Suggested they test for other substances, apart from gas.'

'And they came back pretty soon after that.' Betsy got up to offer more tea and coffee.

'But, what happened after all this time?' I couldn't quite believe this tale. 'I mean... things don't just blow up.' This, after all, had been the main accusation about me. These things don't just *happen*.

'They're not sure.' Ted was finally wearing his glasses to consult his papers. 'Their best theory is the petrol cans deteriorated, and some kind of spark set it off.'

'They said a rat chewing through a flex could do it.' Without asking me, Betsy picked up a fresh teacup. 'You look like you could use this.'

'Obviously, they can't prove that, because there's no trace left of the cable. Or the rat,' Ted said.

'Indeed.' Kenneth held his cup out for more tea, too. 'But some of the fragments do corroborate the theory of basement storage from that era.'

'Good grief.' I breathed out. 'This is a lot to take in.'

'Anyways, Ted and I, we wanted to say how sorry we are for your distress, Maggie.' Betsy was standing opposite me, hands clasped. 'I know we didn't make it easy on you and you must have been worried sick.'

I looked up at her but words wouldn't form.

'She was. Thank you.' Fortunately, Grace found her tongue. Then she put her arm around my shoulder to give it a squeeze.

'We're talking to our insurance company,' Ted said. 'But frankly, Maggie, I don't think you need worry. The loss adjuster sighed a lot. I think that means they're gonna pay up, when they sigh.'

I felt like sighing myself, or possibly skipping that part and just crying. I picked up my tea with two hands. 'Really?'

'Really,' Betsy said. 'It wasn't your fault. It was a freak accident.'

Even though it seemed I was off the hook, I wasn't thrilled with the realisation that I'd been tromping about in the stables, with sufficient petrol underneath to blow us all to bits. It was a lot to take in. I drank half the cup in a few gulps, then asked, 'And your foot? Is your foot okay?'

'My foot's fine, honey.'

As my heart rate finally slowed, I turned to Kenneth. His role in my acquittal had been pivotal. 'Thank you so much. I can't believe... thank you.'

'My pleasure,' he said. 'Nothing I like more than a puzzle.'

'I guess there will be a few more formalities,' Ted said. 'But really, Maggie, you're in the clear as far as we're concerned.'

I choked on a little sob, before managing to squeak my thanks again. A crushing weight – the equivalent of a stable block – had been lifted from me.

Ted and Kenneth shook hands, while Grace hugged first me, then our hostess.

'However, before you go, we do still have one small problem.'

I looked up, dreading a twist in the tale.

But Betsy simply gestured to the coffee table in front of us and laughed. 'Somebody needs to help me eat all these scones.'

We stayed another half hour with Ted and Betsy. The cheese scones disappeared fast, once they didn't have to compete with dread in my stomach. After that, I strolled home on my own, amazed that the huge cloud over my head was lifted. I should share the good news with someone who'd be as relieved as I was.

'Hi, Vincent, it's Maggie,' I said, when he answered his phone.

'Hey up.' His tone was guarded. I didn't blame him for that.

Remembering how wretched I'd been about the explosion, I got straight to the point.

'Fantastic news. It wasn't us. It wasn't our fault. It wasn't even gas.'

There was silence, then he said, 'You mean... the explosion?'

'Sorry, yes, the explosion. It wasn't our fault.'

Down the phone came a half sigh, half groan. 'Thank God.'

His reaction brought a lump to my throat, reminding me of the crushing angst. 'I know, it's fantastic.'

'So, what...?'

'Petrol, they think. From World War II.'

I told him the rest.

'Blimey.'

'Anyway, it definitely wasn't us. They showed me a preliminary forensics report. So there won't be any inquiries about whether I was working alone, or you being there.' I paused to sniff a rose over someone's front fence. 'Best of all, Colin doesn't need to know you were anywhere near the place.'

'Well, well...' He paused. 'That makes more sense now.'

'What does?'

I heard him take a breath. 'I went over to Bedford last week, to the HSE office.'

'What, the Healthy and Safety people?'

'Yeah. I figured I'd let them know, in confidence like, that I was at the job site. Not you.'

'Really?'

'Anyway, they brushed me off, didn't want details. They must have known about this already.'

'Oh, Vincent.' I processed this. He'd gone to tell them the truth, risking his future work with Colin. 'Thank you so much.'

'Never mind that. It's brilliant to know for sure what happened. You've made my day.'

'Me too.' I grinned, picturing his face. 'I'm so sorry for all the trouble.'

'Nah, don't worry about it,' he said. 'But I'm glad you rang.'

'Of course.'

'Listen, I've gotta get back to work, but maybe you'll come for supper soon? We'd love to see you.'

Hopefully, Vincent's scary wife would soften a bit, now the accusation of negligence had been lifted.

'I'd like that.'

After we hung up, I ambled the remaining distance to my cottage. In a daze, I noticed some jam jars were missing, and, sure enough, there were coins in the honesty box. It seemed the universe had decided to smile on me today.

Nonetheless, I've never been so glad to push open my pink front door, and head upstairs to bed.

~ ~ ~

'Of course she's not staying under those blankets. She's coming to The Plough to celebrate.'

When I opened my eyes, I found my bedroom curtains had been flung back. From the way soft light danced on the walls, I deduced I'd slept for a while. I squinted and found Amelia at the foot of my bed.

'Up you get, Twinkletoes!' My auburn-haired friend tugged at a corner of my duvet.

'How did you get in here?' I tugged back.

'Apparently, you were too swept away by the good news to bother locking your front door this morning.'

'She's right. You need to be more careful.' Grace hovered in the doorway.

'Nobody bothers with locks in Saffron Sweeting,' I said, although I knew she was right. It was true that many of the older folk still left their front doors on the latch while they were home, but I'd trundled off to bed and wouldn't have heard if a pack of goblins had moved in downstairs.

'Anyway, you're up now, jolly good show.' Amelia was exaggerating. It was clear I was neither up, nor a good show; I was wearing a ratty shirt and a pair of Colin's old boxer shorts as pyjamas. Note to self: stop wearing ex-husband's underwear.

I sat up in bed. 'What time is it and why are you here?'

'It's party time.' Amelia went to my small and chaotic wardrobe. 'Congratulations, by the way.'

'I told her,' Grace said. 'Hope you don't mind.'

I shook my head. 'Glad it's over.'

'It's not over until we crack open the bubbly, darling.' Amelia's voice was muffled by her exploration of my shirts. 'Tell me you've got some hot water.'

'Why, are we making tea?' In my opinion, tea was always the perfect way to wake up.

But Amelia just hooted. 'No, because otherwise, you're getting a cold shower.'

~~~

An hour later, I found myself at the pub. Amelia had first forced me into the shower (as predicted, only lukewarm), then enlisted Grace's help to kit me out. Consequently, I was wearing my best jeans and a jersey cowl-neck top, in a shade which reminded me of blackberry jam.

'Sorry,' Grace had said, as Amelia set about daubing make-up on me. 'She does this sometimes.'

'You're the guest of honour.' Amelia had pointed with her mascara wand before producing an enormous hairbrush. 'We need you to look radiant. Grace, see if she owns a hairdryer, would you?'

I'd protested, but by the time we reached the pub, I found I didn't mind looking good. My hair would never be entirely docile, but Amelia had done a good job of smoothing the worst of the frizz. My lipstick didn't last long, but the eyeshadow and mascara looked nice. And my long daytime nap had perked up my complexion.

'Did you invite Kenneth?' I asked. 'I must buy him a drink.'

'Yes,' said Grace. 'And he's bringing Violet, because she gave him the idea about the war in the first place.'

In fact, as the evening went on, it turned out almost everyone in the village was claiming some credit in solving the mystery.

'Load of baloney,' Fergus said from behind the bar. 'But we're all glad your name's been cleared.'

I smiled, aware that his takings tonight were far from baloney. Amelia had treated me to champagne, and I bought several rounds of drinks too. Then Ted and Betsy showed up, and the festivities were amplified when they opened a tab for another hundred pounds. Eventually, Violet proclaimed that the Americans weren't made of money, and told the 'stingy sods' to buy their own. She was drinking slimline tonic, which gave her the moral high ground.

'Feeling better?' Grace asked me, when I was halfway through my third glass of wine.

'Much,' I replied. 'Thanks so much for coming today.'

'You didn't need me, as it turned out.'

'No. But that's not the point.' I realised how bereft I'd felt since Finn left, and how much strength I was drawing from my friends in the village. Grace was staunchly supportive and Nancy asked all the right questions. Amelia, although at times verging on bossy, was like a turbine that never stopped producing positive energy.

I was enjoying the mellow satisfaction that came from good friends and great wine, when someone tapped me on the shoulder.

'Excuse me, are you Maggie?'

I turned to find a woman of about my age. Her shiny black hair was piled on her head in a top-knot, and she had a beautiful, long face. Her trouser suit looked too smart for her to be a journalist, but still...

'Er, yes.' My instinct was to deny it, but with fifty people in the pub who all knew my name, my chances of anonymity were slim.

'I brought you these.' She held out a box of chocolates. 'It's not much, I'm afraid, I didn't have time...'

I stole a glance at the chocolates. They appeared to be truffles from Marks and Spencer: one of my favourite indulgences. Then I looked back at her face. Did I know her?

'Er, thanks,' I began. 'But, sorry, I don't think...' I couldn't remember her name. Or anything else about her, for that matter.

'My kids told me what you did. They wanted to say thanks.'

Thanks? For what? Not blowing up Ted and Betsy's stables? Thanks for not ruining Vincent's career? I peered again, certain she wasn't his wife. But my hand reached for the chocolates.

'I'm Tim and Amy's mum,' she said. 'They told me about you.'

'Tim and – oh!' That's why her almond eyes looked familiar.

'I've been working overseas, you see. Mostly in Japan. I was going to help them with it, but...'

'You mean, the treehouse?'

'Yes! My kids told me how much work you've done. They're thrilled. We all are. I've promised Amy I'll climb up there myself, tomorrow. She's going to serve me tea, in her new cups.'

I stared, imagining the joy I would have felt, if my own mother had shown even the tiniest bit of interest in a tea party in our beloved treehouse. Instead, she was too busy having affairs, before finally sodding off to France while I was away studying. I amended my opinion of Amy's mother from uncaring absent parent, to dynamic jet-setting mum.

'Oh, I really didn't...' I chose not to mention their lack of permission for the new structure. Instead, I looked down at the chocolates, embarrassed for misjudging the woman without ever meeting her.

'But you did! If it wasn't for you, they'd still be staring at a heap on the back lawn.' When I continued to keep my gaze averted, she added, 'My grandfather likes you, too.'

I gaped at this revelation, and she winked. 'So, I'm sorry this isn't much, but we did want to say thanks. Of course, if you'd like to send us a bill, that's fine too.'

'Sorry?'

'A bill. For your work on the treehouse.' She looked uncertain. 'I wasn't trying to pay you in chocolates. Just, er, show you the kids are grateful.'

Before I could stop myself, I knocked back the last of my wine. 'You really like it, then?'

She took my free hand and pressed the truffles into it. 'We love it. The kids are ecstatic. You could say, they're over the moon.'

~ ~ ~

I slept deeply that night and woke – with no bedroom guests – when the sun was high.

I pottered around the cottage, flinging windows open in celebration of the lightness in my bones. With fresh eyes, I considered the further improvements I could make to my home. Copious amounts of elbow grease, plus a bit of advice from Grace, would no doubt go a long way.

While I waited for some porridge, I threw old newspapers into the recycling box and tossed suspect products from the fridge. Pleased with myself, I dusted the living room, including the television, and then turned it on, just because it was there.

But Saturday morning wasn't the time for stellar entertainment. On the first channel someone was cooking noodles, and the next was a droning interview with a politician. On the third, I found a golf tournament, broadcast from somewhere hot, where the greens stretched for miles and the emerald grass gleamed.

Colin hated golf, I thought.

And in a flash, I remembered the list. Maybe I could pick golf as my next way of showing he was less important to me than a flea on a hedgehog. Back in the kitchen, I found the list, which I'd shoved in the tea towel drawer after Finn stormed out. There it was, item number eight, golf. Good. I would start by watching the tournament while I ate my breakfast, then investigate where I could take lessons. Somebody in the village might lend me clubs and a few balls.

I made a pot of tea, added the requisite dollops of golden syrup to my porridge, and prepared for a lazy morning. After all, with everything that had happened, I needed some downtime.

Whoever invented porridge surely deserved a Nobel Prize, I thought, as the combination of oats, the syrup, plus caffeine from the tea did their work. The food, and the benefits of ten hours' sleep, might turn me into a new woman. With my feet on the coffee table, I prepared to enjoy the faraway scenery and drama of missed putts and bunker shots on the television.

A tall lean golfer in a pink shirt sliced his way out of the rough, sending his ball through the low branches of a tree.

'And that's how it's done!' said one commentator in his smooth, BBC voice.

'Indeed,' added the other. 'It doesn't have to be pretty to get him back on track. There he goes, taking back control of his game.'

I looked at the little white ball bounce onto the fairway and it hit me. I was sitting on my sofa, spending time on something I didn't care about, just to get back at Colin, who wouldn't even know. And he'd probably think nothing of it, if he did. As for spending money I didn't have, on golf lessons I didn't need, that was ridiculous.

I finished my last spoonful of porridge, and stood up.

It was time to take control of my game.

## Chapter 31

My first stop was Tim and Amy's house.

'I'm so glad you all like the treehouse,' I said to their mother, when she answered the door. 'And I haven't brought you a bill, but would it be okay if I took a few photos?'

If there was even a small risk the council would make them tear it down, I wanted evidence before it disappeared.

She blinked, but recovered. 'Sure. I think the kids are up there now, actually. Can't prise them away from it. Just kick them out, if you want the treehouse without their ugly mugs in your shot.'

'Will do. And thanks for the choccies!'

I'd eaten most of them in the bath last night.

Half an hour later, I popped my head around the door of Hargraves & Co. 'Oh good, you're here!'

Saturday was Amelia's busiest day and I wasn't sure she'd be in her office.

'I have a viewing in twenty minutes.' She barely looked up from her screen. 'Did you want to buy a house?'

'Sorry, no.' I went all the way inside. 'But can I borrow a computer and your colour printer?'

She popped her head around the corner of her monitor. 'If you must.' Then, as I bounded across to the spare desk, 'Goodness, Maggie, you're as bouncy as the March hare.'

'The joys of being found innocent,' I said. 'New lease of life.'

'Yup. Been there. Work is a fabulous medicine, although best used as a short-term cure.'

'Not in this case.' I waggled the mouse, willing the computer to wake up.

'Well, darling, if I'm not back when you leave, lock up, will you? Drop the spare key back to me later.'

'Will do.' I was checking which photos on my phone were the best. 'I'll leave you some of my flyers, too.'

'Flyers? Oh, Lordy, is this something else to bug Colin?'
'No.' I grinned. 'Something for me.'

~ ~ ~

Violet was known for ruling her post office with an iron fist. A couple of years ago, Grace said, there had been rumours in the village of her retirement, but it hadn't happened yet. She'd always been offhand with me, especially if I tried to find the right change and held up the queue. But since she'd helped Kenneth with the petrol mystery, I would try to be nicer to her.

I browsed her shelves and found a dark chocolate Bounty bar, then, with more effort, located stationery supplies. I picked out a pad of cream notepaper and matching envelopes.

Then, I approached the counter and held out my flyer. 'May I put this in your window, please?'

Like many village shops, the post office had a board in the window where people placed postcards advertising babysitting services, lawnmower sharpening, and bikes for sale. Today I also noticed information about pilates at the village hall, a quiz night at the pub, and a bargain price for a beehive, complete with bees.

Violet took the sheet. 'It's large, so it'll cost double.'

Then, as was her custom, she read my advertisement, checking it was appropriate for all ages. Legend claims a licensed massage therapist once tried for a postcard in the window, and Violet chased her out of the shop. I held my breath, hoping she'd see nothing kinky in my poster.

'Treehouses?' she said finally. 'Well, well.'

'Yes.' Butterflies of anticipation rose. 'Custom treehouses, made to measure, big or small.'

I couldn't believe it had taken me so long to think of it. I loved being outside and loved making things. This would be twenty times more fun than unblocking sinks, not to mention bookkeeping. Plus, it was my tribute to Matthew. I planned to donate the profits from my first job to a mental health charity.

I'd done enough research in the last few weeks to know there'd be red tape to negotiate. If people were paying me serious money, we'd have to get planning permission. I'd need a class to brush up my CAD software skills, and I knew my first few projects would need to be modest. No wooden turrets or zip lines, just yet.

'That's very enterprising of you, Maggie.' She came out from behind the counter, wriggled behind the newspaper stand to get to the window, and flipped the board around to pin up my advert.

'How far will you travel?' Violet emerged from the window, dusted her hands off on her rump, and returned to her post behind the counter.

'Travel?'

'Yes, to build a treehouse? I mean, what if someone wants one, but they live in, say, Great Yarmouth?'

Had there been an epidemic of fallen lumber in Great Yarmouth that I hadn't heard about? 'Well, yes, East Anglia would be fine, I'm sure.'

My main constraint was to stay away from conservation areas, where they were picky about trees and I might have to bring in an arboriculturist.

'Good,' the postmistress said. 'I'll pass your number along, then. My second cousin might be interested.'

'Thank you.' I felt another rush of excitement. Being paid to build treehouses would be the bee's knees. 'And Kenneth said you helped unravel the explosion at Ted and Betsy's. I'm awfully grateful.'

'Nasty business, dear. Very worrying for you.'

'It was. So... thanks.'

'All in a day's work,' said Violet, then turned to help her next customer.

~~~

The pub was next to the post office; I considered an early lunch, but didn't want to be disturbed. So I turned the other way, shading my eyes from the strong midday sun.

In the garden beside the library was a large tree with broad branches. It must have stood there for almost a hundred years. Occasionally, I saw a kid nestled at its base, reading, but in general they stuck to the small children's area inside. Today, the garden was deserted and I sank down in the cool shade, my back against the trunk. At least my chocolate bar wouldn't melt.

I folded back the writing pad to the first page, and my pen hovered over the paper for the whole time it took the Saffron Sweeting church clock to strike noon. After a minute more, I forced myself to start. After all, I couldn't exactly make it worse.

*Dear Finn,* I wrote.

*I'm not much good at letters and I don't know if this will ever reach you, but if it does, I hope you won't crumple it up immediately.*

*The truth is, I've realised a bit too late how enormously lucky I was in meeting you. I don't think I was quite ready for someone so wonderful to fall into my life and I behaved like an idiot. You obviously worked out that I hadn't moved on enough from Colin to find my own feet and discover who I could be. So it's no surprise that I made a total mess of discovering who we could be.*

*Losing you was painful but as the weeks have gone by, the pain is getting worse, not better. I notice your absence every single day and realise I took your kindness and patience for granted. I've had some experiences which have shaken me up and I'm starting to see glimpses of the type of woman I'd like to become. And I'm very late in realising that you're just the type of person I'd like to share my days and nights with.*

*Maybe this letter won't ever find you but if it does, I want you to know I'm truly sorry. If you cross my path again, I won't waste my chance a second time.*

*I will always cherish our time together and I hope, more than anything, that you are safe and that you are happy.*

*With love, Maggie.*

Crumbs, letter writing was hard work, and emotional, too. I'd better eat the chocolate bar, in case it did start oozing in my pocket.

Then I read the letter again, hoping it had improved. It hadn't, and I briefly considered forgetting the whole idea. But I reminded myself the new Maggie wasn't a coward. The new Maggie took risks and really, I had nothing to lose. Even if Finn ignored me, at least now I knew what finding real love could feel like.

I settled down and made two more copies of the note, placing each in its own envelope. Then I took out my phone and photographed the original.

Having steeled myself for action, I wanted to deliver the letters immediately, but the weekend was in my way. I kicked myself for not thinking of writing to Finn sooner, and wondered where else I could direct my newly acquired energy.

## Chapter 32

'Colin isn't here.' Keiko opened the door no more than thirty degrees. 'He's at work. In Barton.'

'Oh.'

On a Saturday afternoon? Then I remembered, Colin hadn't believed in weekends being family time. I think he relished getting away from me.

'When will he be back?' I tried to hide my frustration.

She shrugged, and although the door hid most of her, she looked smaller than ever. 'Soon, I hope. We go—'

I waited, but she caught herself and gave an apologetic smile. 'He... he said I mustn't talk to you.'

'It's okay, Keiko, I haven't come to hound you.' I wasn't going to spill his dodgy dealings to his wife without getting his side of the story first. 'Unless of course you want to sell me the treehouse while he's gone?'

It was worth a try, but she shook her head.

'Okay, well, thanks.'

I still really wanted to talk to Colin.

Barton wasn't a big village, was it?

It wasn't. I drove out first along the Wimpole road, hoping to spot Colin's van. Then I tried the high street, had a quick look in the car park at Burwash Manor, and finally got lucky at a fencing supplier.

There was a smell of freshly hewn wood in the car park, an odour I loved. Some of the wood supplies might be excellent treehouse material. Leo – our local master woodworker – had offered a couple of hours of coaching for my new business, so maybe I could bring him out here to have a look.

For today, though, I had a less enjoyable task.

'Oh, for God's sake,' Colin said, as he saw me lurking by his van. 'Are you bloody stalking me, or what?'

I ditched any preamble. 'I know the painting's fake.'

He stopped dead, a few feet from me. 'You what?'

My ex looked tired and was sporting five o'clock shadow. This was unusual: Colin always shaved. Unlike Finn, who disliked shaving and usually had a few days' stubble, Colin took a kind of pride in it. Thinking about Finn's stubble gave me a jolt in my chest, and with an effort I came back to the present.

'Dad's train painting. It's forged.'

Colin's eyes darted away.

'You already knew.' I could tell from his reaction. I'd been hoping there'd been a mistake, that maybe he thought the painting was genuine, but from the way his shoulders sagged, I was certain.

We stared each other down for a few seconds, then he said, '*And?*'

'If you're knowingly selling a forgery, that's a crime.' I wasn't sure about that, but it sounded good. Considering he'd been so keen to pin the explosion at Ted and Betsy's on me, I could enjoy the shoe being on the other foot.

'Haven't you got your own crimes to worry about?' He didn't know the shoe had, in fact, changed feet.

'Oh, didn't you hear?' I feigned sweetness. 'They cleared me. It was a petrol stash, some toff, from the war. Not gas at all.'

He faltered.

'In any case, you know I didn't touch their gas. You know I got professional help. And I know you know who that was.'

When Vincent had told Colin that he'd worked with me, my ex had sworn, and blustered, and sulked. Then he'd kept Vincent on his payroll, just the same.

'I'm not going to be bullied by you, Colin.'

'So?'

'So, back to the painting.'

'*And?*'

There it was again, that infuriating *and*. Had he used that during our marriage? I couldn't remember. And actually, I didn't care.

'*And*, you have to tell the auction house you're withdrawing it,' I said. 'Seriously, Colin, I don't know what's going on here, but you're committing fraud.'

He stepped towards me. I'd forgotten how tall he was; for one awful moment I thought he might grab me and shake me, or worse. But he veered to the side and braced both hands on his van as he stared down at the gravel of the fencing yard.

'I'm not withdrawing it.' From the way his jaw clenched, I could tell he was rattled.

'What?'

He turned then, leaning heavily on his van, and pulled a packet of cigarettes from his pocket. I eyed them in surprise. Colin never used to smoke.

He followed my gaze. 'For Christ's sake, don't tell Keiko.'

'I assume you're not doing that at home, then.' Keiko kept a spotlessly fresh house, in accordance with her minimalist, clutter-free ethos. 'Stinky ashtrays not allowed?'

Colin lit up and took a long inhale. 'It's not just the smell.'

'No, as well as the pong, they're a death sentence in a box.' I was annoyed with myself for getting off topic.

But as it turned out, we weren't actually off topic.

'Yeah.' My ex-husband gave a wry smile and puffed out smoke. He turned his head to blow it away from me, and I took that as a sign his aggression was softening. 'But not for me.'

'Of course for you.' I tutted. He wasn't stupid, he knew the facts.

'For Keiko,' he said.

I frowned. How had we got from fake paintings to passive smoking?

'Her doctors say any kind of pollution is...' Colin fell silent, looking at the ground.

'Sorry?'

For long moments, I didn't think he would continue. More likely, he'd tell me to buzz off, take my nose out of his business, and threaten me with a restraining order.

But after a couple more drags on the cigarette, he said, 'She has a rare blood disease.'

'Who? Keiko?'

He nodded, still not looking at me. 'They say it's incurable. Unless...'

'*Incurable?*' I repeated the terrible word in a whisper. Keiko? That couldn't be. She was young and slim and had her act entirely together, from the top of her shiny hair to her polished patent loafers. From the moss-free roof of her house to the gleaming kitchen floor. 'Are you sure?'

'We've known for months. They've done tests and trials, bounced us from Addenbrooke's to London and back again.'

'I'm sorry...' My voice was as pathetic as my words. Poor Colin. After all, he hated being near doctors. It stemmed from how his dad died, I'm sure.

'Her complications are getting worse. Our last good hope is treatment in the USA.'

'America?'

He nodded. 'We leave in two weeks.'

I let this sink in, drawing circles in the gravel with one toe.

Colin finished his cigarette, and pushed himself upright. 'I have to get home.'

'Right,' I said, my zest for justice in the art world deflated. 'Give her my... well, you know.'

He nodded.

'And what about the painting?' I said, as he unlocked his van and opened the driver's door. 'You know, the auction?'

'Did you not hear me, Maggie? My wife has thalassemia. We're flying to America for medical treatment.'

He shook his head. 'Their hospitals are the most expensive in the world.'

~~~

In theory, the four of us were gathered at Amelia's house to watch the new smash-hit historical drama on Netflix. A duchess and her stable boy were dressing up to rob stagecoaches, and Britain was gripped. But nobody had yet pressed *Play*, apparently more interested in the real-life skulduggery which was unfolding.

'Correct me if I'm wrong.' Grace jabbed with a cocktail stick at the fruit in her sangria. 'But wouldn't that be blackmail?'

'Of course it's not blackmail, it's called *leverage*.' Amelia sounded definitive.

Nancy looked from one to the other. 'And is *leverage* customary in your country?'

'Now look what you've done,' I said to Amelia. 'Nancy thinks we Brits go around holding up stagecoaches and blackmailing ex-husbands.'

Amelia was unapologetic. 'Look, darlings. I can see where you're coming from, but all's fair in love and business. Maggie: Colin has something you want, and you have information to persuade him to part with it.'

'Still,' said Grace, 'twisting his arm to hand over the treehouse, or else telling tales about the painting... seems pretty low.'

I sighed. It seemed pretty low to me, too.

'But Colin is doing something fraudulent in the first place, right?' This was Nancy.

'Right.' I nodded.

'And he was a complete shit to you about that business at Ted and Betsy's.'

'Yep. But he kind of took the wind out of my sails today.' The conversation had not gone at all as I'd planned.

'It truly is awful, about his wife and her condition,' Grace said. 'Can you imagine going through something like that?'

We all shook our heads and paused out of respect for Keiko's illness. I'd looked up the disease Colin had mentioned, and was dismayed by what I'd read.

'Is it true,' I asked, 'that medical treatment is really expensive in America?'

'Hell yeah,' said Nancy.

Grace added, 'It's awful. I mean, it's awfully good, usually, but the bills can be astronomical.'

'So they really need the money...' I stared at my drink.

'Sounds like it'll probably bankrupt them,' Amelia said, then saw the reaction from the rest of us. 'What?'

'You don't have to be quite so pleased about it,' Grace said. 'Even if that means you can swoop in and offer to sell their house for them.'

'They're selling their house already,' I said.

'Or *trying* to.' Amelia smirked, as though she knew something the rest of us didn't.

'Look, the bottom line is, for Colin to sell that painting knowing it's not genuine, is wrong.' Nancy got to the crux of the matter.

'Even if he really needs the money,' Grace added.

'Right,' I said. 'And for me to pressure him to sell me the treehouse, or threaten to shop him... well, that's also wrong.'

Amelia sighed and examined her nails. 'It's a *treehouse*, what's the big deal? And if you give him a fair price, that'll help with their medical bills, won't it?'

I let the remark go about a treehouse not being a big deal. 'I suppose so, yes.'

'So, what are you going to do?' Grace asked.

'I don't know.'

Nancy, as usual, hit the nail on the head. 'I guess it depends how badly you want that ol' treehouse.'

*Chapter* 33

My father used to say that if you give someone three things to do, the world divides into those who will pick the easiest thing first, and those who will pick the hardest. As a teenager, I rolled my eyes, but by my late twenties, when I'd learned a bit about self-discipline, I'd begged him to tell me which way was better.

But he shook his head, and told me I had to work that out for myself.

His enigmatic answer implied it was best to start with the hardest, so I took the three identical letters I'd written for Finn and decided his scary grandmother daunted me most.

Bingo night was Monday; I arrived at the hall early, equipped with no fewer than five Yorkie bars. But I felt a tremor in my step as I entered.

'Will you look here! A young lassie's joining us.'

I hadn't expected a welcome this warm. Maybe this was why Finn had been keen for us to try bingo.

Other voices joined in. 'Are you playing, dear?' 'What's your name, love?' and, 'We've a seat here. Sit you down.'

I hadn't intended to play; I'd thought I could just find Grandma McCarthy and beg her mercy. But, what harm could a couple of cards do?

'We're glad you're here,' said the old gent next to me. 'Cuts the average age drastically.'

'And the average skill, too,' I said, which delighted them no end.

With ten minutes before the official start time, I spotted Finn's grandmother and excused myself to approach her table.

'I brought you some Yorkies,' I tried, as my opening gambit.

'Oh, it's you.' Her reply was far chillier than the reception at my own table.

I took a breath. 'I know you're busy.' After all, she was arranging her glasses, bingo pens and Fox's glacier mints. 'And I know you don't like me—'

At this, she looked up, head tipped back so she could study me through the correct part of her varifocals. But she didn't contradict me.

'Anyway.' I put the Yorkie chocolate bars on the table, reached for the letter, and pressed on. 'If you would consider posting this to Finn, I would be enormously grateful. I believe he would appreciate it, too.'

She looked at the cream envelope in my hand.

'I've stamped it for Ireland,' I said. 'And put his name on it, obviously. You only need to add the address and pop it in a postbox.'

'You're not pregnant, are you?' Seated, she had a view of my midsection.

'Absolutely not!' Life was complicated enough without that. 'I would just like this letter to reach him. I know it's a lot to ask.'

It wasn't a lot to ask, not at all, but I suspected polite deference was best.

Now, Grandma McCarthy squinted up at me. 'Are you playing tonight?'

'Well, I—' What was the right answer here? Would she be more likely to help if I rolled up my sleeves and got my eyes down to bingo, or if I left them to it?

She sniffed and turned away, ignoring the letter. I was about to leave when I caught her wink at her neighbour. Then she said, 'If I win tonight, Maggie O'Moone, then I'll consider it.'

'Oh!' I said. 'Right, er, thanks.' I placed the letter next to the chocolate bars. 'I'll leave this here then, shall I?'

The old bat would probably steam it open later, then throw it in the bin with her leftover fish and chips. But that was a risk I had to take.

'If you wish,' she said. 'Oh, and Maggie?'

'Yes?'

'Next time, bring me Yorkies with raisins in. I like those best.'

Great, I thought: now I was potentially mixed up in both blackmail *and* bribery. Grace would be so disappointed in me.

~ ~ ~

Early the next morning, I arrived at the Blood Donor Centre at Addenbrooke's Hospital. I was compliant with the required waiting time after a tattoo, but only by a whisker.

The hospital smell hit me as soon as the automatic doors slid back. No wonder Colin hated anything medical, right down to getting the flu vaccine. Keiko's treatments must be torturing him, as well as her.

'Sorry, are my hands cold?' asked a pretty nurse with ringlets, as she dabbed the cleaning wipe on my arm.

'A bit, don't worry.' I waited for the sting of the needle. It was the least I deserved.

'There we are, all sorted.' The nurse added tape to my arm to hold things in place for the duration of my donation. 'All right?'

'Fine.' I deliberately didn't look at the blood bag beside me. 'But I do have a question.'

'Mmm?' She was tidying her supplies and dropping sundries in the medical waste bin.

'Do you know Finn? Does he still work here?'

'Finn?' She sounded surprised. I suspected she'd been expecting a query about blood groups or platelets. Then I saw her expression close. 'Er, I'm not allowed to give out any information.'

'I understand.' I tried to look non-threatening. Which wasn't hard, considering I was tethered to a medical trolley with blood pouring from my left arm. 'But I was hoping the hospital could forward a letter.'

I'd parked the letter on top of my bag, which was resting on a chair beside the bed.

She hesitated. I figured, if this pretty blonde nurse and Finn were involved, or if she liked him, she'd tell me to get stuffed.

Instead, she said, 'Stay there.' This was unnecessary, given my predicament, but I was happy to oblige.

A minute or so later, a man wearing medical scrubs arrived. He was a little older, with a neat goatee beard. A supervisor, maybe?

'Hello.' He looked at the clipboard beside me. 'Can I help?'

'I'm not asking you to breach protocol,' I said. 'But I'm a friend of Finn's.'

'Uh-huh.' The supervisor's face was neutral.

'Well, it's very embarrassing...' I glanced at the ceiling. 'We were going out together, I really liked him, and I, er, mucked it up.'

The supervisor cleared his throat, but said nothing.

'I have a letter.' I nodded at the chair. 'I know you can't tell me anything, but if you have an address for him, I've stamped it, ready to go.'

He glanced at the envelope. 'I see.'

'And you're doing brilliant work here.' I waved my free arm at the other donors in the clinic. 'It's so important, isn't it, to give blood?'

The supervisor tilted his head. Was there a ghost of a smile there too? How many pints would it take before he cracked?

'I can come back.' I'd looked up this rule, too. 'If that helps. In sixteen weeks, I can donate again, right?'

Now, he took a step backwards and rubbed his beard with his thumb. 'You could. But we still won't be allowed to tell you anything.'

'I get it, that's fine. You've all been great.' They hadn't, actually, but I had known they wouldn't give out Finn's address to every crazy donor who spilled a few pints. 'So I'll leave the letter there on my way out, okay?'

He shrugged, then wrote something on the clipboard. No doubt a secret acronym for *patient is deranged*.

I forced a smile. 'Super, then. Great. Thank you so much.'

The supervisor nodded and walked away. I lay back, drained not just of blood but of optimism too. Then I studied my arm. How much longer before I could get rid of that blooming needle, and claim my free cup of tea?

~ ~ ~

'I saved you for last because I thought you'd be easiest,' I said to Robyn after I'd explained what I wanted. 'Please don't disappointment me.'

'Well, I'm not fond of being called easy.' She glanced down at the box of Lego she was holding, then gave me a pointed look. 'And you're assuming I even know how to reach Finn.'

'I thought, if you don't, then your brother probably does. They're friends, right?'

I was sure she'd told me that, the day we'd first chatted at the bakery. Hopefully, Finn and her brother were lifelong pals, rather than acquaintances who'd met a few times down the pub.

Another customer came into the shop, a mother offering a carrycot for consignment. I hid my frustration and stepped to the side so Robyn could deal with her. As soon as the door closed, I tried again.

'Please?' I cajoled. 'You're my last hope.' This wasn't strictly true: I didn't know for sure that neither his scary grandma nor the bearded supervisor would forward my letters. But I wasn't optimistic.

Robyn shook her head, but in the way some people do when they're thinking, not deciding.

Finally, she said, 'Maybe I could...'

'Oh, please. I'd be so grateful. Any favour at all in return, name it.' It was almost five o'clock. 'A drink? Cup of tea? Dinner?' Dinner wouldn't be cheap, but it would be worth it.

More head shaking followed, and I entertained the uncharitable thought that she'd learned to do that because her hair was so beautiful and it helped it catch the light.

Then, she stopped. 'What kind of car do you have?'

~ ~ ~

Two hours later, and against all the laws of physics, I'd helped Robyn transport a humongous canvas from her flat in Milton to a wealthy client in Dry Drayton.

I'd sweated, and squeezed, and squirmed to get her artwork down the stairs, and onto the roof of my car. Then, driving at snail's pace with Robyn hanging out of the window to grip the painting, we'd delivered it safely.

'Thanks for all the help,' Robyn said, as we staggered into the nearest pub for pints of shandy and hearty portions of cottage pie.

'I know I keep on about this,' I said, 'but is there any chance you'll be able to get that letter to Finn?'

'Gosh, I'd forgotten all about that. Well, if my brother has an address, yes, okay, I'll try.'

Well, I thought, that was that. I'd done all I could. Three letters might, or might not, be on their way to Finn. I had no options left. I'd have to wait and see.

'Oh, and you should probably know,' Robyn added, with the casual air people often adopt when they feel guilty. 'I tipped off that auction house.'

'Sorry?' I was chasing mashed potato around my plate. 'What auction house?'

'The one selling the forgery you told me about.' She paused, checked my reaction, and continued hastily. 'You see, it's a funny story, I was there for my internship interview and—'

My fork fell with a clang. 'You told them?'

Robyn looked down at her lap, then met my eye. 'Yes.'

I stared at her. 'But how did you know which...?'

I'd never mentioned the painting's name, had I?

'Well, I'd been banging my head against the wall, trying to get an internship with a gallery, and talking to you made me realise I could try small auction houses, too.'

My heart sank.

'So, I managed to get an interview at Brissinghorn & Beem... and while I was there, they mentioned a canvas by Cuneo, and a delay, and it fell into place.'

I was momentarily speechless. She clearly had a head for details that I'd thought were irrelevant.

'Mr Beem was ever so nice. I told him to check the other art for that auction *especially* carefully.'

I'd never realised the art world was so small. 'Did you at least get a job out of it?'

She nodded happily.

'Well done, then,' I said lamely.

I stared out of the pub window, but within seconds, I found my glass was empty. My *leverage*, if I'd been planning to use it, had just disappeared.

## Chapter 34

It was after midnight when I fell asleep, and I was awake again by five.

I stood at the kitchen sink with bleary eyes and a double-strength cup of tea. It was far too early to work on my new business. I was out of sugar and the shops wouldn't be open yet, so jam making was temporarily off the agenda too.

But I could at least tackle that one remaining box from Dad's house.

I dug it out from the cupboard under the stairs, made myself some toast and marmalade, and got stuck in.

There were a few Christmas cards, and a couple of ancient railway magazines, and for some reason, about two years' worth of old telephone bills. But buried deep beneath was a stack of grainy photos, faded now, showing our family when we used to be a family. Dad and me, holding somebody's pet rabbit. Matthew and me, at a birthday party. Even me and Mum, posing in front of tall flowers. I wasn't very old, seven maybe, so this was several years before she and Dad broke up.

And there, almost at the bottom of the pile, was the photo I'd forgotten was ever taken. There we were, Matty and me, perched eight feet in the air, legs dangling, faces radiant. It looked like I was missing a front tooth, and he had acne. But that didn't matter. We were in the place we loved best, a place where life was honest and uncomplicated in a way it never has been since.

We were in our treehouse.

And as the Saffron Sweeting church clock chimed six, I knew I had to make one last try.

~~~

At seven, I phoned Colin, but got no reply.

By half past seven, I was fed up of pacing my small lounge. I'd try to track him down in person: anything was better than stewing here.

I was hunting for my car keys when there was a brisk knock on the front door.

'I was just coming to see you!' I blurted, when I found my ex-husband standing on the front path.

'Well, I found you first.'

'Do you want to come in?'

He shook his head. 'If we stand out here, there's less chance I'll wring your neck.'

I took a pace back, then processed his words and decided outside might be safer. I put my phone in my back pocket and stepped out. 'What's the matter?'

I wasn't being coy, I was struggling to think. It was going to be another beautiful day, but at this time the air was crisp. My brain was grateful for it.

'It was you, wasn't it? Who told them?'

'Told who?' All right, so now I *was* playing for a bit of time.

'Oh, yeah, you're all innocent. You make me sick.'

'Whoa. Hold on.' I raised my voice. Then, for good measure, I planted my feet and lifted my chin. 'What's happened?'

He shook his head. 'As if you don't know. *Someone* spilled the beans to Brissinghorn & Beem. About the painting. The sale's off. Beem chucked it back in my face.'

'Well, good for Mr Beem.' No need to reveal I already knew. 'But—' I raised a hand to stop him interrupting, 'I didn't snitch.' And I wasn't about to drop Robyn in hot water.

But something about that second name, *Brissinghorn*, was niggling me. I was sure I'd heard it in another context, over a month ago. Something Amelia had said?

Colin's face was almost puce. 'You expect me to believe that? You were in a right lather about me selling it, and making money for Keiko's bills.'

'I thought it was wrong, yes! But it wasn't me who told.'

Never mind that I'd been on the brink of reporting it myself. He didn't need to know that.

'Christ, Maggie, if it wasn't you, who was it?'

'People talk, you moron. Probably some bloke you boasted to in a pub.' Colin himself knew he could be indiscreet when he'd had a few. 'Or maybe Mr Beem decided to check up on his partner's judgement.'

Colin gave a little start, and at the same moment, the penny dropped. Amelia's friend, I thought: Bunty Brissinghorn. *She* was the connection.

I took a big breath. 'Maybe Beem wanted to look into the art being sold by the bloke who was *coincidentally* doing loads of work on Brissinghorn's house?'

Colin's shoulders slumped.

'Was that it?' I pressed. 'Did you give them a juicy price on a new kitchen, in return for helping you offload a fake painting? Bargain bathroom, too?'

Not only had I nailed it, but I'd never stood up to him like this before. I could tell from the way his eyes were shifting: he was surprised, and rattled.

'What did you do about the provenance?' I had the upper hand in this conversation, but I was also genuinely curious. 'Did Brissinghorn take the painting, with nothing to back it up?'

'None of your bleeding business.'

'Oh, come on Colin, the game's up.' I sounded like Miss Marple, but I was on a roll. 'You're not trying to tell me you found a receipt or something for it.'

'I'm not saying another word.'

I sighed. 'Look, contrary to what you think, I'm not out to get you. I have my own life now and I'm perfectly happy.'

In that moment, I realised it was true. He wasn't a concern to me any more.

He spat in one of my new lavender bushes, but I could tell the fight had gone out of him.

'I'm sorry your little painting con's been halted, but only because I know you need the money for Keiko's treatments.'

At the mention of Keiko's name, the last of the bluster left him. He must truly love her, in a way we'd never loved each other at all. I understood that depth of emotion, now. I'd never experienced it with Colin. But with Finn, I had.

My ex scuffed his toe and looked down at the path, shrinking by a couple of inches.

'We can't sell the house,' he said finally. 'I mean, we've had no offers. No interest at all.'

'Oh.' I put my hands in my pockets. There was an awkward silence before I said, 'Maybe you need a new estate agent.'

He didn't acknowledge me. 'The bills are piling up, and if I go to America with her, I won't be able to bid for new work. But I can't let her go on her own, can I?'

'Not really, no.' He looked so dejected, I softened my tone.

'The painting... it was... well, I needed the cash so badly.'

I waited.

'And you're right,' Colin said. 'Brissinghorn wouldn't take it without provenance. Bloody stuck-up git.'

In my online research, I'd read about this. Some forgers thought the art world was too hoity-toity, and deserved taking down a peg or two. They thought trading bogus art was a victimless crime.

'So you found some?' I prompted. 'Provenance?'

Colin turned, examining my little jam house. He pulled out a couple of jars and read the labels, before putting them back.

'Keiko... she clears old junk out of people's houses.'

I nodded. I knew this. She was a so-called professional organiser, and more in demand than ever.

'She came home one day with a boot-load of stuff, on its way to the tip. There was a fifties typewriter, and some paper which looked like the same era.'

The real painting, the one by Monkton, dated from 1956. My eyes widened. 'You made up some kind of receipt?'

Colin turned a pot of raspberry jelly in his hands. 'I just banged out something from a gallery in York, to say it was sold to a buyer in Harrogate in 1958.'

'And Brissinghorn accepted that as provenance?'

Colin looked sheepish. 'He wasn't checking too closely.'

There was a long silence. I reminded myself to breathe: in, then out, then in again. Then I did some mental calculations, chewing on my lip as I considered my bank account. Finally, I checked the sky for signs of rain. If this fine weather held, I could postpone my new roof a bit longer.

'I'll give you some cash,' I said.

'What?' His head came up.

I forced myself to carry on. 'I offered you two hundred pounds for the treehouse, remember?' Technically, the conversation had been with Keiko, but I assumed she'd told him.

His eyes narrowed.

'Well, now I'll give you six hundred,' I said. 'Today. Shake my hand, right now, and I'll get you six hundred in cash by the end of the day.'

I saw him swallow. He'd be a terrible poker player. 'You're not still banging on about that—'

'I am,' I interrupted. 'And I'm deadly serious. Six hundred pounds, in your pocket, today.'

You could have heard a pin drop. Then he muttered, 'Seven.'

'Six-twenty.' I'd be living on baked beans for a month, but it was worth it.

'You have to take it down, and transport it. I want nothing to do with it.'

'Fine.' My heart was in my mouth and my blood might have stopped pumping too. I held out my hand to my ex-husband, and as I did so, I realised this was the last thing that tied me to him. 'Deal?'

He shook it. 'Deal.'

~~~

After Colin left, I stood frozen to the front path for several minutes, trying to believe what had happened. Having yearned for the treehouse for so long, I couldn't quite trust that it would now be mine.

The sun was peeping over the trees, and the village was waking up. The milkman had been and gone, but the postwoman would show up soon. The day was upon me.

I took some final deep breaths of the refreshing morning air, noticing a pleasing hint of lavender. My little jam house was almost empty, and the jars Colin had inspected were the last. But there was fourteen pounds in the small honesty box. Good: every little helped.

Then I turned to go inside. It was time to get to work.

Hoping it wasn't too early for phone calls, I set about contacting everyone I knew who might help with the headache of moving the treehouse. Having battled for it, there was no way I wanted logistics to get in my way.

As soon as the bank in Newmarket opened, I popped over there to get the cash I'd promised Colin. I didn't dare take more than five hundred and fifty pounds out of my account, since my gas bill and council tax were due any day. But I had another fifty in an emergency tin in the airing cupboard at home, there was today's jam money, and... yes, I could find the rest from my purse, in twenty pence pieces if necessary.

Colin had said he'd be home by five, and that I could bring the money over then. In the meantime, I hid the cash in the fridge, closing the door with a restless sigh.

I still had most of the day to kill.

~ ~ ~

'Jeez, you look like a refugee from a baking show,' Nancy said when she caught me outside the bakery about three o'clock. 'Your shoes don't match and... is that crushed fruit in your hair?' She peered more closely. 'I bet you didn't sleep, either.'

'I don't care,' I replied. 'I've been making jam all day.'

'Oh, boy.' She sighed. 'What's wrong now?'

'Nothing! Everything's perfect!'

Quickly, I filled her in, although I suspect she didn't appreciate the momentous excitement which accompanied treehouse ownership. Well, some people got all revved up about babies, and kittens, after all. This wasn't so different, was it?

'So why have you got your nose pressed up against Brian's window, like Oliver Twist?'

I grinned. 'Ah, well... I only have seventy pence left.'

Having put aside the cash for Colin, then buying sugar for my jam-making binge, I was down to coins.

'You're messing with me.'

'No. And I'll tell you a secret. Every day, about this time...' I lowered my voice. 'Brian reduces the price of his sandwiches.'

Nancy's eyes widened. 'Seriously? You're telling me you haven't eaten all day? Except for jam tastings, I mean?'

I shrugged. 'I'm fine.'

'No wonder you're tired but wired. Come on.'

She marched me into the shop and purchased two packs of sandwiches, three scones, a macaroon, and a custard tart. 'There you go, you crazy woman.'

'Thanks.' Now the food was in front of me, I found I was ravenous.

'Hold up, whirling dervish!' She grabbed the bag back. 'One of those cakes is for me.'

We parked ourselves at one of Brian's outside tables, and she let me scoff in silence for a few minutes. While I ate, she pulled a work document from her bag and started reviewing it.

As I finally slowed to enjoy the creamy, nutmeg-scented tart, she looked up. 'Better?'

'Fantastic. You're a brick, Nance.'

'Seventy pence...' she muttered, tapping her pen on the edge of the document. 'Good grief.'

I sat back, stomach full, expecting to feel calm and replete. But something was off.

'What's up?' Nancy asked. 'You've wrinkled your brow and you keep darting your eyes around.'

I didn't answer for a few moments. She was right, I had been looking around the village street, trying to identify the niggle which remained. Then my eye fell on her pen, poised above her paper.

'That's it,' I said. 'That's where I've been going wrong.'

'Where?'

'All this time. I've been working off the wrong thing.'

The list of ten things was all about the opposite of what would please Colin, and nothing to do with the things that would please *me*.

'I get it now.' I jumped up, my chair wobbling. 'Thanks so much for the sarnies. And the cakes. I owe you.'

'No problem, but Mag, where are you going?'

'Home,' I said. 'Now. Immediately.'

'More jam?'

'No. Not jam.' I leaned down to give her a quick hug. 'Ink. Lots of ink.' The light had finally dawned. 'I need to make a list.'

## Chapter 35

'What's the one thing harder than *building* a treehouse?' Leo groaned, as five of us sagged in a dishevelled row on the grass outside Colin's house in Burwell.

'Moving a treehouse.' Bella was the only person still standing, and the only one of the group who didn't have bits of leaf in her hair. The rest of us sported bark stains down our jeans, grazed arms and pulled muscles.

'I'm sticking to spreadsheets from now on.' Nancy stretched her shoulders and turned to Peter. 'Next time I claim that women are as strong as men, remind me, would you?'

Once I'd told her about my plan to remove my property from Colin's tree, she'd insisted on being involved. But despite her feisty assertions, she wasn't used to manual work.

Nor was Peter, who was going to have a cracking bruise on his temple tomorrow from a low-hanging branch. He shook his head carefully. 'I wouldn't dare, love.'

'You owe me a lifetime of jam, Maggie.' Vincent wiped his streaming brow before downing an entire can of the lemonade Bella had the foresight to bring. She'd declared herself catering and morale officer for our mission, and it's a good thing someone had stocked up with drinks, flapjacks, and wet wipes. After two hours of treehouse wrangling, the rest of us were a filthy, thirsty mess.

'You're all amazing,' I said. 'I know I'll never be able to repay you.'

I'd freaked out after we'd spent the first hour trying to detach the treehouse from its moorings and move it intact. It turned out it simply wasn't possible – let alone safe – to untangle a structure of that size from the branches it lived in, and lower it to the ground.

And yes, I admit my eyes had welled up when Leo had taken me to the side and explained the inevitable. We'd have to make strategic cuts to the walls.

'No!' I'd wailed, already exhausted. 'We're not chopping it up!'

This was my childhood, my most precious memory. Not to mention my last six hundred and twenty pounds.

'It's not coming out of there in one piece, Maggie.'

Bella had put her arm around me. 'Trust Leo. He knows what he's doing, I promise.'

And of course, he did. We'd had to sacrifice a few of the base pieces, but Leo had pointed out they were starting to rot in any case. And then, genius that he was, he'd found a way to cut the treehouse cleanly into two halves, which could then be man-handled to the ground.

'They do it with whole houses in some places,' he'd told me. 'I stayed at a dairy farm once in New Zealand. They'd chopped their house clean in two and moved the whole thing from one side of the country to the other on the back of a lorry.'

Finally, I'd agreed. Now, we were rumpled but triumphant in our quest to free the treehouse. But it was currently in the road outside Colin's house, in two halves.

'What time's your friend coming?' I turned to Vincent, who had his nose in his phone. 'We said eleven, right?'

Vincent rubbed a hand over his eyes, leaving a smear of bark on his forehead. 'Sorry, sweetheart.' He gestured with his phone. 'My mate texted that he can't come. He's not well.'

'What?' Holy smoke.

'But he says we can still use his van, and the trailer.'

'Okay.' I exhaled. 'Fine.'

'Assuming anyone's qualified to drive it,' Vincent added.

'You have *got* to be kidding me.'

A quick survey of the assembled group revealed that none of us had the knowledge, let alone a qualification, which would let us drive a twenty-seven-ton trailer from Burwell to Saffron Sweeting.

This time, I wept for real. I was hot, filthy, and bone-weary. I'd battled for weeks with my ex-husband to spend the last of my cash on an ancient treehouse, which had then proved harder to move than Jabba the Hutt. Not only that, but we'd had to slice my precious relic in two, and it was stranded in pieces, on a public highway.

'Come on, Maggie.' Bella squeezed my shoulder. 'You've come this far, don't give up now.'

For a minute, I couldn't answer, sniffling and gulping and making inappropriate deals with the devil. Then I remembered the list I'd made, the new one. So I wiped my nose on my T-shirt – it was already ruined, after all – and addressed the little group.

'Okay, folks. Don't abandon me now. Phones out. Call everyone you know. Wake them up, call in favours, do whatever you have to do.' I paused for breath. 'Ask them if they, or their neighbour, or their kid's ballet teacher – anyone at all – knows how to handle an HGV. I'll be a free handywoman for a year, to any of you who finds me a driver. Let's get this treehouse home.'

~~~

There's a saying that we're all connected to everyone else on earth by a few degrees of separation – something like six, I think.

So it shouldn't have been a huge surprise that when our group jumped on the mobile network with one specific question, a driver was found before the morning was out. Having overseen the loading of the treehouse in Burwell, I got a lift with Nancy so I could be in the village for its arrival.

The wait seemed interminable and despite assurances from both the driver and Leo, I wouldn't believe it until I saw it with my own eyes.

The long low trailer rolled past the Saffron Sweeting duck pond, hooting its deep, baritone horn to greet the small crowd which had gathered. Word travels fast in Sweeting, and we'd announced the event to most of the village, when we'd phoned in search of a driver. The big white van and orange trailer, complete with the halves of the treehouse trussed on top, came to a juddering halt outside the pub.

The driver leaned down from the cab, auburn hair catching in the breeze. 'I must say, darling,' she hollered, 'it's a lot less hassle to treat yourself to new shoes when you're depressed. Try it, next time?'

'Amelia,' I said, not bothering to dash away the tears which formed in my eyes, 'where the hell did you learn to drive that thing?'

Our village estate agent, tastemaker, and femme fatale grinned back at me. 'A stag weekend. On Salisbury Plain, had an absolute blast. Mostly, I drove the tanks, but the other chaps enjoyed the lorries. Anyway, darling, they're all much of a muchness, aren't they?'

I shook my head. I was pretty sure it wasn't a muchness at all, but the treehouse was here. Amelia had once again revealed layers of herself the rest of us could never guess at.

'Oh, and look who else I scooped up on the Cambridge road. He was thumbing a lift.'

Amelia nodded at the passenger seat and for the first time, I noticed a person sitting next to her. But the sun glinted off the windscreen, and I couldn't tell who it was. A moment later, the door opened, and long legs emerged from the high opening. As they slithered to the ground, I saw that they were attached to Finn.

'Hello, Maggie Moone.'

He wore a baseball cap pulled low over his eyes, and more stubble than I remembered.

Truth be told, he looked a bit rough around the edges.

I put one hand on the van, to steady myself. 'Hi.'

We were several feet apart, but I saw him bite his lip. 'I was planning to tell you, you look beautiful,' he said slowly. 'But, actually, you don't.'

I looked down, and recoiled in horror. If Finn looked rough, *I* was an unmitigated dog's dinner. My clothes were drenched in sweat, my hair was a hedgehog's nest, my face was smeared with goodness knows what, and I'd wiped my nose on my shirt.

'How... are you here?' I managed, still clinging to the van. Today, of all days, I wasn't sure I believed my eyes.

'My car broke down. But as Amelia said, she scooped me up.'

'I mean... I thought you'd gone back to Ireland?'

'Ah, yes, you're not wrong there.' From his back pocket, he pulled a crumpled envelope. 'But then this arrived.'

Finn took a step towards me, and I held my breath. Was that one of the letters I'd begged others to post?

'And then this one came.' From another pocket, another envelope.

Hope bubbled inside me. I recognised the stationery.

'And this one made three.'

He was standing right in front of me, but I found I was no more able to touch him at this distance, than if he'd been in Limerick. I looked up at him, willing myself to say something sensible.

Or, failing that, anything at all. 'Oh. So...'

'So it seems, I couldn't stay away.'

He reached out his hand and brushed my arm. At his touch, my tongue loosened.

'I'm so sorry,' I said. 'I made such a mess of things. I didn't see how lucky I'd been to meet you, until you weren't here any more.' I gulped in a breath. 'I know that list was ridiculous, and insulting. I can't tell you how sorry I am. I'm not wasting my time on that any more.'

'So I see.' Finn jerked his head to the treehouse on the trailer, and I saw that the crowd of villagers had dispersed slightly. Some were still loitering on the pavement on the other side of the road, Grace and Amelia amongst them. Then my attention was pulled back to the gangly Irishman in front of me when he said, 'My ego got in the way. I should have given you more time, not tried to rush you.'

'You didn't try to rush me.' I laughed. Nobody could have been more laid back than Finn. 'You should probably have rushed me some more.'

'Is that so, Maggie Moone?' He closed the gap of mere inches between us and put his arms around me.

'I'm a mess,' I squawked, even as my heart rate galloped.

'No you're not.' He bent his head and brushed my lips with his. 'You're beautiful.'

My whole body softened into his and I neither heard nor saw anything for long moments.

Eventually, he drew back, keeping his eyes glued on my face. That was when I remembered our onlookers.

'Isn't that nice?' called Violet, who would never win prizes for discretion.

'Good job you gave that scruffy hitchhiker a lift, Amelia,' came another voice I didn't recognise.

At this, Amelia herself stepped forward. 'Look, darling, I can see you're terribly busy.' She paused theatrically for the other villagers to laugh on cue. Then she pointed at her cargo. 'But I don't think this thing will actually fit up your lane. So where would you like it?'

After making hasty, provisional arrangements for the treehouse, I turned back to Finn. 'What now?'

He gave a gentle smile. 'I could walk you home, Maggie Moone?'

So we strolled home together, his arm around me, saying nothing. For that short walk, it was enough to have the warmth of his body against mine, to know our strides matched in length, and to sense him breathing in and out with every step we took. But there was an invisible barrier of caution between us. We still had talking to do.

My cottage, always compact, shrank the moment Finn stepped across the threshold. I was acutely aware this was the last place we'd seen each other, and the ghost of harsh words hung in the air. Was he back for good?

'It looks nice.' He glanced around. 'More settled, somehow.'

My new clock ticked proudly on the mantelpiece and above it, I'd hung *Chasing the Train*. Colin had included it with my treehouse purchase, saying he never wanted to set eyes on it again.

But I didn't want to discuss my decor.

'Finn, I treated you horribly.'

Dammit, why couldn't I find more powerful words? Words to tell him that a list scribbled drunkenly on yellow paper didn't negate what happened next. A way of explaining that the initial seed may have been careless, worthless even, but that the roots and branches and leaves that grew from it were no less beautiful.

'I was... jealous,' he said, standing just inside the front door, as if he wasn't sure he was staying. 'I mean, I didn't trust that your heart was free.'

'I messed it up,' I replied. 'It wasn't until I lost you that I knew I truly *was* over Colin.' I took a breath, hoping the risk of saying this would be worth it. 'I know what love feels like, now.'

Finn stared at me, his amber eyes dark.

'I'm sorry.' I lowered my own gaze.

Next moment, my magenta front door closed with a thud.

Finn pulled me into his arms, far more tightly than our meeting in the high street. 'Shh. It doesn't matter. I'm back.'

I nestled into his neck, feeling the firm pressure of his hands on my back, knowing that if he chose to never let go, I'd be okay with that.

Finally, I found the courage to whisper, 'Back for good?'

'If you'll have me.' He kissed my temple.

We stayed there, in the middle of my living room, for long minutes. The church clock chimed two, and still we didn't move.

'So, you *were* in Ireland?' I asked eventually.

He nodded. 'My sister had emergency surgery. I was helping out with her kids.'

I asked the necessary polite question. 'How's she doing?'

'Long way to go, but they say she'll be fine. Thanks.'

I dropped my eyes again. 'I would have liked to have known... that you were okay.'

This was as close as I could come to saying: *not hearing from you tore my heart out.*

Finn sighed. 'To be honest, it helped me have a good long think.'

'I can't believe all three letters reached you.'

'What, you only sent three? I was hoping there were more.'

I laughed, and claimed another kiss. 'That was so nice of your grandma and friends, to send them along. I didn't think they would.'

'Maybe romance isn't dead after all.'

~~~

Despite Finn's claims that I was both beautiful and kissable, I was mortified by my chaotic and grubby state. 'Promise you'll wait, while I take a shower.'

He rolled his eyes. 'If you insist.'

When I came down, I brought a pad of paper with me. 'Look, I know this is probably a sore point.'

Finn sat forward on the sofa, and looked at me warily.

'But there's something I want you to see,' I continued.

'What is it?'

I went over to him and sat down, tucking one leg under me so I could angle my body towards his. 'I'm hoping it'll help show I've got my priorities straight now. Well, more straight, anyway.'

'Okay.' He took the paper from me. 'And this is...?'

I inhaled, reminding myself I loved Finn and trusted him. Showing him was no big deal. Having looked into his eyes today, I was sure he'd understand. 'It's my list.'

~~~

Ten Things Maggie Loves:

1) *Brightly coloured front doors*
2) *Lavender*
3) *Treehouses*
4) *Making jam*
5) *The Shipping Forecast*
6) *Chocolate truffles*
7) *Clocks which tick*
8) *Swimming*
9) *Television baking shows*
10) *Finn*

*Chapter 37*

One thing I'd learned this year: the residents of Saffron Sweeting will embrace every opportunity for standing around in the street to gawp. The day of the explosion, this drove a spike into my gut. But today, as the small crowd spilled out of the modest garden by the library and into the street, their gossipy gathering filled me with pride. Someone had organised an old-fashioned cart to sell candy floss, and a stilt walker moved amongst the crowd, juggling and entertaining the little ones.

'And finally.' Kenneth puffed out his chest as he finished a mercifully short speech. He was looking dapper in a paisley waistcoat, which coordinated with his socks. 'On behalf of the Board of Directors of the Saffron Sweeting Library, I call upon the generous donor of our new treehouse, and the woman who got her own hands not only dirty but bloodied in bringing it here for us. Maggie, will you please do the great honour of cutting the ribbon!'

I stepped forward to the trunk of the huge tree where I'd written my letters to Finn. It looked pretty different now.

A foot or two above my head, the treehouse nestled in its broad, low branches. Its new door featured a cut-out star shape, and there were working shutters at the windows. Its roof was crowned with a decorative crescent moon, and the newly built ladder was sturdy enough to withstand frequent foot traffic from young readers. We'd even added a basket on a winch, to help get books up there safely.

Leo had spent hours with me last week, making sure the treehouse could withstand a small hurricane. And the Parish Council had dipped into their special fund to install springy safety matting around the base of the tree.

I didn't know who'd had a gentle word with the people at the planning department. It could have been Amelia's friend, Scott, who worked in property development and had a boundless old boys' network. Or it might have been the genial architect from the new firm with offices above the beauty salon; in fine weather he spent every lunchtime reading outside. But planning permission had come through remarkably fast.

We'd tried to festoon the treehouse with bunting, but settled for looping it around the tree trunk itself. Made from the pages of old books, it glowed gently in the soft September sunshine. I paused to admire the treehouse again in its new home, then raised the large drapery scissors we'd found in Peter's antique store. With a satisfying snip, they sliced the ribbons.

A cheer went up from the assembled villagers. I turned to Kenneth, who, to my surprise, hugged me. The excitement of being Master of Ceremonies must have loosened his usual starched demeanor.

'Well done!' called Violet, coming over to shake my hand. Then she returned to her station at a trestle table displaying children's library books themed around treetop adventure. I'd been amazed to see titles including *The Treehouse Fun Book*, *The 39-Story Treehouse*, and my own personal favourite, *The Magic Faraway Tree*.

The chairman of the council thanked me for my endeavours. 'Oh, no, it was a village effort,' I replied, thinking of all the friends who'd helped me untangle the treehouse from Colin's. Not to mention those who'd supported me in untangling my own affairs.

Colin, of course, wasn't here. He and Keiko had only recently returned from her month-long treatment at Cornell's medical college. Before they left, they'd sacked their previous estate agent and hired Amelia. She pulled out the stops and got them a reasonable offer on the house even before their plane lifted off from Heathrow. Now that the treehouse was no longer part of their property, I was delighted for them. It was a much better way to finance Keiko's bills than dodgy art.

Amelia, who'd been taking photos, lowered her phone. 'Why don't you scoot up there and show us how it's done, Maggie?'

I shook my head. I'd worn a skirt for this special occasion. It was a long one, but still... a better excuse was apparent. 'Too late, the kids have beaten me to it.'

Around a dozen children were thronging at the base of the ladder, where Grace and Bella restrained them from a mass ascent.

'Two at a time!' Grace said, in her firmest voice. 'No, Randy, *wait!*'

Bella was gripping little Amy's T-shirt to stop her making a break for it. 'Just a minute. When they come down, you're next.' She looked at me and rolled her eyes.

I grinned back. 'This was your idea, don't forget.'

It was Bella who'd suggested that since the treehouse clearly wouldn't fit anywhere at my cottage, and the pub garden already had swings for the kids, that a special bolt-hole for young readers might be welcome. Kenneth, to my surprise, had embraced the proposal.

'Oh, yes, what a superb idea,' he'd said. 'It's often clear to me, some children like to find the most secluded place possible to read.'

The riot of ground-level children was distracted then by the arrival of Peter's business partner, who had offered his services making balloon animals. And Brian, from behind a table loaded with lemonade and shortbread, began calling out his wares to the adults.

'Nicely done, Maggie Moone.' Finn's gentle voice came from beside me. He'd stayed in the background during my few minutes of fame.

'It looks great, doesn't it?' I felt a lump in my throat, not for the first time that day. 'I'm so glad the treehouse has a proper home.'

'I can tell,' he said. 'You look happier than I've ever seen you.'

I smiled gratefully, then turned to him. 'It's not only the treehouse.'

'Is that so, Maggie Moone?'

Nodding, I reached up for a quick kiss. Last week, Finn had moved his things into my cottage, the final impetus for me to donate belongings from my old life. Since then, we'd made both jam and soup together, and he was well on his way to convincing me we might be a permanent team.

With reluctance, I brought myself back to the present, acknowledging a few more well-wishers. Ted and Betsy were amongst them, both intrigued by the impromptu party forming around them.

'How's your new business?' Ted wanted to know.

'Pretty good, I think. I have one definite customer – in Great Yarmouth – and two more who are interested.'

My custom treehouse service would take time to grow, but I was prepared to be patient.

'Good job!' Betsy hugged me. 'Come for dinner soon.' She looked at Finn, whose arm was firmly around my waist. 'Both of you.'

I thanked her and watched as they headed for the refreshment table. Then our attention was pulled upwards, as the tree and treehouse now contained far more than a pair of children. Amy was perched on a branch, Tim was attempting to scale to greater heights, and at least three other faces peeked from the door and window of the treehouse itself.

'You wouldn't believe those two have a treehouse of their own,' I murmured to Finn.

'And you seriously think anyone's after taking a book up there?'

I considered this. 'When it calms down a bit, they will. I know from experience, sneaking off up there to read will be a treat for some of them.'

'I wouldn't mind sneaking off up there for something else.' Finn dropped his head to kiss my temple, squeezing my arm as he did so.

I tutted and shook my head, but my heart brimmed with joy.

~~~

At dusk that evening, when the party was long over, Finn and I took a final stroll around the village.

'You'll never sleep otherwise,' he said. 'With or without the Shipping Forecast.'

We passed the shadowy malt house, and paused to listen to an owl. The windows of the bakery were shuttered, Amelia's estate agency was in darkness, and it seemed the whole village was at rest. Outside the library, my footsteps slowed. Finn sensed my change in pace, and stopped too.

'Can you give me a moment?' I glanced at him, then nodded upwards. 'On my own, I mean?'

He squeezed my hand, then let go. 'As long as you need, Maggie Moone.'

In the last of the September twilight, I shimmied up the ladder to the treehouse. I'd swapped my skirt for jeans, but even if I hadn't, by now I was used to nipping up and down.

The moment I stepped inside the treehouse, it was as if the outside world melted away. Below, I'd barely been aware of a breeze, but up here, there was enough to sway the structure. I took a long inhale, noticing the smell of old wood, plus some newer timber that we'd used to reinforce it. Kenneth and I had talked about miniature reading chairs, but at present, the space was empty, save for the plaque I'd commissioned.

*In loving memory of Matthew Moone.*

He would never have the opportunity to scramble up the ladder behind me, to retreat from a world which even then was starting to make him feel different and unwelcome. He'd never curl up beside me again in this treehouse, finding escape in his adventure novels while I wrinkled my nose at an unfamiliar word in my own book. My brother was gone. But at least now, a new generation of children might enjoy their own corner of solitude, reading, and perfect peace. Maybe, just maybe, my own kids would play here one day too.

I waited another minute, listening to the creak of the tree as it held me gently in its arms. Then I turned, ducked through the doorway and lowered myself down the ladder with as much grace as I could.

I could barely make out Finn's features in the darkness, but I could see his strong silhouette, waiting patiently, ready and willing to put down fresh roots with me.

'Okay?' he asked, as I paused at the bottom of the ladder.

I nodded, trusting he could see me in the shadows. 'Yes. All okay now. Let's go home.'

I gave the tree trunk one last pat, then turned to take his hand.

The End

# From the Author

Independent authors like me rely on reviews from readers to help spread the word about our work. Please consider adding your review of *Ten Things My Husband Hated* to Amazon, Goodreads and other online forums.

At the end of this book, you'll find the first chapter of *Saving Saffron Sweeting*. Set in the same village, this is the first in the Saffron Sweeting collection. You can learn more and purchase it at: https://mybook.to/sweeting

I love to connect with readers through my website and social media. Visit www.paulinewiles.com for news, bonus materials and special promotions. You can also sign up for my newsletter to be notified of new releases and receive two free bonus guides: *50 British Foods to Try Before You Die* and *60 Things to Know Before Your First Trip to England*.

# Saving Saffron Sweeting

# Chapter 1

I was balanced on an eight-foot ladder with a mouth full of curtain hooks when I realised that my husband was cheating.

The individual pieces of the picture suddenly came together, making terrifying sense. I blinked hard, then stared at my knuckles, which were now white from gripping the ladder. But the image wouldn't subside. The picture I saw was James with another woman.

I was hanging curtains in my client Rebecca's bedroom, and the project was almost complete. This was great, as she'd been excited to give the room a whole new look after she'd recently come to the end of a long relationship.

'I'm ready to move on. Grace, I want a totally fresh look,' she'd told me when we met to discuss how I could help her. 'Something luxurious, maybe a little sensual. I don't plan on being single forever.'

I was still new in the design business and it was a huge deal for me not only to land a new client, but also one who had money to spend and some kind of clue what she wanted. My first few months had been a real struggle and I was starting to question my talents. Other business owners had stressed the importance of tapping my personal network to get things rolling, so James had spread the word around his office. Apparently, he had done a good job of promoting my abilities to Rebecca, his company's marketing manager. She had been great to work for and seemed appreciative of my suggestions. The only slight issue was that in the last few weeks she had been anxious to speed things up and get the bedroom completed.

Eager to please, I had been beavering away and attempting to charm my suppliers into hurrying. After getting the curtains up, I planned to hit the shops for accessories, and then the room would be ready for whatever action she had in mind.

My work had been interrupted by a knock on the front door of Rebecca's condo. I'd opened it to find a bubbly young woman, who presented me with a pair of pink stilettos.

'Oh!' she said. 'I was hoping Becca would be home. Can you let her know Kerry returned these?'

'I think she's at work,' I said, taking the shoes. 'I'm her bedroom designer.'

'Ooh, you mean the love nest? Can I see it?'

'Er, it's not finished yet,' I replied. 'I expect she'd rather show you herself.'

Kerry shrugged. 'Okay. I'll catch up with her.' She turned and was a few steps down the hall before she added, 'And tell her I want to hear all about Vegas and this James guy. He sounds delish!'

My mind was still on the curtains. I'd shut the door and put the cute shoes down, before returning to the bedroom.

Climbing back up the ladder, I thought, No wonder Rebecca wants to hurry this room. She's met some man in Las Vegas and needs her bedroom back. I was stretching to try to hook the edge of the curtain to the last ring on the pole when the dark feeling began to slither over me.

Did the ladder wobble? Had one of San Francisco's famous earthquakes nudged it? Or was the lurch, the sway, the feeling of my stomach dropping to the new wool rug, due to something else? I checked the new tear-drop chandelier hanging above the bed. As a British transplant to the Bay Area, I had spent the first couple of years diving under our dining table at the slightest tremor. But by now I had learned that if the light fixtures weren't swaying, the seismic jolt was all in my head. The glass drops of Rebecca's chandelier stared back at me steadily, not even winking, let alone dancing.

I had the presence of mind not to swallow my curtain hooks as I took a huge gulp and slid down the ladder. I slumped onto the new and naked mattress as I thought about my husband's recent conference trip to Las Vegas and how edgy he had been since. I remembered our paths crossing briefly in the kitchen, the morning after his return.

'How was it?' I'd asked, digging through the drawer for my favourite cereal spoon.

'Okay, I guess.' He reached for the tea bags.

James seemed dispirited and I thought perhaps the industry analysts had given his company, a mobile security start-up, a tough time.

'Are you home this evening?' he wanted to know.

'Probably,' I called over my shoulder. I was already heading to my computer to check whether anyone had emailed for decor advice. Even at that hour, my mind was firmly on my fragile business.

But that day I'd been called by a potential customer to discuss her family room and, as was typical, she could only meet me in the evening. I was hard at work researching inspiration pictures when James came home, and within minutes I headed out to my appointment. After more than an hour of fruitless discussion on the merits of contemporary versus rustic style, I drove the forty minutes home across the Dumbarton Bridge to find my husband was already asleep.

With an uncomfortable feeling, I also recalled the previous evening, when he'd come home from work early and asked to talk to me, but I'd been flying out of the door to my women's networking group. This had been the pattern of life recently: we seemed to pass each other fleetingly, our schedules never lining up for longer than it took to brew a pot of tea.

And now I had learned that Rebecca had hooked up with someone called James in Las Vegas. My James had been acting oddly since he had returned from there. Keep calm, I told myself, it's probably fine.

But it wasn't fine. The third and ugly part of the truth was literally staring me in the face. Rebecca's favourite colour was purple and despite some reservations on my part, she had been adamant about using a strong shade of aubergine. We'd finally agreed on a sophisticated tan for three walls, painting the dramatic colour as an accent behind her bed. And although James usually showed precious little interest in any of my decorating ideas, we had been talking about Rebecca's project just before his trip, when we'd been in the kitchen long enough to empty the dishwasher together.

'How is your client list coming along?' he'd asked, shaking leftover water from a wine glass.

'Slowly,' I'd replied. 'Rebecca's bedroom is nearly finished but I don't have anyone lined up after her.'

He didn't say anything but had stretched over my head to put some plates away.

Happy to talk about my work, I'd let my brain run on. 'I hope it all comes together okay. That accent colour was such a bold choice.'

He'd pulled a slight face. 'Yeah, purple always reminds me of something my grandad would have had.'

I had dropped the topic, as I'd learned during our years together that James based most of his interior design dislikes on the vivid avocado and orange combinations in his grandfather's house. He thought any room featuring retro patterns or an accent wall was hideous.

Now, I leaped off the mattress as though it had bitten me on the behind. I was convinced I hadn't mentioned purple, aubergine or any other arty description for the colour behind the bed.

*He knows what colour this room is. He's been here.*

I was out of the house and into the car before I knew it. Days later, it occurred to me I should have stuffed Rebecca's hollow curtain poles with frozen shrimp. Of course, the clever moves always elude me at the time.

~~~

By the time I arrived at the Palo Alto office where James and his team were trying to create the next Silicon Valley success story, all dignity had abandoned me. I think my tears were already beginning as I lurched through the front desk area, empty because the company was too small to have a receptionist. In my haste, I then collided with the *foosball* table, which appears to be a required toy at every start-up with venture capital funding.

I spotted my husband – cropped, dark brown hair, shirt half untucked as usual – hunched over his keyboard, at the end of an untidy row of T-shirt clad computer coders. This gaggle looked barely old enough to have gained admission to Stanford University, let alone already graduated.

James looked up and noticed me. Surprise crossed his face, but was replaced with something I assumed was guilt. I could see how deep the lines in the middle of his forehead were getting these days, and how weary he looked.

'Purple,' was all I managed to utter at first. Terrific. Millions of wives over the centuries have faced this situation and all I could say was *purple*.

'Grace –' He stood and took my arm, trying to get me to sit.

I wrenched myself free. 'How did you know her bedroom is purple? How did you know?'

'Listen.' He shook his head. 'It's not what you think'.

Okay, so *purple* may not have been eloquent, but at least it was original. I saw red – as well as crimson, magenta and every shade in between.

'How could you?' I hissed. 'I know what's going on. And all the time, I've been decorating that sodding room!'

'Please,' he glanced sideways at the line of coders. 'Calm down!'

Fingers had frozen over keyboards. Curious youthful faces were turned towards us: James was a popular boss.

'You knew her bedroom is purple because you've been sleeping with her, haven't you? You've been sleeping with my client!'

'No, look, it wasn't like that.'

'No, you look. Look at this purple and tell me you've never seen it before.' I pulled the paint sample from my purse and unscrewed the lid. Dark and liquidly sinister, I waved it dangerously close to his computer.

'Okay, okay, I'm sorry. Please – calm down and let me tell you.' By now his dark brown eyes were wide with panic.

The whole office had fallen silent, but I saw that not everyone was watching us. Instead, some of them had turned to the far side of the room, as Rebecca stood and began heading our way. I realised most of them knew she had a part in this drama. And what about Rebecca? Was she half expecting this to happen? There I was, a total mess inside and out, and she appeared to be perfectly composed.

She came closer and I caught the eye contact between her and James. He had now turned paler than I'd ever seen, including the time he got food poisoning in Turkey and couldn't stand for three days. As she walked behind the desks of her co-workers, most of them didn't seem to know whether to freeze or flee.

'Look,' she said, 'let's not do this here.' Not a blonde hair was out of place.

'Where would you rather *do it*?' I snapped back, but my voice was quivering. 'Your bedroom? With my husband?'

James reached for me again, but seemed to change his mind and let his hand drop. 'I know you're furious right now, but it was just one stupid mistake in Vegas,' he said quietly.

'I don't believe you! You've been in her bedroom!' I was looking wildly from one to the other, sick with the thought of them wrapped around each other.

'Well, actually,' Rebecca had the nerve to put her hand on his arm, 'it's probably best that you know, Grace. It wasn't a mistake.' She glanced at me and I noticed for the first time an intense determination in her face. 'I'm so sorry, we didn't plan it this way. It happened after I hired you. But we can't help how we feel.' In her strappy beige sandals she was nearly as tall as James, and she barely needed to lift her pointy little chin upwards to gaze at my husband adoringly. 'The thing is, I care about you and I want to be with you.'

A collective gasp flew round the office, almost loud enough to drown my yelp of pain. I could sense the techie crowd reaching for their phones to post *Wild and crazy work love triangle* on their Facebook pages. I felt like I'd been whacked in the ribs with a cricket bat, but I registered through my tears that James was shaking his head in defeat. The little pot slipped from my fingers before I could think of throwing paint in their faces. Instead, it added a permanent souvenir of the demise of my marriage to the carpet and his Hush Puppies. Rebecca sidestepped smartly and her sexy sandals escaped the shower. Too bad.

Failing entirely to live up to my name, I turned and fled with as much poise as a double-decker London bus.

~ ~ ~

We spent the next two days in an ugly blur of sobbing, shouting, and silence. Not all the tears were mine: James followed me straight home and begged me to hear his side of the story. I heard but I didn't listen and I certainly didn't believe his lame attempts to blame his cheating on a drunken night of clubbing at the conference in Las Vegas. Did he really think I was that gullible?

He tiptoed around me for the first evening, then slept in our guest room and left early the next day. That was worse than the awkwardness of him being in the apartment: I knew he was going to see Rebecca and I was tormented by the thought. I wasn't even sure he'd come home again. But he did, to find me curled up on the sofa with a blanket, in pointed denial of the California sunshine outside.

'Will you please talk to me?' He approached hesitantly. 'I know this was really, really stupid but I need to tell you my side of things.'

'You mean you've got something original to say? Because up to this point, it's all looking like one big cliché to me. You cheated, you got caught, you're a lying bastard.'

He sat down at the other end of our Ikea sofa and I immediately tucked my legs under me, as if it would burn me to touch him. 'Grace, I didn't lie to you, I was trying to tell you!'

'Well, you didn't try very hard.' I could feel my eyes welling up yet again.

'Look, ever since I got back, I've been trying to get you to sit down.' He did at least have the decency to look distraught. 'But you've been so caught up in your business recently – there wasn't a good moment.'

He was staring at me intently and I could see the beginning of tears in his own eyes. He clearly hadn't shaved that morning and his shirt was even more of a crumpled disaster than usual.

'Well, excuse me for turning my back for five minutes to try and make some money.' I was firmly on the defensive, one hundred per cent the injured party. 'And in case you hadn't noticed, I was slaving away to finish a project for the woman you're sleeping with!'

'I'm not sleeping with her. It was just one time. One stupid bloody time. I'm so sorry.'

'I don't believe you. You knew about that goddamn purple wall.' I was looking around wildly, seeking my escape route. I didn't want to be in the same room with him.

'All right, so I happened to see her bedroom! That doesn't mean anything.'

'No, it means everything.' I was sobbing now. 'It means I'll never trust you again.'

I wish I'd had the panache to storm out of our apartment in an expensive cloud of Chanel perfume. I wish I'd owned a Louis Vuitton bag to grab on my way to check into a luxury hotel, where I'd instigate a passionate revenge fling with a nineteen-year-old bellboy. Unfortunately, I clambered off the sofa with pins and needles in my legs and tripped over my blankie instead. Then I trailed soggy tissues across the floor and locked myself in the bathroom, where my only company was a dog-eared copy of *National Geographic*.

I had followed my British husband – and his job – from London to California, but my own attempt at the American dream had flopped. I'd been working crazily, had failed to see my marriage falling apart, and felt like a total fool.

I certainly couldn't afford to kick James out and stay in our apartment on my own. My so-called business was barely breathing. I had no idea how many months or years of scraping by might be ahead of me, if I attempted to build a list of design clients who weren't going to thank me by stealing my husband. Did I have the energy to move out, find a job, and rebuild my life in the fast-moving world of Silicon Valley? What the heck was I doing in this country, anyway? All I wanted was to crawl under the bed covers and hide, preferably with a packet of imported Cadbury's biscuits.

In the small, mocking hours of the next morning, I found myself unearthing a suitcase from the closet. With safety, seclusion and comfort food as my primary motives, I booked a flight home to England.

~ ~ ~

# To continue reading

To continue reading *Saving Saffron Sweeting*, please visit:

https://mybook.to/sweeting